WITHDRAWN
WORN, SOILED, OBSOLETE

By Charlie Price

Dead Connection
Lizard People
The Interrogation of Gabriel James
Desert Angel
Dead Girl Moon

Dead Girl Moon

CHARLIE PRICE

DEAD GIRL MOON

SQUARE
FISH

FARRAR STRAUS GIROUX
NEW YORK

SQUARE
FISH

An Imprint of Macmillan
175 Fifth Avenue
New York, NY 10010
macteenbooks.com

Square Fish and the Square Fish logo are trademarks of Macmillan
and are used by Farrar Straus Giroux Books for Young Readers
under license from Macmillan.

Our books may be purchased in bulk for promotional, educational,
or business use. Please contact your local bookseller or the Macmillan
Corporate and Premium Sales Department at (800) 221-7945 ext. 5442
or by e-mail at MacmillanSpecialMarkets@macmillan.com.

Library of Congress Cataloging-in-Publication Data

Price, Charlie.
    Dead Girl Moon / Charlie Price.
        p.   cm.
    Summary: Grace, a scheming runaway, JJ, her foster care sister, and
Mick, the son of a petty thief, become entangled in the investigation
of a teen prostitute's murder in a small, corrupt Montana town.
    ISBN 978-1-250-04004-6 (paperback)   ISBN 978-0-374-31753-9 (ebook)
    [1. Murder—Fiction.   2. Runaways—Fiction.   3. Foster home
care—Fiction.   4. Political corruption—Fiction.   5. Montana—Fiction.
6. Mystery and detective stories.]   I. Title.

PZ7.P92477Deg 2012
[Fic]—dc23

                                                    2012004992

Originally published in the United States by
Farrar Straus Giroux Books for Young Readers
First Square Fish Edition: 2015
Book designed by Jay Colvin
Square Fish logo designed by Filomena Tuosto

10   9   8   7   6   5   4   3   2   1

LEXILE: HL630L

In memory of Tony Pusateri,
who set the mark for graciousness and generosity

Dead Girl Moon

GRACE LOVED A SONG called Dreamtrails by Dirty Mittens. The music haunted, the lyrics told her story. Walking a highway of dreams, every guy, every girl with her own, as fragile as porcelain, as powerful as hate.

Grace wanted to be untouchable, independent, in charge of her own life.

Mick wanted a real home, a real town, a real team, and a girl to share it.

JJ wanted the moon. And Mick.

The dead girl wanted glamour and attention, really, if she'd admit it, wanted Hollywood and movie stars. Instead, she got naked and stiff in a river.

Grace didn't think anyone got what they deserved. Except possibly Gary, but that was pretty harsh deserts. Who knew? Maybe in a few years they'd look back on this and say they learned something. Maybe. Or maybe they'd just be glad they lived through it. But the murder, the kidnapping, the things she'd done . . . those had left Grace rethinking her options.

Maybe college.

Wouldn't it be funny if she became a cop?

1

AT THREE IN THE MORNING, when everyone else is asleep, you can hear your brother's lungs expanding. You can smell the rum and cola on his breath. If your eyes are used to the dark, it's surprising how well you can see. The crinkles in his ear. Sideburns, acne lumps on his cheeks. The edge of his hairline where you're going to plant the hammer. How hard will you have to swing it to break through and still pull it out again?

Grace lowered it to her side and let it move back and forth to get a sense of its momentum, raised it shoulder high and rotated her wrist in a short arc to gauge its heft. Calculated. A medium-hard swing and the weight of the tool should mash through the bone into the goo. He was passed out on his favorites: booze and Oxy. He wouldn't wake. Wouldn't make a sound.

The second brother would be harder to kill. She'd probably have to get him in the bathroom. Before too long he would come home stoned and go in to pee before he went to bed. So Grace would hide behind the door. Smash him in the back of the head, low, base of the skull. Even if he lived, he'd be a zucchini.

And then? No more gang rapes in the Canby house. No more

two-on-one late at night when the parents were blitzed and snoring. And, when Mom and Dad were gone for hours taking Caitlin to a soccer match, no more bringing the buds in to play wrestlemania. Caitlin? She'd never have to fight and lose and feel . . . she'd never have to go through what was making Grace a murderer.

Two-handed, she was thinking. Didn't want the thing to slip. She raised both arms. Hesitated. A breath to get ready. Found herself looking at the world map on his far wall. Lowered the hammer. What if she just left? Just left for good. Took all the cash in the house. Her brother's stash in his sock drawer, her mom's folding money in the purse on the breakfast counter. Emptied her dad's wallet that was sitting on the top of his dresser. Left and never came back.

It was a good idea.

Starting in sixth grade, her older brothers, eighth and ninth graders, got on her and wouldn't get off. Nights after her folks went to bed. The boys told her they'd hurt Caitlin if she said anything. Grace stayed quiet, fought them. The more she fought, the better they liked it. Finally she told her mom.

Her mother, several drinks into the evening and tired from another day's pressure cooker at the advertising agency, went in and gave the boys a lecture. A lecture! And then forgot about it. Thanks, huh? When the boys reached high school, they began bringing their friends into the mix.

If she killed her brothers, she knew what would happen. Her

mother would blame her. Grace would go to jail. Exchange one maggot life for another.

After you ease the screen door shut, it's easy to walk out of the neighborhood at four in the morning. Dark clothes. Stay near the trees and shadows if anyone drives by. But don't run into some insomniac doofus walking his poodle. Main streets are harder, more police cruising, so use the alleys when you can. The freeway ramp? Find one a few blocks south near the warehouses where trucks will be rolling. Got to wait near the entrance, near cover, so you don't get surprised by a patrol car. Thank god for the bushy oleanders. Cover blond hair with a ball cap. Jeans and denim jacket. Tennies. A boy? Right? Flip the brim to the back and you're ready.

Grace thumbed a refrigerator rig before dawn.

The guy was eager for company, talked nonstop. Wife problems. Didn't make Grace for a girl.

Grace could feel her energy draining but the guy took an exit. Roused her, surprised her. Highway 37. Grace relaxed again. He was going north to 5. She didn't want her voice to give her away. Made it deep. "Sacramento?"

"Citrus to a bunch of independents," he says, eyes on the road. "Redding in about four hours, Weed—other side of Mount Shasta—in six."

Weed. That made Grace smile. Majorette, B student, gone to Weed. Off the grid. They'd never find her.

• • •

By the time they pulled into the docking bay at Bounty Food in Weed she wasn't so sure. The police would check bus stations, put out a bulletin north and south on 5 figuring she might be hitching. The grocery store was on an intersection: Business 5 and Highway 97 north. She caught a ride with a younger guy driving a flat rig up 97 into Oregon.

He tipped to her early on. "Pretty risky. A girl on the road." He sized her up while they climbed the long grade out of town.

Grace shifted a little so he couldn't get such a clear profile.

"How old are you?"

Don't ask her how she knows, but she knows where this is going. Reached for her pack between her feet. Put it in her lap.

"I got time," he says, "and fifty bucks for a little affection."

Grace ignored him.

He slowed and took a turnout bordered by fir, brought the truck to a stop. Undid his seat belt.

Grace found the door handle. When he leaned toward her, she jerked the hammer out of her pack. Watched his eyes widen. She was out the door before he could move.

Before dark she was on another refrigerator truck. This one going nonstop to 395 and Spokane, Washington. The driver, a quiet older man with a picture of his middle-aged wife and six or seven kids magnet-stuck to his dash. He doesn't say two words the whole trip. Pulls off for a nap outside of Pasco. Grace slept like she was in a coma.

2

THE SPOKANE BUS STATION is downtown, one block off 395. The trucker is going to a warehouse farther north.

He stopped, let Grace off on the corner. Spokane was cold beyond what she'd known in California. The bus station was poorly lit and full of people in shabby coats, carrying cheap suitcases. Here and there a kid with a duffel, probably heading to college or back to the army.

Grace sat on a wooden bench next to a woman wearing layers of clothes, a striped serape over head and shoulders. Mexican? South American? A long way from home.

Time to take stock. She had two complete changes of clothes but no warmer jacket. She'd find a heavier wrap at the Salvation Army. She had almost three hundred dollars in cash. Enough for meals and at least a week in a bare-bones hotel.

An hour's exploration told her she was wrong. Only enough money for three days if she wanted to travel at the end. And she did, by bus. Wanted to disappear. Away from the I-5 Corridor, so she'd go east. She asked around. Heard: "Missoula's cool. University stuff happening all the time." And Billings, "Biggest city. Lots of business. Two colleges." Both good towns, large enough to have jobs, opportunities. "Take Interstate 90."

The day she left, she picked a newspaper off the bench while she waited. Read that a girl named Grace Herrick had been killed in a car accident coming back from a party. Good enough. From now on she would be Grace Herick, drop one "r" so nobody could bust her alias. Get new ID wherever she landed.

She bought a ticket to Missoula under that name. There were two buses waiting in the parking bays. Grace avoided people. Didn't want to be remembered. Waited to board until the driver was distracted putting a heavy suitcase in the luggage bin. Went down the aisle to the back, covered her head, wouldn't surface until she felt motion. At the outskirts of Sandpoint, the driver announced the town name and the final destination, Calgary, Canada. That can't be right.

She moved to the front and asked the driver about options. If you take the wrong bus? There weren't many. No bus station in Sandpoint. Even if there were, the ticket back to Spokane and on to Billings costs more than she has left. The driver told her Highway 200 would get her to Missoula, let her out at the intersection.

She'd hitch. She made it easily around the top of Lake Pend Oreille but her luck ran out past the Montana border. She was stranded outside someplace called Heron for hours and then got a ragtag series of short rides in ranch pickups. Each guy warning her: Don't do this. Too dangerous.

After dark it got pretty chilly. She found an empty barn near the highway. Next day, a woman in a GMC towing a horse trailer let her out by the hardware store in Portage, Montana. Grace was almost broke. Didn't want to risk another night out in the mountain cold. Inside the hardware store, a cashier told her Social

Services was two blocks up, one block over, black-and-white sign out front.

Grace had been to civic buildings back home in Marin County for parking tickets and registrations. Didn't like them. Remembered they were sterile, impersonal, but she was broke now. Looking for help. The lobby fit her picture. Antiseptic, worn gray linoleum, metal folding chairs along one wall with magazine-strewn end tables on either side.

A dumpy middle-aged woman wearing a headset looked up from something she was reading. "Help you?"

"I need work and a place to stay," Grace said, wishing she'd checked herself in a bathroom mirror before she started this, knew she looked like she'd been jumping trains. The woman half stood and leaned over her counter, appraising. "Runaway?" she asked, pursing her lips.

"No."

The woman sat back to her reading. "Main Street across from the hardware store. Human Services. See Mackler."

Dismissed.

Mackler's office was more plush than Grace expected. Maroon carpet. Polished wood trim and accessories, velour couches. Attractive woman at a desk in the center of the room looked Grace over. Frowned. Said, "What?"

"Work and a place to stay," Grace said. Hated feeling needy.

"Name?"

"Grace Herick, one 'r.'" It got easier all the time.

• • •

Mackler escorted her into a large office with a flat screen TV on one side, two recliners on the other. Went to a short refrigerator beside his desk, took out bottles of water and gave her one without asking. Began with "What can I do you for?"

Grace answered the same she'd told the woman earlier, but her mind was running. Two-bit town, one main street, middle of nowhere. Sleazy guy playing at his job. This couldn't really be Social Services. More like the talent agency she'd seen for models back in California. But lame.

Mackler wrote a couple of words on his desk pad, picked up the phone, turned his back to her.

Grace couldn't hear the conversation.

Finished, Mackler asked her if she needed to use the restroom.

The tone of his question made Grace's neck sweat. She shook her head.

He told her to have a seat on the couch. Left her in the office.

A few minutes later another man walked in. Introduced himself as Sam Hammond. Expensive haircut, pressed slacks, tassels on his loafers. He asked Grace questions about herself.

She was polite but vague. "I'm from Washington. Lost my home. Lost my job. I need a place to stay and I need work. Do I have to say more than that?"

Hammond looked her over: hands, hair, clothing, shoes. "Smile for me?"

Why? Grace shot him a look, thought the request was

ridiculous. Then got it—her teeth—did the family she was raised in have money for braces.

"Education?"

"High school," Grace told him. "I got good grades."

Hammond continued to study her, picked up Mackler's phone.

Twenty minutes later another man came in. Said, "Hi. Gary Stovall. Hammond gone?"

Grace nodded.

"Mackler?"

Grace shrugged. Had no idea where that man went.

"Got a bag?"

Grace showed him the pack.

"You can stay with us," he said. "Like a foster child, until you're eighteen. Tina and I have a girl your age, JJ. You'll probably like her. Hammond'll give you a job in a few weeks when you get settled."

Grace hadn't told anyone her age. Just turned sixteen. She wouldn't have gone anywhere with the other men. This guy was different. Gary. Maybe forty. Long and slender. Brown ponytail. Red plaid cotton shirt, rolled-up sleeves, old jeans. Logger boots. Had a soft smile to match his voice. Kind eyes. She'd go with him and pay attention. Learn how to play the game in this town.

She knew something sly was going on here. Portage. Nothing was official. No paperwork. Seemed like Hammond was the man,

Mackler his flunky. This was a place she could figure out. Way less horrid than home. And she might be able to make some money in this town. Grow up.

Grace Herick. Businesswoman. She could play that. She just had to stay tough.

3

GRACE EXPECTED GARY TO HAVE A CAR. He didn't. At least not one he was driving. They walked about six blocks to an alley off Main that quickly became gravel on its way toward a bank of willows and the Clark Fork River. About a hundred feet in, the alley widened into a big dirt parking lot bordered by two trailers. The one to her left, freshly painted, cedar deck that overlooked the river. The one on her right, downstream, rusty and dilapidated. She couldn't believe that was the one he headed for.

Past a junker car, they walked up weathered two-by-six steps that led to the small plywood porch and front door. When Gary opened it, Grace made an effort not to wince at the smell: old garbage, unwashed clothes, maybe even a whiff of urine. A slack-faced woman sat on the couch facing the door, a drink in her hand.

"That's my wife, Tina," Gary said, "and JJ's around here somewhere."

The woman turned from the small TV she'd been watching.

"This is Grace," Gary said. "She'll be living with us for a few months."

Tina nodded. Lifted part of her mouth in a smile. Went back to the TV.

Grace heard a noise to her left. Sitting on the floor, ankle cuffed to the kitchen table, was a boy nine or ten years old.

"That's Jon," Gary said. "He's on a time-out."

The boy stared at Grace, unfocused, uninterested.

"JJ!" Gary yelled at a back bedroom to the far right.

No response.

"Oh, right. She's in school till three-thirty. You'll meet her. Let me show you where you're staying." He headed toward the bedroom he'd yelled at.

At least this room smelled clean. Smelled like some kind of incense, actually. The double bed took most of the space. A small closet was surprisingly empty of clothes: a couple of pairs of jeans on hooks, T-shirts on a high shelf, a raincoat and a wool mackinaw on hangers. On the left side of the bed a makeshift dressing table with a brush and a hand mirror. The two-drawer bureau that doubled as an end table held a gooseneck lamp and a book. Grace picked it up. *Babe Didrikson Zaharias: The Making of a Champion.* Man or woman? She had no idea, never heard the name.

There was room on the right side of the bed for her pack. Looked like someone had either just built or just cleared a board-and-brick bookcase, two shelves, so Grace could lay out her clothes if she wished. She sat on the bed corner, stomach empty and growling. Should she run? What had she gotten herself into?

• • •

JJ woke her. Said hi. Smiled. Shook her head. "Welcome to the palace."

Grace sat up. Didn't know what to say.

"I'm JJ, right? I've been living here for years. How do you think I feel?" When Grace didn't respond, JJ went on.

"It could be worse. Gary's nice enough except the way he handles Jon. Tina's a zombie, 24/7. Jon's hell. Avoid him. Gary cooks okay. Cooks a lot. He tokes around the clock so he's always hungry. You got to be careful not to put on weight like me. I'll trim down when softball starts."

Grace was trying to get up to speed with this girl. Younger, clearly. Almost Grace's height. Built sturdy with big shoulders, big wrists, short spiky black hair. Dark eyes, full lips, olive skin a little like Tina's. Reminded Grace of a tree cutter her dad had hired back in San Rafael last summer: strong, pretty without makeup, mannish figure. Grace checked her for a chain on her wallet or a wad of keys clipped to her belt loop. Checked for a nostril ring, tongue stud, tattoo. The girl looked butch but maybe she was . . . a jock?

"Yeah, I know," JJ said. "Not much to look at, but I got a few brains and I got your back, so get to know me."

4

IN THE MONTHS THAT FOLLOWED, Grace learned that Portage was a sewer, rotten with secrets and deals. She learned that Sam Hammond ran the town with partners: Mackler, the director of Human Services, for sure, probably a judge named Bolton and a banker named Greer. Maybe also a highway patrolman named Scott Cassel. She learned that Hammond had something going with Cassel's older son, Larry. Twenty-five, no experience, and suddenly he was the town's new building inspector. The day she met Larry, she learned something else. He fancied himself a Casanova.

Hammond hired runaway girls. He'd arranged for Human Services to make her Gary Stovall's foster child. Until she turned eighteen, if she stayed, the Stovalls would make an extra six hundred dollars a month. *Like a beat-up single-wide full of dope and booze was a "suitable" placement!*

Grace told JJ very little about herself; nothing that was true, including her real age. She did say that she'd appreciate JJ's help learning how to fit in here.

From JJ, Grace learned Gary repaired electronics for a living out of the trailer. Had an arrangement with the hardware store, Hammond's, to pick up and refurbish radios, TVs, surround-sound systems, but his real money came from selling the weed he grew hydroponically in an insulated shed a couple of blocks above Main. JJ told her she'd lived with the Stovalls since her mom, Tina's sister, died several years ago. Told her that Tina's drinking had made her a turnip by the time she'd had Jon, the Devil Boy, and that neither Gary nor Tina could deal with him. Something was wrong with Jon. He was wired and mad practically all the time. When he got real bad, Gary would keep him cuffed and medicated. JJ didn't know what to do, afraid what would happen to all of them if she told the police. Grace already knew in her bones that Jon had no future. Psych ward, jail, or death.

From Grace's real family, the only person she ever thought about, the only person she ever missed, was her sister. Caitlin had been a good athlete like JJ. Taller and leaner, a different body entirely, but she'd been blunt and funny and she lifted Grace's spirits when they spent time together.

Turned out JJ was fourteen, an eighth grader, but she'd been bumped up to a combo of freshman-sophomore so she could attend high school and play on the girls' sports teams. Softball in particular. The Portage Trappers had a chance to take state for the next two years thanks to a remarkable junior pitcher. JJ was the only girl in town good enough to catch her sixty-mile-an-hour fastballs and risers.

Grace was polite to Gary, avoided Tina and Jon whenever possible, and steadily developed a low-key friendship with her younger roomie. At school, Grace was busy making grades. Told them when she enrolled that she'd been homeschooled and should be a junior. Standing with her, Gary nodded, and the guidance counselor accepted it. So leaping grades like JJ, she had a lot of work to cover. Of course she was the new girl, but socially she managed a quiet entry because she didn't try to make friends. Aloof, disdainful, she seemed older, above it all. The girls bad-mouthed her among themselves and were happy to ignore her. The guys wanted a new conquest and her persistent lack of interest left them mostly bewildered.

5

GARY WAS RIGHT. Hammond came through. Six or seven weeks later, post-Thanksgiving, he gave her a job waitressing after classes in his downtown café. Gary gave her the news, sent her over after school in early December. She walked through the door into a medium-sized dining area bordered by an L-shaped counter, four booths along the opposite wall, six tables in the middle. The place was well-lit, warm, and smelled like butter and burgers.

A guy came out through the service door, lots of gray in his wiry hair, stomach bulging against a stained apron, all business. Pointed to the two waitresses standing behind the counter, a pretty young Latina, Ramona, and a tall, stacked blonde, Evelyn. They nodded, kept their distance. He said his name, Cookie, and showed her the pantry/locker room. Handed her two cheap white tops that looked like they'd fit. "Wear black pants," he said. "No jeans."

Grace wasn't sure what to say. Hadn't had a job before. Thought he might ask her age.

"Five to closing. Don't be late. It's a good shift. Dinner. You're hungry, you can eat something after. Pay every second Friday. Do good, move to full-time this summer."

Should she ask how much she'd make? Didn't seem like it.

"If this place is slow, you'll go to the motel couple of blocks down to finish room cleaning. Start tomorrow. You need something, ask." He left her and went to the wide stainless-steel grill and griddle, took a spatula and turned browning potatoes. Saw her watching him. "Breakfast all day," he said. "You can leave that way." He nodded to a back door. "You drive here, that's the parking lot."

It was dark when Grace got back to the street. Most businesses were lights-out. Old-fashioned streetlamps gave Main a coziness in spite of the wind chill. The cold clean air made Grace dread returning to the funk of the trailer.

Grace was a quick study, learned to keep the orders straight, smile, boost tips with subtle flirting. Such a different person from school! Made her feel like an actress. Better, she started to earn real money. Ramona moved to day shift, Evelyn stayed swing. She and Grace made a pretty good evening attraction. More truckers and ranch hands every night.

Turned out ideal. Café was gossip central and the motel provided some of the juiciest confirmations. Grace added another layer. Undercover intel, gathering news she could put to use when opportunity presented.

Within days, Mackler was waiting for her at the sidewalk when classes let out. She saw him, walked wide to avoid him, but he cut her off.

"How's it goin'?" Though the temp was in the thirties, he'd loosened his tie, suit coat over his shoulder, chewing gum.

Grace faced him. "I'm working for Hammond."

"I know. I got you the job."

"Thanks."

"Yeah." He looked around casually like he was checking to see if anyone was paying attention. "Want to do something? Go for a drive?"

It was sunny, no wind, snowless patches on the southern hills were golden.

"I'm working for Hammond," Grace repeated.

"Yeah," Mackler said. Left it at that.

"I have to go."

Mackler cut his eyes to a late-model Audi parked by the curb.

Grace shook her head, walked around him. Didn't look back.

She hadn't gone a block before she felt someone close behind her. She wheeled, thinking to slap the creepy bastard and get it over with.

Not Mackler. Two jocks in letter jackets. One handsome enough to be an actor. Probably six feet, medium build, curly reddish brown hair to his collar. The other, bigger, bulky, black crew cut.

"You one of Mackler's?" This question from curly-hair, with a mean smile behind it.

Grace shook her head. Guy was hot but reminded her of her second brother.

"Going to the game tonight?" Bulky grinned at her. Even his teeth were big.

"Football . . ." Grace didn't catch on.

"Basketball. Tim and I start. How about it?"

Grace didn't smile. Not ready for this. "I work," she said.

The guy nodded. "You stuck up? Think you're chill?" He waited for a response. Didn't get one.

Grace left them standing there.

"I'm Cunneen. My man's Tim Cassel," he yelled at her back. "We deal with bitches."

By February Grace had settled into a steady routine: school, work after, studies before bed. She was staying low-profile, making good money, and the friendlier she got with Cookie, the more dirt she heard about the town's inner workings.

Yesterday and today winter had taken a short break and Grace enjoyed her walk home, the late-night stillness, her breath like smoke in the cold air, stars blinking through leafless branches. When she reached the trailer, she was expecting to lie down on the bed and quietly finish her homework. Wasn't going to happen. JJ was all wound up, bopping around the small room like a puppy.

"We got a new neighbor," JJ said, grinning.

Grace thought about the old woman across the lot. She moved? No, Gary would have said something.

JJ plopped on the bed and patted next to her for Grace to sit. As soon as she did, JJ popped up again. Grace hadn't seen the girl this animated.

They didn't have any classes together but she knew JJ was low-key at school, always by herself in the halls. JJ had grown up in Portland, had gone to a huge elementary school until her mom died. When she'd had to move here to Portage, she'd never really adjusted, never shared any of the cowboy culture. JJ'd complained that she wasn't pretty enough to be courted by guys or sought by girls for their cliques. Her sports ability wasn't glamorous. Worse, living in this trailer, this cesspool, it wasn't like JJ could invite new friends over.

Grace remembered the afternoon she herself had arrived. JJ'd been openly glad to have a roommate nearly her age. Finally someone to talk to, and JJ could be funny, but tonight was something else. Grace thought she knew what. "A boy, right?"

"Damn straight. He's tall and quiet, like big but gentle, but not soft, you know. Nice eyes."

"Hey, simmer down, homegirl. How do you know all this? Did he take a personality test?"

"No, G, I just know. I spent the last hour with him at the river."

"So he's a fisherman? A stalker? A hobo?"

"He just got here. He's in that place on the corner by the alley."

"The shack behind the hardware?"

"He's going to play football next year."

"That explains it. Jock to jock connection."

JJ blushed. "It's not like that. You have to meet him . . ." JJ's mood shifted as she said that and looked at Grace. Looked at her lying back on the bed now, in her dark pants and white waitress top. "Crap!" JJ seemed to want the word back but it was too late.

Grace got it.

"I won't," she told JJ. "I'm not even interested. Don't want a guy. At all."

"Doesn't matter," JJ said, sitting on her side of the bed, picking up her hand mirror, putting it down. "He'll see you. And from then—" JJ stopped herself. "Anyway," she said, "he's cool. No, he's real. You'll like him."

Grace didn't know what to say.

JJ stretched out, turned on her reading light, picked up her book, energy gone.

7

MICK WOKE TO HIS DAD tugging on his arm. The man didn't have to say a word. Mick knew. He also knew arguing was a waste of breath.

"Ten minutes," his father said, and then he was gone and Mick could hear him rummaging in the kitchen.

The boy scrambled up, took a deep breath, tried to get his brain working so he could check his room. First things: pulled on his jeans and a sweatshirt, got his heavy snow jacket out of the closet along with the shopping bag he always kept packed. Unplugged his CD alarm and tossed it in the bag. Tossed in the book he was reading. Looked under his bed for his magazines. Couldn't find them. His dad must have taken them.

"C'mon!" The man walked past Mick's door on the way to the garage.

The boy turned a complete circle. Most things he had cared about—watch, first-base mitt, his mom's picture—had already been left and lost in earlier moves. Mick saw the souvenir bat from a Boise Hawks game they'd gone to this past summer. Took it. Good memories, good weapon. He jammed his feet in his snow boots and that made him think of his sneakers. He found them behind his door as he heard the car start. The home phone started ringing.

"Leave it!"

That reminded Mick of his cell. He found it in his shirt pocket on the chair by his bed, pulled the charger out of the wall plug and shoved it and the shirt in the shopping bag. He was sticking the cell in his jeans when he heard the garage door go up.

"Now!"

That was always the last warning. Sure enough, a car door slammed. If his dad left him . . . he made it to the passenger side as the car started to roll. They were out of the driveway when his damn phone rang.

"They must have gotten your number," his dad said, holding out one hand and steering with the other, taking the corner too fast, fishtailing.

Mick put his phone in the outstretched hand and his dad

threw it as far as he could out the driver's-side window. The man felt on the seat beside him, came up with a paper sack. Pushed it at Mick. "Sandwich," he said.

The cell phone. The only tie Mick had to the kids he'd met here. For a minute it felt like his father had ripped off Mick's arm. If they'd been going slower Mick might have jumped from the car to look for it.

The boy wasn't sure what time it was but the lack of neighborhood lights and the absence of traffic made early morning a good bet. He didn't feel like eating. His stomach was rumbling like it did when he thought his dad might be arrested. Mick put the sack back on the seat, belted up, zipped his jacket all the way to the neck, and closed his eyes. Crap! He felt in his pockets. No idea where his gloves were. He sat hating himself. Stupid. The last thing he remembered was leaning against the cold window glass looking out at winking ranch lights in the meadows near the turnoff to Riggins.

Not such good things happen when your dad is a thief. Your mom might leave. Mick's did. You might move way too much. Might not have any friends. You might be afraid a lot. Nervous. Like something bad could happen anytime. Like cops. And if they take your dad, then what? Where do you go? Think they could still find your mom after six or seven years? His mom hadn't even called. Might not have kept the same name. Might be remarried. Might have a new family. A new son.

• • •

Mick awoke after dawn to the memory of his dad hustling them out of McCall in the dead of night. Same old thing. Something had gone wrong or somebody had ratted and the cops were onto him. So far he'd stayed a jump ahead. After a few minutes Mick caught a road sign. They were driving up Montana 135 heading toward Plains. His dad noticed him looking.

"Going to Portage," the man said. "Couple more hours."

To their right a dark river slid along the canyon, to their left, rocky bluffs climbed skyward. His dad said pay attention, they might spot a bighorn sheep. The man drove with both hands on the wheel, kept a constant check on the rearview mirror, didn't break the speed limit. Couldn't afford to be pulled over. "It's going to be different this time," he told Mick. "Swear."

His father didn't look at him but Mick thought it was kind of an apology. His dad told him he was tired of hustling, tired of nomading around. He thought he had a good job waiting for him at the Conoco in Portage. Said he'd called and set it up the week before when he'd been worried a local investigation was getting too close. He told Mick he was done "finding" things. Caused too much trouble. Never made that much money with it anyway.

Mick listened, kept looking out the window.

The past twelve months Mick had gone to three different high schools. His dad said Portage had a good one, two or three hundred kids. Mick knew something his father didn't and Mick wasn't going to tell. This time Mick was going to make a close friend, somebody he could stay with if his dad got in trouble again. Mick was going to have a whole junior year in one place. He was strong enough and fast enough and he was going out for sports. He was done skipping out. Better off alone if that's the way it had to be.

An hour or so later they crossed the Salish River, tooled past the tiny airport, and drove the length of town, east to west. It was big enough to have the stores you needed, small enough to walk where you wanted to go. Main Street showed wall-to-wall colorfully painted buildings, front sidewalks shoveled clear of snow.

On their way back through, when they took any narrow street south toward the river, the paving ended quickly in a scrabble of shacks and beat-up trailers. The broken siding, patched roofs, plywood windows were a big contrast to Main Street. The town was fakey, like a movie set. Maybe that was a fit. He and his father looked right on the outside, but inside? Not so good.

8

MICK'S FATHER RENTED THEM A PLACE down one of those gravel alleys, a "studio," he said. Actually it was a ramshackle room with rickety walls and no insulation, cobbled on behind Hammond's Hardware. When they moved in, they found the pipes were clogged or frozen and the plumbing useless, but his dad had already paid cash. The deal didn't include refunds. For a few days they would have to do their business and take spit baths after hours up at the Conoco. Until April, they'd have to wear most of their clothes all the time. That would make entering school as a new kid even harder. Mick would look and smell homeless.

• • •

At first they would be pretty careful. His dad had a new rule. No more phones. Didn't trust them. Thought all the companies collaborated with law enforcement. They'd keep scanning for unmarked cars or any sign they were being watched. After a week or two they could probably relax. Mick didn't know how much he could trust his dad's promise, so he got to know the neighbors right away.

JJ, Janice Joplin Stovall, was the first person he met. Ran into her the second night in town when he walked from his shack across the parking area to the river. Sitting on a stump between the willows and the water, she'd been hidden from his sight line. He pushed through branches and there she was, staring up at the moon, her breath making steam. Mick thought she was a boy when he first saw her. He'd never told her that. Short, stiff dark hair, hands tucked in a vest over a black hoodie, dark jeans, high-tops. Mick was thinking halfback or safety, or even a wrestler.

He stepped toward her, rocks clacking under his weight, and she turned to look at him. She said hi. Girl, he saw then. No makeup. Smile. It struck him. She wasn't afraid. He knew what he looked like, over two hundred pounds, bushy brown hair, scar on his face. She turned back to moon-gazing. Mick studied the river and they were still for a while.

She didn't look at him again after that first time, but she didn't frown or edge away. Didn't seem like she minded his interruption. Felt like he was welcome to join her. Eventually they did a couple of those first-time things. Him, Mick Fitzhugh, just moved here, the corner place behind the hardware store. Sophomore this year. Her, JJ. The downriver trailer. High school, fourteen.

Mick looked at her more closely. Yeah, her face looked young, but something about her seemed older. Maybe her build. Like she lifted or worked out.

She told him she lived with her uncle and aunt, Gary and Tina. Said Gary repaired TVs and electronic stuff for the hardware and private customers. Said Tina didn't work. JJ rolled her eyes. Guess there was a story to go with that. Maybe he'd hear more about Tina later. Also said Tina had a ten-year-old son, Jon. Told Mick watch out. Jon was trouble.

They were quiet again after that. In a couple of minutes she said there was one other person in the trailer. A foster girl that came a few months ago named Grace, a junior.

Mick nodded, said huh from time to time to let her know he was listening. He didn't tell her much about himself, wouldn't say anything that led to questions about his dad or why they moved all the time. Word gets around. His father'd drummed that into him. As for Mick, he didn't have anything to say worth hearing. He read a lot? He wanted to play ball? That sounded lame. He couldn't think of something he'd done that he was proud of. He could think of several things he hoped she'd never find out. Him telling her that he was ready to settle down, make this town his home? Too weird. Really, there was nothing to say.

Before they went back to their places for the night, she

pointed at the moon. "This one's the Snowcone," she said. Mick didn't understand. Didn't know then that she named each one.

At the edge of the bushes, he checked the parking lot for cops before he left cover. Old habit. Silly, probably, but he was still a little gun-shy. When Mick thought about it he didn't see how anybody could have followed them here. He knew his dad didn't ever tell getaway plans. Always used cash. No way to trace them except for the car, and his dad had lifted Montana plates from an abandoned wreck outside of Plains.

WITHIN DAYS MICK HAD MET everyone in their compound. His front door looked across the flat dirt lot to willows edging the river. The Stovalls' trailer sat downriver a hundred feet to the right, an old Chevy station wagon with flat tires parked to the side of its porch. Gary and his drunk wife, Tina, their son, Jon, JJ, and Grace, all squeezed in the single-wide. Gary seemed decent enough. Stoned. Did his electronic work on the foldout kitchen table. Kept his jays in a ziplock beside him along with Visine for red-eye. Mick didn't know then that he made most of his money on weed, selling ounces out of his kitchen.

Tina was beautiful. Or had been beautiful. Now she wore housecoats, forgot to comb her hair. Slurring and sleepy whenever

Mick saw her. Mostly stayed on the living room couch in easy reach of a drink and a small TV. Jon had a short daybed just to the left of the front door. Gary could work and watch him at the same time. Gary tried to keep the kid quiet with meds. Jon learned to cheek them. Made for a daily battle.

JJ and Grace shared the bedroom off the living room; Gary and Tina had the one on the other side of the kitchen. One big happy mega-baked family, except JJ didn't use and if Grace did, she hid it.

Left from Mick's front door, directly across the lot from the Stovalls, was Ms. Crabtree's double-wide. Her trailer had an elevated deck where you could see the black water of the Clark Fork and the tree-covered mountains beyond. She told Mick to call her Dovey and invited him in for a cookie. She looked older than rock. Said she'd been Sanders County clerk since the early seventies. She was easy to talk to, soft-spoken, unhurried. Said she'd thought about sending some banana bread over but didn't want to intrude. Asked what Mick's dad did, and accepted "mechanic" without more questions. Mick could tell by the way she looked at him, her steadiness, she would be a hard lady to fool. Must have seen a lot over the years.

Grace Herick, he'd run into after school. Nice! She was sharp-faced, with dry straw-colored hair, and some freckles. Not pretty, exactly, but she looked you right in the eye like she was daring you to give her any grief. Didn't smile much. Had a don't-tread-on-me attitude with sarcasm or a mini-smirk that made it seem like she could be wicked. He tried not to stare or get caught staring, but the more he looked the more attractive she seemed. Her gray eyes? Her lean strength? Something. She moved right . . . From the start, Mick wanted to get on her good side. And he could relate. She was more guarded than he was.

10

A COUPLE OF WEEKS after they moved in, his father asked if Mick had seen a red Chrysler hanging around. The kind with the big wheels. That was a new one. The other times they'd just watched for police-type vehicles.

"Why do you care about a car like that?" They were walking up to Skinny's, the burger place on Main, for dinner.

"Nothing really. Jerk-off on that construction back in McCall has one. Thinks I owe him money."

"Do you?"

"Don't owe anybody anything." He coughed and spit in the weeds. "No problem. Just asking."

His dad was getting edgier all the time. Jumpy. Mick thought it was the pills. His father called it medicine but he never saw a doctor. When he drank on top of it, he got mean. Mick had asked him to stop a while ago. The man said no. Said it kept him alert.

Around that same time Mick ran into some trouble. Grace never joined them, but JJ and Mick had gotten a little better acquainted walking to school together in the mornings. They also had the same third-period keyboard class. He kept his book in her locker since it was nearby. They were side by side, putting their texts on the shelf, when JJ fell into him.

"Hey, Lezbo, got yourself a new bitch?"

Mick untangled to find a guy with long brown hair and a letter jacket facing them. Close beside him a kid that looked like a lineman. Mick didn't know either one.

JJ turned to the guy. She'd kept hold of her book, and the way she was gripping it, Mick thought she might fling it. She was beet red; angry or embarrassed, Mick couldn't tell which.

"Don't worry," the guy said. "I won't tell your secret."

Mick punched him hard in the sternum, knocked him back a foot.

His face showed a second of pain before it morphed to hate. The goon beside him started for Mick but the kid with long hair grabbed his arm, stopped him. "I'm Tim Cassel," he said. "Don't tell me your name. I won't remember it." He made a show of looking Mick over carefully. "Nice scar," he said. He cut his eyes to JJ. "Hope you and your pussy find love." He waited then, Mick thought, to see if either of them would move. When they didn't, he wheeled and strode off with his buddy. Over his shoulder, said, "Be seeing you."

Mick was vibrating.

JJ got his attention. "Don't," she said. "His dad runs the Highway Patrol in this county. He's got an older brother puts people in the hospital." She touched Mick's arm for a sec. "Let it go," she said. "That guy doesn't matter." She put her book in the locker and left without another word.

Next morning on the way to class JJ thanked him. "I'm like an outsider," she said. "Too young to do the Bachelorette thing. Guys in this school want to date up." She was walking carefully to avoid the patches of ice on the sidewalk. "Plus I'm not the sexy type most guys like, so I'm pretty much invisible, except to creeps."

Mick glanced at her to let her know he'd heard.

"Basically, Tina's out of it, Gary's either working or corralling Jon. Nobody but you and Grace talk to me. That dyke crap from Cassel? You were there for me. Appreciate it."

That was the most open she'd been with him. Felt like an honor.

Starting that day, guys Mick didn't know began calling him Zip or Zipper. He didn't get it and then he did. The scar. From time to time somebody would trip him in the halls or shove him on the stairs. They were good at it. Sneaky. Mick never saw for sure who it was.

He brought his souvenir bat to school and stuck it in his locker. Last year his dad had asked him, made him, help with a couple of jobs. In a warehouse theft, the two of them got in a pretty big fight with a burly security guy. Mick learned. Helps to have something besides your fists. Thinking about it, he hoped he never got in that kind of situation again. On the other hand, he'd be ready if Cassel decided to bring it. Turned out it wasn't Cassel and he wasn't ready.

11

MICK EDGED INTO CLASSES the rest of the winter, bore down in the spring hoping to finish sophomore year with a B average. Tried track that spring, shot and discus, but didn't do either well enough to earn a letter. Did get to see the lineman, Cunneen, in action. The big kid lifted more weight than anyone else in the training room and his effort and strength paid off. He usually won the shot at meets, won or placed in the discus. The other guys deferred to him, gave him a lot of room, tried to make him happy. The king and his court.

He generally ignored Mick, referred to him as The Zip, and was only civil when coaches were present. At the end of most practices Cunneen was joined by Tim and an older man, clearly an ex-jock, for what looked to Mick like football drills. The three of them laughing, chumming around, made Mick jealous. If he played well enough to start next year, maybe somebody would pay that kind of attention to him.

JJ played school softball. Okay bat, great glove, and big enough to block the plate. No wonder he'd thought she was a guy. Mick was surprised how aggressive she could be on the field, given how quiet she was in class. Not your ordinary girl, this JJ. She was good, but they gave the MVP to a blond junior pitcher. Grace and Mick met at JJ's games when his own practices didn't interfere.

When JJ had no game, Mick loved walking home after track

practice. Low sun on the nearby mountains. The fresh breeze off the river carrying the scent of new hay from ranches east of town. He'd be showered, clean, tired from the strength machines and the three-mile jog that coaches demanded from most of the weight men. *Home,* he was thinking. *Portage makes a good home.* He didn't hear the car pull up beside him, didn't notice until the doors closed.

Three guys joined him on the sidewalk. Looked a little old for high school. Had probably been jocks a year or two ago. Now they looked a little softer, like maybe they drank more than they played.

The smallest one stepped in front of him. "Hear you got a big mouth."

Mick didn't say anything.

"Think you're tough." The little guy kicked for Mick's nuts.

Mick caught his foot. Lifted and the guy toppled. Mick didn't see the punch that got him in the neck or the foot that jammed him behind the knee. He was down and getting hurt. Couldn't pick up the blows, covered up while they kicked him. It didn't last long. At least he didn't think so. A boot to the back of the head made him woozy.

When he got to his knees, blood dripped on the sidewalk. Nose or lip, Mick couldn't tell which. The sore knee made it hard to stand. Took him a minute. He was stiff but he could walk. Slow at first, then better. By the time he reached the studio, he was good enough. He washed up, fixed his mouth with superglue, butterfly-bandaged the gash on his forehead. Couldn't fix the black eye.

He left his dad a note saying he'd gone to the library. Didn't want to hear the words of wisdom. "Wait till they're not looking and bash their heads in." Not much help, really, if you wanted to keep living in this town. Was this payback for punching Tim Cassel? For not kowtowing to Cunneen? Or was it just another kind of initiation to a small cowboy town where new people paid dues, one way or the other.

It didn't matter. Mick healed quick. After that, the school year moved along without major trouble. No cops in the yard. No red car. No more fights. No sign that hell might break through the earth's crust and melt Mick's life. Well, one thing. Early May. Quickly forgotten.

Getting ready to leave for school Mick heard loud voices. Never a good sign. He eased out of his place, located the argument on Dovey's porch. A black Lincoln Town Car sat just to the side of her steps and a large man with a blond crew cut was pointing his finger at Dovey and shouting. Mick's first thought was some kind of shakedown. Dovey? Loan? Gambling debts? Not likely. But what then? Who could be trying to lean on this woman and why? The car had no logo, no insignia, the guy was wearing dark pants and a blue shirt. No clues there.

Dovey's eyes shifted to Mick as he walked toward her. The man caught that and turned. Mick hadn't recognized him from behind, but this was the guy who'd been doing football drills with Cassel and Cunneen after track. The ex-jock. He reminded Mick of a TV sports announcer: handsome, strong features, white teeth, cold blue eyes. Mick had to make himself keep walking.

"That's far enough, pal, none of your business." The man seemed to grow larger as he spoke, as if he could puff up intentionally.

Mick guessed the guy was around six four, two forty or fifty. Bigger and harder than anyone Mick had confronted. He continued walking to the edge of the car. "I need to talk with Ms. Crabtree," Mick said. "It can't wait."

The man turned back to Dovey. "That list is *my* job. Court order if I need to." He moved down the steps, quick, agile, got in his car and drove away without another glance at Mick.

Mick had to move to keep the fender from hitting him. When he made it to the porch he could see Dovey's face dark with anger, jaw set. He waited for her to speak. When she didn't he asked. "Who's that?"

"Larry Cassel. Lieutenant Cassel's older son." She shook her head as if to shake away the annoyance. "Long story. The end of it's he's the new Tri-County building inspector. Don't ask how he got that with no contractor's license or building experience. He wants a list of construction projects going back five years but he won't get it from me. News travels. He's already reviewing old projects asking for new fees. Cardwell's going to have to bring the state in like he used to with Hammond's father."

"He's Tim's brother?" Mick said.

"Yes, six or seven years older and stay out of it. He threatens but he won't hurt me." Her face softened. "I appreciate you coming over to make sure." She smiled. "How about a brownie?"

12

BEST TIMES MICK HAD WERE OUT at JJ's river spot. Fine May evenings, shirtsleeve weather, at least a couple of times a week. Grace was at work. It was just the two of them, talking, teasing, her watching the sky, him the water. Gradually, JJ opened up. Told him about her real mom.

JJ found out her mother used to be wild in high school. Partied a lot till she got pregnant and her guy walked out. After she had JJ she got real depressed and never seemed to pull out of it. Stayed single. Worked, but never left the house, evenings or weekends. Only thing her mom did was read and watch TV. The woman filled JJ's head with fairy tales about princesses and knights, Snow White and Disney stuff, right up until she died of quick-hitting cancer. Five weeks and she was gone. JJ got shipped to the Stovalls, her mom's sister, Tina.

On one of those river nights, JJ swore Mick to secrecy. He imagined rape or something with Gary. Wrong. JJ wanted to talk about the moon. As soon as she said "moon," Mick thought, *Great, she's crazy. Tina's crazy. Jon's crazy. It's rubbed off.*

During the time he'd known her he'd seen some strange things. Nobody looked at the moon as much as she did. Mick mentioned it to Grace. Grace made that motion, circling her ear with her finger. "I love her," Grace said. "She's my homegirl, but she's nuts. La-la land. Baseball or boonies, no in-between."

Mick had seen JJ walk down the main street, the highway, at night looking at the sky, totally distracted. Not even aware of cars or the possibility of being hit. She'd look out the window in class and not hear the teacher call her name. No way was she stupid. But she was . . . what? A little disconnected sometimes? Lost in space? When she started talking about the moon, Mick realized it was true. She could get lost in space. Literally.

That particular evening, JJ began by looking at him, right at him. "When you stood up for me with Cassel I felt . . . thought maybe you'd understand."

Mick never did. Not really, but he listened.

JJ told him that after she came to live with the Stovalls, she'd only left Portage once, years ago, and that was on a trip to Missoula with Gary. That time he'd finished his business early and took her to the city's planetarium for a treat. It was the only real museum-type place she'd ever seen. When the lights went out, the projected sky was black with little dots of light for the constellations. Nebulae reminded her of finger paintings, but the moon . . . the moon they showed was huge and white. Glowed like magic.

That was when she learned that the moon's far side always faced away from the earth, hidden, secret. Like the fairy tales her mom used to tell, JJ began daydreaming about a place even the astronauts missed. She imagined a castle among the far side's craters, a palace with spires and banners and crystal and gold. Thereafter she'd always paid special attention to the moon, particularly its dark areas, and she had started naming the different shades and shapes. "Ivory Moon, Tea Cup Moon,

Dapple Moon, Cue Ball, Pepper, Buttonshine . . . things like that."

She told Mick, if the moon came out during the day, it was a Ghost Moon and had special power. Then she got quiet and looked at him for a moment or two, searching his face, he believed, to see if he was going to laugh at her. He didn't. He didn't know what to think. He also didn't know what to say. *Thanks for telling me?*

"I wanted you to know," she said finally, "the moon's like my totem. Gives me energy."

Mick wished she hadn't said that. Thought she was trusting him with too much deep stuff. Thought maybe she was . . . he didn't want to go there . . . having a crush on him? It scared him a little.

He had to do something. He smiled. Pointed at the sky. "Which moon is this?" he asked, avoiding her eyes.

13

IT WAS OBVIOUS to Mick that Grace was also different. Way different. Far more like a woman than a girl. On the times she joined them she kept a distance, listened but didn't have much to say. Mick kept looking for ways to warm her up. She was pleasant. Nothing more.

He asked her once if guys like Cassel ever bothered her.

JJ was with them, smiled.

Grace shook her head.

"Not after she kicked Bobby Teague," JJ said.

Grace looked down.

Was she embarrassed by JJ's comment? Mick couldn't tell.

"Bobby got a cheap one. Pretended like he was yawning and brushed her boob with his elbow."

Not a term Mick had heard before, but he knew what JJ meant. There were hundreds of ways to cop a feel.

"Grace kicked him." JJ grinned and bit her lip. "Hard."

Mick shot a look at Grace. Head still down. This story was revealing something, making her uncomfortable. If she'd had a knife, would she have stabbed him?

"Bobby went down," JJ said, reaching over to brush Grace's hair back behind one ear. "Nobody jacks my sister. She's got a rep," JJ said, nodding her head to emphasize the point. "So do you."

Grace cut her eyes at Mick, but he couldn't tell if JJ'd told her about his run-in with Cassel.

"Hey," Mick said. Hoping for a rise out of Grace. "Nice work. Be my bodyguard?" He winced as soon as he said it. Sounded sexual. Sounded stupid.

Grace didn't bail him out. Said, "Talk about somebody else."

Watching her, the way she carried herself, the way she measured what she said, her willingness to get violent, Mick had a feeling. Something's happened to her. He wondered if he'd ever learn what it was.

14

GRACE LIKED WORK. Anything was better than that trailer. She and Evelyn talked when things were slow.

Evelyn said she was leaving this pit as soon as she could. "I got A's in Speech," she told Grace, like that was a big accomplishment. "I exercise first thing every morning. I could be on TV or one of those reality shows? I'm thinking Seattle first, but maybe I'll just go straight to L.A."

Right. Grace mostly listened.

"When you go on full-time, let's not split tips." Ev, thinking out loud.

That was okay with Grace but she wondered why.

"Just give Cookie and the dish guy five percent each night."

Grace nodded.

"I'm thinking I'm going to charge for dates."

Did that mean what Grace thought it meant?

"Lots of traveling guys want company. I'll meet them afterward." She looked around to be sure Cookie wasn't listening. "Don't say anything."

"What will you charge?"

"I'm thinking a hundred. Is that too much?"

Like Grace would know.

• • •

A week or so later, Grace could see, as soon as she walked in, that Ev was edgy.

"What?"

"Ramona split."

That wasn't such a shock. Grace thought the girl might be illegal. Mona had a great smile, was real polite, but other than food, didn't speak much English. "Move? Her folks get a different job?" Grace asked.

"I don't think so. I don't think she had a family. She's just gone. Surprised Cookie. I had to cover her morning. He'll get somebody else by tomorrow."

Grace didn't think any more about it at the time. She did keep thinking about Ev's new sideline. Particularly as certain customers seemed to come in regularly to set up a get-together. In this town it was like evening entertainment. Town movie theater usually showed B-grade crap; there were no music clubs except local CW bands in bars on weekends.

Larry Cassel was a regular. He had wide shoulders and a strong chin and his eyes were an interesting mix of merry and cruel. Evelyn was cool toward him, didn't smile at him or give him the coy looks she gave potential customers. Grace teased with him but declined offers of dates, at least for the time being. He was a big spender, porterhouse-rare kind of guy, and always left huge tips. He wasn't as hot as he thought he was, but still.

Another regular was the new mechanic from the Conoco. Never ordered more than pie and coffee but gave Ev and Grace his undivided attention. If you can smell like a man, he did. Grace liked his heavy beard, hard arms, gentle hands the way he cradled his cup and held his utensils. Where Larry talked a mile a minute, the mechanic had few words and never wasted any. He was too old for Grace . . . but still.

The more familiar she got with the school scene the better Grace could see that Cunneen was too dim to serve any purpose but pest control. Problem was, if she used him, then he'd become the pest. Tim Cassel was probably the pick of the crop but he was a boy compared to his older brother and Grace had bigger plans than a high school kid could deliver. The new boy? The mechanic's son, Mick? Nice enough but clueless. He was right there, thirty yards from the trailer, handy. Grace thought at some point he might be useful. She knew she had his nose but couldn't return a drop of his interest. JJ liked him. They were like three planets not even orbiting the same sun.

15

SOMETIME END OF APRIL, early May, a few weeks before school closed for the summer, Cookie told Grace that Hammond wanted to see her. Pointed to Hammond's office on the other side of Main in the next block.

Around five, before the dinner crowd, Grace redid her lip gloss, put on a fresh top, and crossed the street. The outside of the

Hammond Real Estate and Insurance building was a snappy gray with carefully detailed trim colors. The same style as its neighbors but much better kept. The interior office area was upscale, large plants, sunshine lights, leather chairs, and two desks for the sales representatives. The front door had been unlocked but there was no one working. Grace didn't know if that was common or if people had been given the evening off. At the back, a glass wall, blinds drawn, with a dark wood door at the far side, Hammond's nameplate in gold script.

She knocked.

He was half sitting against the front of a fancy glass-top desk, smiling, casual.

She closed the door and stood beside it, not sure what to expect.

"Thank you for coming," he said, gesturing to a plush leather couch behind an ornate coffee table to Grace's right.

On her left along the far wall a full bar glowed with hidden lighting, mirrored back, liquor and wine bottles standing on the marble shelf, a mixing area beside a variety of glasses on the countertop. Behind him, what appeared to be a large picture window showed an icy blue mountain lake resting between snow-covered peaks. A photograph, she decided. Grace sat, feeling self-conscious, wondering if she should have buttoned her top a little higher.

"Drink?"

She shook her head. Swear to god, something in his eyes reminded her of home and she hadn't thought about that for weeks.

Hammond moved behind his desk and sat in a black mesh captain's chair that looked space-age but comfortable. "Are you open to the occasional piece of extra work for extra pay?" he asked. "Not waitress money," he amended. "More, depending on the task."

Grace didn't trust her voice. Hated feeling outclassed. Made every effort to project the face of a businesswoman. She nodded.

"You'd like to know what I have in mind?" he asked, comfortable, familiar with managing unequal relationships.

"Yes," Grace got out, but not as clearly as she wanted.

"Like a courier," he said. "While you're working in the café. Exchanging paper, an envelope, unobtrusively when you deliver their food. Monitoring things there and when you're over at the motel. Reporting anything unusual to Cookie. Simple, really. Another pair of eyes, another pair of hands. If the work goes well, we might agree to more sophisticated tasks." He studied her as he spoke.

Grace pressed her knees more tightly together. Wanted to ask, Why me?

Hammond anticipated her question. "Ramona used to handle these duties until she had to move on. Cookie tells me you're the next best candidate." He brushed something off his slacks. "Sound good?"

Grace knew she was being invited to join Hammond's underground network. It was an easy decision. She'd have a bigger stash when she took off again. Plus, she might learn things that could be worth even more down the line when she was ready to leave. "Good," she said.

"Cookie'll tell you what I want," Hammond said, putting his

hands behind his head, grinning like perhaps his wants could be interesting and fun.

"Good," Grace said again, annoyed with herself for not managing a more sophisticated response. She stood quickly and left before anything else had a chance to happen.

16

THE "COURIER" WORK WAS TOO EASY. Grace didn't understand why Cookie didn't do it himself. Wondered if this was illegal, was she being set up to take a fall? In the last two weeks she'd also been given local people to keep reports on, another snap, and she wondered why Hammond hadn't recruited Evelyn to do that work. She'd been here longer. Nevertheless Grace was making more money, even part-time, than she'd thought possible. Don't kick a gift horse.

Cookie stopped her before she could pick up table four's meat loaf order. Was she ready for something a little different?

Sure.

He told her to bring a dress to work, heels, makeup. Get fixed up and go out with a man after her shift ended tomorrow.

Okay, but that created a problem. No dress, no heels, no makeup. Didn't want to admit that to Cookie. Curious to be part of another level of Hammond's operation.

Thought about it during the afternoon. Thrift store? Judging from its window display, she doubted that Rags to Riches had anything suitable. Tina? Tina had put on thirty pounds but she probably used to be about Grace's size. Would she still have any outfits? Should she ask or just look? What was that rule? Don't ask for permission; do what you want and ask for forgiveness?

Gary and Tina pretty much stayed in the central room all the time. He rarely left the trailer, she never, so how would Grace search their bedroom? Maybe she could catch him when he was distracted with Jon, whisper with a little beg in her voice. Ask if she could go in their bedroom and look through some of Tina's old makeup to wear for a work picture tomorrow.

Gary and Tina were in their usual places, Jon at Gary's feet. JJ was at the river. Gary said yes, said don't bother Tina, said she wouldn't mind.

In their bedroom, Grace was repelled by the wad of clothes, mostly underwear, on the floor on Tina's side of the bed. Went to their closet first. Gary's shirts, one pair of khakis hung cuffs on top. Mostly Tina's slips and housecoats. Way on the side, a couple of rayon dresses. She held up the black one with orange and yellow flowers. Probably short enough. Pretty deep V in the neck but it could work. She brought it closer, smelled it. The front was musty but not too bad. Smelled the armpits. Ancient deodorant, a little white crust on the inside. It would do. Searched the bottom of the closet, gagged over more dirty clothes, but found a pair of medium heels, gray, no, black but covered in dust.

Next to the dresser. Nothing usable. End table on Tina's side.

Top drawer had a cellophane pack of tissues, half-empty bottle of face cleanser, Q-tips. Grace guessed Tina had trouble standing to do this stuff in the bathroom. The vibrator under the ratty washcloth surprised her. Tina seemed too spaced for sex. Bottom drawer, old movie magazines, a tangled mess of necklaces that the woman had probably given up on. So where? Bathroom? Theirs was across from the bed, set off by a folding door. Medicine cabinet had maybe thirty over-the-counter med bottles and some scripts in Jon's name. Scissors, tweezers, rusted bobby pins.

Finally, between the toilet and the wall, a plastic container holding a pile of ancient makeup: dried and cracked tubs of base, broken eyeliners, tubes of lipstick mostly in garish colors that only zombies would wear. Grace was able to salvage a dark eyebrow pencil and a soft red lip gloss that looked unused.

Now, how to get the stuff out past Gary and Tina?

Grace pushed her black jeans down, wrapped the dress around her waist and pulled the jeans over it. Opened the bedroom window, pitched the shoes out. Carried the liner and lipstick and flashed them at Gary on the way across the trailer, mouthed thank you. He smiled, stuck his thumb up, none the wiser.

Grace hung the dress in her closet, hoping the wrinkles would fade. Opened her bedroom window and went out to get the heels and toss them inside before JJ came back. She'd pack them to work tomorrow, try them on there.

Even in the pantry, the outfit looked pretty good. Not a style Grace had ever worn before. Drapey, kind of sexy. Grace solved the deep neckline with a safety pin. At closing, Cookie had her put on the outfit and get a ride with Larry Cassel to a local bar a block north of Main. He'd let her out and she'd walk around to the side parking lot. A guy in an older model Cadillac would flash his lights and she would get in. The man would probably start kissing her. As soon as he got grabby, Grace would scream and Larry Cassel would walk up and knock on the window. Ask the guy what was going on. Ask Grace how old she was. Grace would say . . . what?

"Tell him fifteen," Cookie said, not realizing how close he was to the truth.

Larry would threaten a citizen's arrest and Grace would jump from the car and hustle back to the street, where Cookie would pick her up and drive her home. Pay for five minutes' work? Three hundred dollars.

17

WHEN SCHOOL ENDED, Grace started a new work rhythm. Go to the motel at one, clean rooms for a couple of hours, take a break and go to the café for evening shift, four to closing. Usually got a day or two off mid-week. That left late evenings to go out a little on her own, mornings to sleep late after JJ went to work. Good time to make some alliances. Build a little backup if she came to need it.

She began with Tim Cassel. Away from school he acted a little more mature. Plus, he had a cool Mustang convertible, enough money for burgers and beer, and a hard body that Grace considered acceptable. From a distance. Which wasn't easy. The boy didn't like no for an answer.

Next, she edged a little closer to Larry Cassel, who, contrary to his reputation, had been surprisingly thoughtful and, by Grace's standards, was practically rich. The Lincoln was cushy and if it was the night before one of her days off, they sometimes tooled all the way to an Indian casino on Kalispell Lake for a midnight dinner and gambling. She could see he wanted her, but he seemed willing to wait. The statutory thing again.

Fitz Fitzhugh was all sweat and business. If his tips hadn't been so extravagant she would never have given him a try. Weird, right? Mick's father. Fitz had a way of looking at her like he knew her, like he could see what kind of person she was under that actress smile. He took her out in the country, turned up the car radio and taught her basic swing dancing. He was rough, and his kisses felt like sandpaper, but he always stopped when she asked. He drank a boatload of hard liquor. Grace thought the pills he took kept him upright. He offered some to her but she was afraid to try them.

The second time he went out with her he really surprised her. "Want to shoot a pistol?"

That was a new one. They were south of town on a wooded ridge that overlooked the Clark Fork and the power plant. Grace looked at him to see if he was serious. Should have known. He was always pretty serious. Raised her eyebrows.

He bit his lip as if reconsidering, but wound up reaching

over into the backseat, to his leather jacket, and bringing out a folded brown paper sack. "This one's too big for you," he said, unwrapping a dark square-shaped handgun. "Got a .32 in the back's more your size."

Grace nodded. "Sure." Could be fun.

He set his pint of bourbon on the roof of the car, opened the trunk, lifted the spare tire, and pulled out a smaller package. Like a miniature copy of the first, but silvery with black grips. Returned to the trunk and came out with a six-pack of empty longnecks. "Targets," he said. "Nobody close. People who hear'll think coyotes."

Grace set her beer on the hood and accepted the gun. Easy to grip but way heavier than it looked.

"Pistol," he said, "revolver's the kind you can see the bullets." He reached up and touched her chin. "Just as soon you kept this between us," he said. "Not even Mick. What we do is private. You okay with that?"

Grace nodded. There was something dangerous about this guy. Where Hammond was slick and organized, Fitz was rough and lone-wolf. Neither were regular citizens. Hammond was teaching her scams. Who better than Fitz to teach her to shoot?

It took a while but she finally broke a bottle.

Fitz clapped. "Have to take a second job to keep you in ammo," he said, smashing her to him in what he considered a hug.

18

EVELYN DIDN'T TAKE HER EYES off the highway as she dug in her purse for the cell phone. A few hours after dark the big ranches had finished their day's work, loaded their trailer rigs with cattle and hay, and sent them rolling toward Bonners Ferry or Sandpoint. Those big trucks and tired drivers could be all over the road and you had to be careful. She flipped the phone open, listened.

"Hey, I just saw you ahead of me."

She thought she recognized the voice.

"Going home," she said. "Long day."

"Pull over for a sec, I got you a present."

"Uh, give it tomorrow. I'll be at work."

"Can't. Really, it'll take less than a minute. Pull over at that dirt road with the mailbox."

Evelyn thought it over. In the past couple of months she'd been given several presents and most she'd been able to sell to girlfriends in Plains for more cash. Could be anything from a bracelet to an iPod. She put the phone away, knowing that her brake lights would signal her decision, and concentrated on spotting the unlit gap in the tree cover. Tiny rocks pinged off her undercarriage as she edged off the road and moved forward to give the trailing car room to pull in.

Looking in the mirror all she could see was the glare of his headlights. She tried to see if she was right about the voice, but he kept in the headlight shine as he walked toward her. All she got was the dark silhouette.

He stopped before he reached her window. "Come on out. I don't want to reach it through."

"Only for a minute."

"Sure."

She opened the door and swung her legs out, started to stand and got jerked off her feet as he tugged her the rest of the way out. She got a whiff of alcohol as he pulled her close.

"Wha—"

He hit her hard in the ribs and doubled her over. Pulled her upright immediately.

She got air and tried again. "Why are—"

He shook her, making her teeth rattle. "You think you're so goddamn—"

It was a reaction. She didn't even think as she slapped him as hard as she could, right in the face. She didn't see his return punch coming but she felt it ruining her jaw and then a blinding pain in the back of her head.

He was not expecting her to crumple. He grabbed her by the shoulders, hauled her up and shook her again. Her head rolled side to side with no resistance. She was out cold. He looked at her more closely, held her up in front of him. She was limp. Worse, she didn't seem to be breathing.

When he lowered her to the ground he noticed the dark spot on the window. More closely, he saw ooze and a bit of hair at the top corner of the car door that had been left open in the tussle. If the back of her head hit that when he punched her . . . He touched the point. Blood. On the metal edge and on the rubber insulator, and drops, the first one he'd already seen, inching down the window. He knelt and turned her head to the side. More blood, a lot of it in her hair and down her neck. Put his ear to her lips. Nothing. To her nose. Nothing. Hand on her diaphragm. Nothing.

Shit!

Still kneeling beside her, he looked both ways. Headlights just coming around the curve maybe a half mile ahead. He took her wrists, pulled her away from the road and over to the far side of his vehicle. Jumped in, jammed off his headlights, started his engine. Jumped out and ran to open his passenger door. Lifted her into the seat. Hustled back and made a right turn onto the dirt road, goosed it and coasted, engine off now, into a nook in the trees. Hit the parking brake hoping it wouldn't flash his rear lights. Seconds later the eastbound car whirred past.

When he ran back to the highway, it was clear in both directions. He had at least thirty seconds. He slid into her seat, started her car and reversed it into the unpaved road, peering through her rear window to guide him. In the nightglow he was able to pick up the lighter color of the graded dirt as he moved maybe a hundred yards down until another recess presented itself. He put it in drive and wheeled the sedan forward far enough to conceal it from the highway. Where did this road go? He may have been on it fishing once or twice, thought it went in another mile or so to a ranch and barn not far from the Clark Fork. It would do.

He grabbed her purse and coat and ran with them, opening

his door and tossing them in on top of her. Got in. Got out and ran back to her car tearing his shirt off, then his T-shirt, and used that to wipe down her door handle and steering wheel and gear shift with a swipe at the keys. Ran back, made a U, and headed west on the highway.

He was breathing so hard the windshield was fogging. He lowered the windows and the cool air braced him, like a slap, getting his attention. Brief picture: Standing holding the bars in a cell the size of a coffin. Not him. That wasn't going to happen.

First, dump the body. He knew just the place. He'd read that bodies bloat with gas, bob up to the surface. Not this one. He had a tire iron to puncture her stomach. Second, clean up. To get it right he knew he'd need help, knew he needed to make a call. When there was no answer he left a message. Cell phone to cell phone, private, he told what happened, where he was going, and what he was going to do. Give a heads-up so help would be ready.

19

SOME PEOPLE WENT LOOKING FOR TROUBLE. Mick's dad said no need. Trouble will find you. Okay. Sixteen years old, Mick knew trouble. Lived with it, ran with it. Made it through the worst times. With any luck at all, he was done with trouble.

At the beginning of summer, Mick got a part-time job stocking and doing warehouse work for Hammond's hardware store and the nearby feed store. Started saving money for school sports fees.

Grace continued working for Hammond's motel and café as a maid and waitress, just upped her hours. JJ got a job mornings with county recycling. Queen of the cans!

Turned out Grace usually got Tuesdays off, and a couple of days a week neither the feed store nor the hardware needed any grunt work, so there were some afternoons that Grace, JJ, and Mick hung around together.

In mid-July Mick had an idea. Simple. Obvious, really. Maybe a great idea that would speed things up between him and Grace. The three of them had all afternoon off. Time enough to go to a private swimming place up on the Salish River. Mick figured if JJ went, Grace was more likely to come along.

A tiny glitch: Jon. The ten-year-old overheard Grace and JJ talking while they were getting ready. He threatened to run to the Conoco and tell Mick's father that Mick was taking the Pontiac without permission. Extortion. Okay, it might mess up their privacy, but on the other hand, maybe it would make Mick seem more generous and mature. Truth, he was dizzied by the idea of Grace in fewer clothes and agreed to take the kid.

As they piled in the car, Mick noticed the girls didn't seem to be carrying bathing suits and didn't seem to have any on under their jeans and shirts.

Grace caught him looking. "Don't have any," Grace said. "We'll swim in our clothes."

"You don't have to get your clothes wet," he said, letting his imagination run.

"They'll dry," JJ said.

They drove past the popular swimming area on the Clark Fork under the bridge at the east end of town and took Salish River Road north to a spot JJ'd shown him an earlier time he'd "borrowed" his dad's car. Almost nobody ever drove that road in summer when fishing was poor.

Two miles past where the narrow pavement turned to dirt, the road got steeper, trees thick on either side. Even in July, the shade in the small canyon let the bordering grass stay green. They parked at a curve and walked about a hundred yards back to a cliff-faced bend that created a pool a few feet deep. It was maybe forty feet across, with weak current until you got to the end of the hole and the water took off again. Private, bordering on cozy.

JJ had a blanket for them to sit on and a beat-up life vest for Jon to wear so he wouldn't drown. When they got to the gravel beach, JJ and Jon began fighting over the vest. Jon wouldn't wear it. JJ tried to make him. Jon flung it into the current and it disappeared downriver. Case closed. Grace said well then, he couldn't go in the water. Jon pulled away from JJ, ran and jumped in, clothes and all. Another case settled. Mick told JJ and Grace to go ahead and let the kid drown. Be less trouble in the long run. Jon didn't hear that. He was already diving, looking for trout.

Mick took off his shirt and lay down on the blanket to warm up before going in that cold water. Grace shed her jeans, sat down beside him in shirt and briefs. That might have embarrassed JJ, because she started walking, following the riverbank upstream.

Grace watched her leave. "She'll be back in a while," she said, nodding at JJ.

The river made its own sweet noise, and Mick was lying close enough to Grace to hear her breathing. Such a good day, such a good idea. Sunny, warm, pure brilliant, and he'd made it happen. He tried not to stare at Grace. Mostly kept his eyes on the water. Pictured her, instead, in his mind's eye. Began imagining what it would be like if they were a couple. What it would be like to kiss her. Pretty exciting. A little too exciting. He needed to calm down. Mick didn't have much experience with girls. Better to keep his eyes closed for a while and put his mind on something else. Football? He wasn't sure it was possible.

Jon's yelling jerked Mick into the present. Jon, the little dickwad that blackmailed Mick into bringing him along. Right away Mick figured Jon was caught in the current, getting swept away. He scanned and saw the kid across the river tugging on a log in an eddy. Mick shouted at him to stop because the thing could drown him; could catch on his clothing and roll him under. Mick could see there was already something stuck on it. A rag or a mop.

But he was wrong. Jon had hold of a body.

IN A SECOND A LOT CAN GO THROUGH YOUR MIND. You watch junior year go down the drain. You give up the idea of playing football. You drop the dream you're going to get together with Grace. You see your friendship with JJ disappear. And then a hope fights its way in. An idea. With a little bit of luck, you could skate around this. You could get out of here without being seen. You could say we were never here. You might not even have to lie. You could just return Dad's car and shut up. You're not in a hole. This didn't happen.

Mick had never thought much about luck. His dad said you make your own luck. If Mick had thought about it before, he'd have said today was his lucky day, his dream come true. JJ, Grace, and him swimming. Anything could happen, most of it good. Might even get a kiss. Or more.

Grace's scream yanked him back to the present.

He'd frozen, watching Jon struggle to drag the thing to shallower water. Mick didn't move till Grace yelled at Jon to let it go, to get away and come back here. That got Mick started and then he was yelling, too. "Don't touch that!" Mick was splashing through the water to grab him.

"Just a sec!" Jon didn't turn around, busy tugging. "It's caught on something. I almost got it."

Mick could hear Grace clambering behind him. He reached Jon first and pinned the boy's arms. The body washed around, rubbery-looking. It was a girl, high school or college. Grace reached them and helped Mick break Jon loose. Half wading, half swimming, they pulled him back to the beach side of the river.

"Let me go, damn it!" Jon was kicking at them. "I almost had it. It's hung up on something."

Mick held Jon while Grace began picking up anything they

had brought. Her jeans and his shirt, a beer can that didn't even belong to them.

Mick put his face close to Jon's. "Listen up! We got to get out of here. If the police think we had anything to do with her, even finding her, they might search our places and then everybody'd be screwed big-time."

Jon looked at Mick for the first time. Considering. He finally got it.

"Crap!" Jon said. "I was going to save her."

She didn't stink yet, but Mick knew the girl was way beyond saving. He didn't say that. He said, "Help us make sure we got everything."

Mick saw Jon picking up bits of glass and pieces of paper while he brushed away their footprints on the beach, his mind racing. What if the police believed they did it? What if the law searched their places and found his dad's stash, and guns, and the stolen tools that connected him with thefts in other towns? What if cops found Gary's dope and who knows what else they kept in that trailer? Their folks would go to jail and Mick and Grace and JJ would wind up in juvie.

Behind him, Grace's voice broke into his thoughts again. "JJ!"

Right. JJ had split when Grace took off her jeans. Walking somewhere. They all began yelling her name, hoping she wasn't too far away to hear.

21

WHILE JON WAS SWIMMING, JJ was trying to shed her disappointment about Mick and Grace. She had headed away from the gravel beach, upriver past the huge dark rocks that reminded her of buildings, some of them thirty or forty feet tall, carved and polished, and hard to climb but she'd done it before. That day, no, she was just meandering.

In a small clearing she crossed drag marks to the river's edge. There were gouges in the soil and some broken branches close to the riverbank. A big raft? There was a large enough gap in the brush that something like that could be launched. In the dirt near the edge of the water a bright glitter caught her eye. Kneeling, she found a black jewel, square, inlaid with a silver design, a small diamond in the middle. Never seen anything like it before. It was small, about the size of a stamp, but it was elegant, like something a king would wear. She shined it on her shirt and put it in her pocket.

As she stood again, she saw a slender ghost moon hanging above the western ridge. Its faint glow in the daylight sky lifted her thoughts, back to the familiar daydream, up through evergreens, up above the sparkling river, up through the clouds, her outstretched fingers trailing in the thin blue sky, until space turned dark and the moon became a huge powdered disk.

She didn't imagine looking down, didn't want to think of her friends holding hands or kissing. That would drop her, hard, to the canyon floor.

When she reached the moon, she didn't stop at the glowing part. She never did. She sailed around to that far side nobody sees. She glided to her castle with its stone walls and towers and pointed spires, through the huge arched door, through the great hall under the flickering torches, up to the throne in front of the tapestry. And there, she turned. And sat. And waited for someone. Waited because the throne was wide enough for two, wide enough to lie down with someone and begin a kingdom. She knew it was a fairy tale, but she let herself stay there. Chose to be there. Chose the castle. Safe, comfortable, her other home.

She couldn't stand to be around Grace and Mick when he was flirting. Couldn't stand to watch Grace tolerate him. Couldn't stand to see him so oblivious, to see him sniff around Grace like a dog. It was pathetic.

At some point the yelling broke through her dream and she had to shake her head to clear the images before she could move. She guessed it was some kind of trouble with Jon. She skirted the boulders and took the road back toward the car. Close, she saw them cleaning up the beach area. That made no sense.

"What happened?"

"Found a naked girl!" Jon, proud as punch.

Mick was all business. "Get in. We'll tell on the way."

JJ shrugged his hand off her arm. "Who? Show me."

Jon grabbed her hand and led her to the water's edge, pointing across the stream to the still eddy under the cliff.

Grace came behind them, getting hold of Jon by his wet shirt. "Doesn't matter who," she said, nodding across the water. "We got to go."

JJ shaded her eyes. "Is that Cassel's girlfriend?"

That question echoed above the noise of the river. Mick might have grimaced. Not something he wanted to hear.

Grace shook her head and began tugging Jon back to the car. The kid was grinning like the information was a wad of dollars.

22

AT THE CAR, Jon was jabbering, full of questions. Grace pushed him into the backseat, hopped in, and pulled the door shut, shushing him the whole time. Mick jumped in the driver's seat and cranked the engine while JJ piled in beside him, slamming the passenger door. He made the U-turn, stopped, got out, and smudged the tire tracks they'd made parking. It didn't come to him that he might be wrecking other tracks as well. He tore out, dust barreling behind them.

"Cassel's!" Jon crowed.

Grace shushed him again, harsh.

"Killed her," Jon getting the last word. Obnoxious.

"Killed?" JJ asked, looking at Mick.

"We don't know," he said. "Could have drowned."

"Everybody shut up," Grace said.

Her words held while the engine burred and the gravel sprayed and rattled against the car. After a few minutes they got on the pavement and the noise settled, but there was no more conversation on the ride home.

When Mick pulled off Main and into their dirt parking lot, Grace kept hold of Jon to keep him from jumping out.

"Nobody says a word about this," Grace said. "We went swimming right where the main highway crosses the river. Right under the highway bridge there. We never drove up River Road." She was looking right at Jon when she was saying this. "Promise."

Jon pulled his arm out of her grip and scowled. Finally nodded his head.

JJ didn't move.

Grace and Jon got out, walked to their trailer.

Mick turned to look at JJ. "You got something to say?"

She kept looking forward.

"JJ?" he pressed her.

A tear slid down her cheek. "You're hopeless," she said. "Blind, but it doesn't matter now."

She was wrong. It did matter. Mick should have asked her what she meant. Should have asked her what she was thinking, but he was preoccupied. His mind on what he was going to do next.

Mick waited until JJ was inside the Stovalls' single-wide before he drove off to find a pay phone and call 911. He wasn't going to give them his name. Just the real location so the girl could be retrieved and given to her family.

JJ's words about the floater being Cassel's girlfriend had really upped the ante. Mick guessed she meant Tim, the son, but she could have meant the father. After their school run-in last spring, JJ had told Mick more about Tim's dad. Scott Cassel—Montana Highway Patrol officer, based in Portage with particular jurisdiction over the roads in Sanders County and the surrounding area. The man had a reputation. Nobody in a fifty-mile radius messed with Scott Cassel.

Years ago, according to Gary Stovall, a speeder tried to shoot him when he approached the guy's car to give him a ticket. Gary says he was tough before that. After that, he was just plain nasty. Nasty enough that his wife left him. JJ said she moved across the country. His older son, Larry, was on his own, but his younger son, Tim, was stuck with him. *He* could beat the boy, but no one else was allowed to.

Tim would graduate next year. This year he'd been suspended a week for drinking at school. Barely kept out of jail, so far, by the influence of his dad and Mr. Hammond. Everybody Mick knew was afraid of the Cassels. He thought any of them might be capable of hurting a girl and, if things went wrong, if she made them mad, maybe even killing her.

23

LUCK. FATE. You can have good sense most of the time, take precautions, make good decisions, make a few mistakes and correct them, but once in a blue moon you screw up at the same time that other things go wrong—little things. Maybe Mick had just made a few mistakes, all at once. He could see that it wouldn't take too many small things to turn his bad luck into a train wreck.

He'd gone to the river park on the east end of town and reported the body. When he got back, he parked his dad's Pontiac where he remembered it had been. His father noticed these things. People, not so much. Unless they were a danger to him. Being a crackerjack mechanic made it easy for him to get jobs. It also fit his hobby, restoring old cars. The Poncho was his latest, a '72 Bonneville four-door hardtop that ran like NASCAR and looked like a rusted Batmobile. Ratmobile. The body and interior were always last in his dad's restoration process and he rarely got to them before he was on to the next car.

Dad, Tighe "Fitz" Fitzhugh, got home a little later than usual, carrying a heavy sack.

Groceries.

"You didn't work today?" He set the sack on the small table where they usually ate. Lifted out a bag of crushed ice and put it in the cooler on the floor. "Better use that milk tomorrow," he said. "I'm starting to smell it."

He pulled a Bosch rotary hammer drill and a heavy-duty DeWalt power saw from the tote.

Definitely not groceries.

Fitz looked out the door to see no one was watching, and then held the saw up to the light, inspecting it. "Barely been used," he said. He looked around for a place to put it and decided on the canvas duffel where he stored car tools. Saw Mick looking.

"Just left it lying around that work project up there." He gestured with his head toward north Main where the local chiropractor was adding a room to his office. "Must be broke," he said. "I'll fix it later."

Broke. Right. His dad was starting again, in spite of his promise. Mick wadded up a poem he'd been working on. Why bother? And he still hadn't met anyone to stay with.

Years ago, drunk and reminiscing, his dad had told Mick he'd started "finding things" in the army. "Just a little touch now and then to boost my pay." Usually, his father maintained the fiction that he found things, broken things that others discarded.

Sometimes Fitz ignored that idea like he'd never said such a thing and stole big. The pickup from the mall parking lot, electronic gear from the warehouse where they'd fought the guard, the tool trailer and generator from the construction site.

Mick knew from past experience that since his dad wasn't doing any carpentry work himself, he could have that saw and drill sold by tomorrow afternoon . . . unless he was planning to wait and boost the whole battery-powered outfit and move it for a kit price.

Mick never figured out why his dad pretended about the little stuff. He had made Mick go with him twice, so it wasn't for his son's benefit. Maybe he couldn't quite admit it to himself, the kind of person he was. And Mick . . . could he admit it? Could he live with another family and be done with the man?

"You didn't work?" his father asked again, sitting down on the cooler and turning to face Mick.

"Stores didn't need anybody today. Restock doesn't truck in till tomorrow."

"You going to make enough to be ready for school? Think they might be charging for extra stuff now." His dad didn't usually give him money, like that would undermine Mick's independence.

"Don't need much," Mick said, "only extra is football, far as I know." He already had five or six hundred dollars in checks under his mattress and thirty or forty cash under his pillow.

"Well," his dad said, "you're big enough for football."

"We found a body today." Mick didn't know why he told him. Probably just to goad him. His dad being so smug about stealing—stuck in Mick's craw.

"The hell!"

"Girl," Mick added, "maybe drowned, or maybe worse. We cleaned up after ourselves and left. Too late to do anything for her."

"We?"

"Me and Grace." Mick didn't know why he left JJ and Jon out. Oh. Yes he did. If his dad asked Grace, she'd automatically lie to him. The other two wouldn't. "East, under the highway bridge on the river," Mick finished.

"Didn't tell anybody?" his dad asked, again checking out the front door to see if they could be overheard.

Dovey's trailer was about a hundred feet away, but sometimes she was in the parking area picking up trash the wind had scattered. As clerk, she did most of the paperwork for the justice of the peace and the sheriff's office. She knew everything that happened in the whole county and his dad thought she was nosy as hell.

Mick shook his head. He didn't plan to mention the 911 call.

"Don't say another word. Don't beg trouble."

Mick had known that would be his father's position.

"Let's eat," his dad said, standing abruptly and jerking the cooler open. He grabbed the borderline milk and set it down too hard, sloshing some on the table. Snatched the lunch meat and package of cheese, pitched them alongside the milk. "Get the peanut butter and that grape crap."

Mick hurried to retrieve the sandwich fixings. His dad was mad. Mad at Mick, mad at the body, mad at the world. Mick didn't get it. If his dad had stayed put and just worked, he could have had his own shop by now. Maybe even his own home. You don't make money stealing. Can't ever fence it for what it's worth, but arguing with his dad had never changed anything.

Fitz's credo was live by your wits. If you're smart enough to find it and keep it, it's yours. Boasted that he'd never been arrested. "Dumb crooks get caught."

Was it the drugs that screwed up his dad's thinking? Lots of thieves got caught. Got jail time. For what? Nickels and dimes. His dad had a streak of outlaw in him. Gave Fitz pleasure to poke the law with a stick. Mick could feel it. Just a matter of time before "luck" ran out and one or both of them went to jail. Mick could kiss his life goodbye. What was a college degree from a penitentiary worth?

After the meal, Fitz left in the car, a familiar pattern. Making connections to sell what he took, Mick guessed, but his dad could have been looking for people who sold his kind of pills. Or maybe he just went to different bars, drank and played cards. Usually Mick smelled liquor on his dad's breath in the morning. Did his dad go looking for women? Did he give them money?

Mick was surprised to think that in several major ways, he hardly knew the man. As Mick got older, he and Fitz had sort of evolved into roommates. His father came and went, did as he pleased, rarely told Mick what he was thinking or doing. If his dad fled again, Mick wondered if he'd even miss him.

24

MICK ASKED GRACE TO GO UP to Skinny's with him to see if there happened to be any news about the body. JJ went, too, but at a distance. She wandered behind, looking at the sky and the illuminated signs along the highway.

He could smell the french fries cooking a hundred yards away. Knots of kids were hanging out together around the building, swatting bugs and sipping Cokes. As Mick got close, he could hear the buzz.

"From Plains . . . last year . . . Evans? Edmonds? . . . graduated . . ."

Mick glanced at Grace. No sign. Had she seen the girl before? He knew he hadn't. They stood around. Listened. Mick bought a coffee and shared it.

"Sounds like she could have worked in the café. You know her?" Mick talked low, right in Grace's ear. He wished he'd visited the café. At least once. Bought a cup of coffee. Watched Grace work. Left her a good tip.

"I might've seen her. Probably not," she whispered back, but she didn't meet his eyes.

He knew right then she was lying. Didn't he? Wanting Grace, acting cool to impress her, kept him from asking more questions that could have made a difference. Mr. Hammond owned the Rock Point Motel and Grill on the north end as well as the motel and café in town. He was somehow connected with county social services, assisted with foster care placements, and provided a fair number of jobs to teenagers. He liked to hire good-looking girls. The more Mick thought about it, how could Grace not have at least met the girl?

"Didn't she even look familiar?" he asked.

"I didn't really look at her," Grace said. "Too creepy." She shook her head. "Nobody's safe," she said, annoyed.

A girl in the group of kids next to them said, "You got that right," not realizing that Grace was talking to Mick.

They'd been whispering, maybe not soft enough. Mick looked around but everybody seemed zeroed in on their own friends. He took Grace's hand and they edged a little closer to one of the bigger groups, blending, catching the news. ". . . Drowned? . . . waitress . . . reputation . . ."

He tried one more time. "Think one of the Cassels killed her?"

If Grace heard him, she gave no sign.

Mick remembered JJ and scanned the crowd. Spotted her sitting out by the highway on the concrete block that anchored the drive-in's sign. Waiting for the sliver of moon to clear the clouds, watching traffic, the kind of thing she usually did. JJ was right. She was almost invisible. She didn't usually join in and nobody paid her any attention.

A quick movement at the edge of the parking lot drew his eyes. Younger kids, squirreling around among the trees in the nearest yard. Mick could see the flash of Jon's face darting in and out among five or six others. He didn't tell Grace. She would think she needed to do something about it, grab him and haul him home or something. Mick knew that wouldn't work. Jon would hit her and run off until she gave up trying to deal with him.

In a corner of Skinny's in the same direction, Mick saw Tim Cassel and his lineman buddy, Cunneen, talking with some other ballplayers and a couple of cheerleaders. He and Grace continued to comb the crowd but avoided that bunch. Nobody at the drive-in seemed to know who the dead girl went out with, or what her dad did for a living. After another fifteen minutes, they collected JJ and went back home, knowing that they'd hear a lot more in the days to come.

Not telling Grace or JJ about seeing Jon was another mistake, one more little thing that caught up with him.

25

JJ LIKED TO WATCH the night traffic, follow the patterns of moving lights. More, she was happy waiting for the moon to clear the clouds, sneaking around like it had a secret. The evening sky had a washboard look, clouds thin, stretched by high winds. The moon made a soft glow traveling above them, peeking from time to time through small rifts. This moon . . . Banana? No, it was more special than that. A bright curve, pointed on both ends . . . like sideways horns. Longhorn Moon.

Her concentration was interrupted by something stinging the side of her thigh. Horsefly? She brushed her leg. Felt it. Inside. In her pocket. She drew out the dark jewel she'd found by the river. What could it have come from? A necklace? A ring? And how long had it been lying by the river? Who lost it? A fisherman? A rafter? Did he even know it? Could it be a woman's? Didn't seem like that kind of jewelry.

She looked at the stone more closely but the light wasn't really bright enough. Square, dark, glossy, the silver inlay a "V" with a small sparkly gem in the very middle. The pattern reminded her of a logo, or a crest, like in her castle. Or Egypt, that god-eye shape. She didn't think she'd seen this exact design before. She'd have to ask Gary.

Another thought. When she'd seen the body, it looked like a girl she'd seen Larry Cassel talking to three or four times. Once, basket to basket in the grocery store. Another time the girl looking in his car's passenger window as if he'd just honked at her. Last week, him smiling at her as they stood on the sidewalk in front of the café. That's why she'd said Cassel's girlfriend, but she had no idea whether it was true.

She held the jewel up in Skinny's neon illumination. Sell it? It looked valuable, exotic. Too beautiful to trade for cash. A wedding ring? No. Nobody had such a dark wedding ring. That was probably bad luck or something . . . and in that moment she had another thought. Could the jewel belong to the dead girl? Upriver, right by the water. But if she took it to the police, she'd have to tell them the whole story. No, she'd better ask Gary.

26

WHEN THEY GOT BACK TO THE COMPOUND, Mick was too restless to sleep. His dad was still gone. Mick lay on his bed, tried to read. Gave up and went to look at the river. Once in a while at night you'd see otter playing in the current. None tonight. Just JJ. Mick sat on the ground near her and stayed quiet, imagining that she never spent time in the trailer if she didn't have to.

She spoke first. "That girl. I tried to sleep but I kept seeing her."

"Up at Skinny's they said she was from Plains," Mick told her. "Waitress. Grace said she didn't know her."

"Somebody could kill me and nobody would notice," JJ said, picking up a small rock and throwing it in the river.

"No way. Me, Grace, the Stovalls. You don't think she drowned?"

JJ shook her head. "Alone, naked, no car? You think somebody could have dragged her to the water? Upstream a ways? Pushed her in?"

"Maybe. Did you see something?"

"Maybe." She looked up at the sky. "I need to ask Gary . . . I don't even know who my father was," she said.

Mick was losing her. Did the dead girl spin her out?

She went on, "I don't know how come I can play softball. Gary played catch with me maybe five times total. Think my real dad was a ballplayer?"

He didn't know what to say.

"I just tried it at recess one day and I could do it. I was as surprised as everyone else. I'm pretty good, but you came to the games. I don't think the girls on the team even know my name."

It could have been true. Mick never saw anybody but the coach talk to her.

"I was chubby until seventh grade and then I grew taller. Everybody in my classes for years? They didn't notice." She shook her head. "Nobody would take me . . ."

He saw tears in the corners of her eyes.

She gave him a weak smile, rose to leave.

Mick felt bad for her. Girl who didn't think she was pretty enough to kill. "What kind of moon is this?" he asked, shifting his look to the sky.

"Waning," she said. "Past gibbous."

Mick thought "gibbous" was a monkey. He didn't say that. "Name?" he asked.

She smiled again. "Um, Longhorn Moon," she said. "Or maybe it should be Death Moon. Dead Girl Moon."

She was right about that.

Mick reached out and touched her arm to stop her. He told her how he got his scar that went from the corner of his mouth to over by his ear. How he'd had it since he was ten. How he got it from one of the motels he and his father lived in after his mom split. How he was running, chasing a butterfly and not looking down, and tripped on a small brick wall the owner had put around a tree, probably so people wouldn't back their cars into it. How he fell headlong and crashed his face into the edge of the bricks and cut the whole side open. How his mom was long gone, but he still missed her.

"Zipper," she said.

Somehow Mick didn't mind it coming from her.

He still didn't tell her that his dad was a thief. He didn't think to tell her about seeing Jon when they were up at the drive-in, and he didn't talk about Grace. Mick liked JJ, but it wasn't the same. Grace had something he wanted. Mick was afraid to put a name to it.

27

THE HIGHWAY PATROL got the car and the probable site of the killing. Tuesday morning the ranch owner living at the end of the dirt road with the mailbox made his daily trip to town. Saw a red sedan in the narrow clearing. The car was small, not likely used by hunters, and the man thought little of it; someone walking a dog or taking pictures in the woods, whatever. That afternoon on his return trip he was surprised to see it still there. Lived down this road twenty years. Never seen a car parked in that spot.

The river was nearly a mile away through impassable brush. No ponds in the area. Not a destination by any means, so what was the car owner doing? He stopped, listened, walked to the car. Had a feeling. Stolen? A suicide with the body thirty feet into the woods? He called the Highway Patrol.

The first responding officer leaned in, saw the keys still in the ignition, and became very careful. Looking more closely, he saw spots and a dark stain at the sharp edge where the driver's window joined the frame. He backed away and radioed Cassel, his lieutenant, who immediately phoned the Missoula office for crime techs.

The tech team arrived by late afternoon. The car's door handle and steering wheel had been wiped clean of prints, but what was almost certainly blood remained on the window and doorframe. Following the tire prints, the traffic expert discerned the car had first been parked or stationary out by the highway and moved from there back to the nook in the trees.

A careful search where the car was first parked yielded a disturbed area where a scuffle might have taken place, a dark patch, still damp, probably blood, and a small off-white button from a shirt. The car itself, a ten-year-old Subaru, was registered to a man in Plains who told authorities that it was his daughter's car and that she commuted to Portage for work. He said she hadn't returned home last night and that he and his wife had assumed she was staying over with friends.

Mick's 911 call set the county sheriff's investigation in motion. Within forty minutes Sheriff Paint with his camera and a deputy carrying fishing waders were at the gravel beach on the river looking across to the body. Living this close to rivers and lakes, Paint had dealt with batches of drownings over the past thirty years. When his deputy got the girl to shore, Paint didn't notice the head injury, but the puncture wound in the stomach was obvious. Not drowning. He, too, called the state police in Missoula for crime scene help and found his was the second request from Sanders County in the past hour.

The fact that the body was snagged on a submerged limb on the far side of the river didn't necessarily mean that the body had been dumped there. Paint knew there was no access to that side for miles, plus objects in the water naturally drifted from one bank to another, depending on how the currents caught them. Since the body had apparently not been in the river all that long they decided to search the west bank, the roadside bank, upstream. It was close to dark by the time the state investigators arrived. They set up lights over a large perimeter and began a grid search of the beach area.

Six a.m. Wednesday a team member located the probable dumping site approximately a thousand yards upstream from the gravel beach. Examination led to a puzzle. Marks at the riverbank indicating the girl had been disrobed there and then dragged or pushed into the water. Underneath the willow and berry cover at water's edge a deputy recovered blond hairs and white thread.

Broken branches, bent vines, and gouged earth in the immediate clearing suggested a struggle had taken place. There was surprisingly little blood on the ground, given the nature of the stomach wound. The signs of violence were inconsistent with the Highway Patrol's initial report that the girl was probably killed miles away on Highway 200. They had most of the blood there, so how did a dead girl put up such a fight here?

Three sets of footprints were identified, the larger ones entering from the west, probably from the nearby road, the smaller size nine from the south, but it was impossible to discern the gender of the print makers or to follow the prints past the small clearing as the area was too rocky.

Not nearly enough information to narrow the search for a killer.

28

YEAH, SHE LOOKED FAMILIAR. Evelyn. Evelyn Edmonds. Pretty, eager, stupid. Ev and her sex scam. Actually, Grace had thought the plan might work. Not a bad idea, but such a small town. What were the odds somebody wouldn't catch her, bust her, or cut in on her profits?

Grace had watched the girl wink and linger with several of the male customers that ate alone. Truckers and tourists mostly. Evelyn would ask where they were staying, make a plan to meet. A few local guys, too. Some high school guys got wind of it and tried to make a deal, Tim and Cunneen in that group, but Evelyn shooed them off. Wouldn't take that big a risk. Maybe statutory if she got caught.

At least once a month, Hammond and his group—Bolton, Mackler, and Greer—came in for a meal. Cookie had filled Grace in. The Gang of Four, Five if you counted Scott Cassel. Teammates from high school, what, twenty years ago? Buddies that had returned after college and built a small empire. Sam Hammond used his inherited family money to start several operations that figured regularly in the town's gossip.

Since he left Cookie alone to manage the café, Grace didn't see Hammond all that often, and except for the monthly get-togethers, she never ran into most of the others. Mr. Highway Patrol stopped in for lunch once in a while.

At the partners' get-together in late April, Grace had waited their table while Evelyn did her thing on the other side of the room. The men made a study out of minding their own business, but they caught the game. For all Grace knew, they ran girls of their own. She'd heard a lot of whispering about kickbacks, gambling, blackmail, even prescription drugs from Canada made available to preferred hardware and feed customers.

Seemed to her like a pretty good setup. Hammond owned several businesses, ran real estate, brokered loans, sold commercial insurance. Bolton the main judge in municipal and superior courts, Greer the banker, Mackler at Human Services controlled the labor pool and was in a good position to obtain insider info about local families. The lawman, Scott Cassel? Grace wasn't sure. Larry Cassel, Scott's older son? She heard Hammond used him for collection work. Grace had been waitressing enough to learn more secrets than a priest or a hairdresser.

Not long after that particular dinner, Judge Bolton's car was waiting in the parking lot when Grace got off work. Waiting for Evelyn? That had been Grace's guess. Then another coincidence. A few days later, Greer's car.

Grace had decided to use the girl as a canary. Keep an eye on her. If Evelyn dropped over, the air was poison.

Since that time, she'd done Hammond's bidding once or twice a week. Cookie always paid her in cash. And, as Hammond had mentioned, when the arrangement continued to go well, Cookie relayed new assignments. She began keeping a more detailed log of the dates when a particular man or woman ate in the restaurant or visited the motel and who they accompanied. She was given a tiny voice-activated tape recorder to hide and later retrieve in specific motel rooms the days that she did cleaning. Occasionally she received phone numbers and instructions to use a sexy voice to call particular homes, quizzing wives about their husbands' whereabouts.

Grace figured this was a small sampling of Hammond's arsenal to bring resistant businessmen around to his way of thinking. She heard that Hammond had much harsher ways at his disposal to put pressure on people. Cookie and others said Larry Cassel played that role.

In a way, Hammond had inspired her. Using her continuing silence as a lever, Grace got Ev to agree on a "finder's fee" for every customer Grace sent her way. Grace heard a concept she liked—broaden your income stream. She could do that.

But Ev's killing had come out of nowhere. Grace was more than surprised, she was rocked. Scared. She'd imagined that Ev might be told to quit her sideline . . . or even arrested, but murder? Grace hadn't seen that coming. It shook her to realize she had no sense of her own risk level. Was she next, or was she suddenly in a position to make even more money? She had no idea, and her stomach had been churning since she recognized the girl in the water.

Now Grace wondered whether that pretty Latina girl had left

on her own a few weeks before. The girl she replaced as courier? Ramona no-showed. Hadn't said a word to anybody about leaving. And nobody raised an eye. Cookie got Evelyn to cover the day, found another girl to take the rest, done and over. Just like that, she was gone like Evelyn would have been if Jon hadn't found her.

29

THE DAY AFTER THEY FOUND THE BODY, Wednesday, Grace made herself go to work. Bonnie, Ramona's replacement on breakfast shift, was still there, finishing the lunch crowd. Ev had worked with Grace Monday, Grace had Tuesday off, so how was Cookie going to handle Ev's murder? One way or another he knew about it. The whole town was buzzing.

At one-thirty a new girl came in, bone skinny, black slacks, white top, hair back in a twist. Cookie brought her over, introduced her, and dismissed Bonnie. Like before with Ramona, no mention of anything about a change.

Grace was left standing behind the counter with the girl, fighting nerves that were getting worse like the old days, when her parents told her good night and left her alone to get ready for bed. Grace made herself focus, made herself talk to what's-her-name . . . Meryl. Weird name. She looked fifteen, undeveloped, tall, thin, dark circles around her eyes that didn't come from makeup. The girl put both hands on the counter, looked at them, took them off. Put one foot on top of the other. Unsure what to say or do. Grace remembered feeling that kind of awkwardness. Not so long ago, really.

"Lived here long?" Grace folded a counter towel, tried to seem polite, not nosy.

"I'm from Lonepine," the girl said. It rushed out like she was relieved to have a chance to say something.

Grace didn't know where that was. "So what're you doing here?"

"Things weren't good at home. I . . . my caseworker gave me . . . I got sent here for placement."

"Great. That's kind of how I started. How'd you get this job?" Grace already knew the answer.

The rest of the day Grace kept expecting Cookie to pull her aside, say something. When he didn't, her worry ratcheted another notch higher. Business as usual in the café when the customers couldn't seem to talk about anything else but the killing? Grace was having trouble remembering orders, trouble carrying things.

The new girl gave her a look. Asked her, "Want some help?"

Grace ignored her. Left late afternoon complaining of a headache.

30

MICK GOT HOME FROM WORK A LITTLE AFTER FIVE, sore from lifting and carrying bags of seed, crates of nails, rolls of metal fencing. Unload them, shelve some, stack the extra in the warehouse. Nine hours straight. Okay with him. Get in shape for football.

His hands were stiff and clumsy and he was having trouble turning the pages on his library book when he heard tires crunching on gravel. Figured his dad had gotten off early and was firing up the Bonneville to go somewhere.

"Hey! Come back here!"

Not Dad.

A glance through the window showed him a black Mustang. Tim Cassel standing in front of it clapping a heavy black-metal cop's flashlight against his open hand, smiling like he was planning to enjoy swinging it. Beside Tim, holding an ax handle, the smaller nut-kicker guy who'd attacked Mick after track with the two other apes. When Mick got up for a better look, he saw JJ, facing them, backed up against the porch in front of her trailer. Jon was peeking out from behind the screen door.

"You been spreading manure." Cassel, loud enough for the neighborhood to hear. He was a couple of inches taller than his buddy but they both weighed about the same, a little under two hundred.

Nut-kicker had a neck like a barrel. Whacked the ax handle on the ground, raising a flash of dust.

Mick wondered if Mr. Stovall had a gun. He knew his dad had guns, but they were locked. Mick grabbed the putter Fitz used for a walking stick and went outside.

"Back off!" Mick came up to them on Tim's side, holding the putter down by his leg.

"Well, well, Zipper Woods," Tim said. "I heard you were in it, too."

"Get out of here," Mick said, stopping about fifteen feet to their front, between them and JJ. "We don't have anything going with you. Nothing. Zero." His voice slipped on that last word. Croaked. He could smell himself, rank, like fear had an odor.

"I never talked about Tim," JJ said, behind Mick. "Never think of him."

"Not what I hear, Bull Butt." Cassel hitched his jeans like he was readying to move quick. "You're saying couple, me and that Edmonds girl."

"Never did," JJ said. "Git before you do something even stupider."

Mick stayed on the balls of his feet, ready for Cassel's charge. Heard the Stovall trailer screen door slam. JJ going in, he hoped. If she was safe he could move behind the broken-down Chevy. Avoid a bloodbath.

"Can I help you boys?" Gary Stovall's voice, pleasant as could be.

Mick kept his eyes on the bullies, ready for their next move.

"Your kid's been telling lies about me," Tim said. "Apology won't cut it. Lesson's got to be learned."

Mick could imagine Scott Cassel saying those same words. Or maybe the other guy's dad, knocking him to the floor and punishing him in ways that wouldn't show at school. He knew about that. His own dad had beat him a few times.

They were glaring, breathing hard, pumping up to hurt somebody, and Mick could feel them getting ready to spark.

"You fellows know what this is," Gary said. "I know you do."

Mick wanted to turn around and look but he didn't. They might throw something.

"You think it's not loaded?" Gary asked. "Triple-aught, full choke," he said. "Blow a hole right through you and your ride, and I don't care if your father is Wyatt Earp."

"You wouldn't shoot us, you junkie piece of shit."

Probably Tim talking, but Mick had spaced out, getting ready to move.

Gary didn't say anything.

Then Grace's voice. "Sheriff's coming!"

Might be yelling this through the screen.

Gary again: "You want to explain this to your dad?"

They stayed in place for a few more seconds and then Tim turned on his heel.

The other guy was in the car before Tim finished saying, "We'll be back."

31

"YOU WANT TO COME IN HERE A MINUTE?"

Mick turned to see Gary on the front steps of his trailer, holding a 12-gauge. He followed the man inside and had to keep himself from gagging. The odor was thick. Toilet, sour laundry, old garbage. The trailer was almost always like this.

Tina was on the couch, lying down, napping with most of her legs showing.

Gary tapped her on the shoulder. "Could we have a minute to figure something out here?" he asked her quietly. "You can rest in the bedroom. I'll go turn on the fan."

Tina had trouble gathering herself to get up. JJ moved to help her stand and took her arm, steadying, as they followed Gary to the back. When Tina was off the couch, a new wave of smell was released. Mick didn't know how the others could put up with it.

Jon peeked his head out of the bathroom and closed the door again.

Gary came back in a minute, walking behind JJ and Grace. As he passed, he opened the bathroom. Jon yelled. Gary didn't say anything, reached in and tugged Jon out by the arm, towed him to the kitchen table, where he sat on the bench and pulled Jon down beside him. He broke the double-barrel open, took out the shells, and stuck them in his shirt pocket. Leaned the gun on the wall behind him.

JJ and Grace stood facing him. Mick was still standing just inside the front door.

"I need to hear something from somebody," Gary said. He was his old self, quiet, low-key. You'd never know he'd just backed down two creeps with clubs. He took hold of Jon and aimlessly sorted through some diodes or some such on the table. After a little bit of silence he looked up at Grace.

"I don't know," she said. "I haven't said word one about the Cassels. I know what they're like."

Gary's gaze moved to JJ. He'd seen her flinch when Grace said "Cassels."

JJ was shaking her head. "I didn't say he did anything," she said.

Gary turned to Mick, clearly puzzled.

Mick was equally stumped. JJ had asked if the dead girl wasn't Cassel's girlfriend. It was just a question. He couldn't imagine JJ talking about what they'd found to anybody else. She hardly spoke to anyone outside the compound.

"Uh, I remember hearing that maybe a Cassel had something to do with the dead girl," Mick said, looking briefly in JJ's direction, "but I didn't tell anybody. Not even Dad."

"The dead girl," Gary repeated.

"The girl they found in the river yesterday," Grace explained.

"You all know anything about that girl?" Gary asked.

Nobody spoke.

Then Jon. "JJ said Tim Cassel did it," he said, his eyes shining like somebody was going to get in trouble and he was going to enjoy it.

JJ's eyes cut toward the front door. She shook her head again.

Mick tried to remember. Tim? Didn't she just say Cassel's girl-friend? Maybe he didn't hear right. He hadn't been as close as Jon. Mick couldn't think what to say that wouldn't make things worse.

"JJ," Gary said, looking at her. "Did you say anything to any-body about the Cassels killing that girl?"

"I said 'Is that Cassel's girl?' is all. Once. Yesterday. I . . ." She tilted her head to include the rest of them as if they could help her.

"Not to nobody else?" Gary asked her. "Not a word?"

JJ shook her head. Eyes on the floor now.

"You believe that?" Gary asked all of them.

Mick nodded.

Grace said, "I do."

"Guess that only leaves one," Gary said, turning to look down at Jon.

"Bullshit!" Jon yelled. "JJ said Cassel did it. I heard her, up on River Road."

Mick was thinking about seeing Jon. Running with those other kids. And Jon would want to impress them. And some of them had older brothers and sisters who knew the Cassels.

"Who'd you tell?" Gary asked, gently pulling Jon to stand up.

"Nobody!" Jon said, starting to twist his arm against Gary's grip.

"He told the kids he was playing with up by the drive-in last night," Mick said. He knew it was true.

"Liar!" Jon screamed. He tore loose from Gary's grip and flew toward the front door.

The kid surprised Mick. He thought he could grab him but missed. Jon crashed out and was gone.

"Guess that explains it," Gary said. "You all want to help me hide some dope down by the river?"

Gary was busy collecting it from hidden compartments all over the trailer when Mick's dad knocked on the door.

"You lose this?" he asked Gary. He had Jon by the wrist and Mick knew his father's grip. Jon wasn't struggling.

"Yeah," Gary said. "You got anything you don't want the law to see, you might want to get it out of your place pretty quick. And then, maybe you and I better make a plan."

Part of the plan was Mick's dad taking JJ and Jon for a long drive so they wouldn't be around for questions if Scott Cassel showed up that evening. Mick knew JJ would be uncomfortable going in a car with his dad. His father made nice with her but JJ could read people. She told Mick, sorry, but she thought the man was missing something. Hollow. She didn't trust him.

Mick could understand that, but at least Fitz had kept Mick. His mom hadn't.

That evening, watching the three of them drive away, Mick knew that the way his dad had just dealt with Jon scared JJ.

Jon had been squirming and refusing to leave. His dad said he needed to talk to Jon alone and pulled the kid inside their place. Mick stood by the car with JJ. When the man and the boy came out a minute later, Jon was quiet, wooden. Didn't say a word when Mick's dad opened the car door.

Jon's eyes looked like he'd gotten soap in them, pink and irritated, and there was a trace of blood on his lips. He was more than scared, he looked stunned. Mick hadn't seen the kid like that before. He'd never seen him give up or quit arguing so quickly. What did his dad do to produce that effect? Mick had an idea. His father had scared the daylights out of *him* a couple of times.

"You okay?" JJ asked the boy.

Jon didn't look at her, didn't move or answer.

Mick's dad got in the car and cocked his head back to hear better. "What's that?"

"Nothing," JJ said. "Just thinking."

"No harm in that," the man said, putting the shift in drive, and they were gone.

MICK HAD TIME ALONE to ready himself for a visit from the law since his dad and the Stovall kids didn't figure to be back until after midnight. His dad had moved the "broken" goods, weapons, and drugs somewhere, probably in a hidey-hole off a country road. Mick had seen his dad unearth these stashes in other towns when they had to flee in a hurry.

Lieutenant Cassel arrived after dark. Mick heard the cruiser roll into the lot. Heard the man bang on the Stovalls' door. Saw Gary let him in. From his window Mick got a glimpse of Tina sitting upright on the couch.

Cassel knocked on Mick's wall a half hour later. The officer was big enough to fill the door and his face was red like he'd scraped it shaving. Mick smelled Right Guard and leather and tobacco.

"You're . . ." Cassel consulted a small spiral notepad he was carrying in his left hand. His gun was on the right side. "Fist-hugh?"

"Fitzhugh," Mick said. "Mickey Fitzhugh."

"You got a big mouth," the man said, raising his eyes to meet Mick's. "Tell me what you did to the girl."

Gary had coached them. *"Never answer more than he asks. Say as little as possible. Be polite. Look him in the eye. Don't look away when you're lying. If he gets nasty with you, take it. He's just trying to scare you into a mistake. Broken-record your story: Don't know the girl, swimming under the highway bridge yesterday, didn't hear about anything till you went to Skinny's last night, worked today. He asks who you were with, say Grace. Leave JJ and Jon out."*

"What girl?"

"You going to be smart with me?"

"No, sir."

Silence.

He took a couple of steps closer. "Live here alone?"

"No, sir. My dad's the mechanic up at the Conoco." Was that saying too much?

"Where's he?"

"I don't know. He sometimes plays cards over in Belknap."

"Upstairs? At the store?"

"I don't know."

"Did the girl tease you?" he asked. "Make you mad? Was it an accident?"

Mick couldn't think what to say that would back Cassel off.

"Do you understand English, boy?" Cassel took another step closer.

Behind him, at the door, Gary's voice. "Hey, Mick, you done yet? We're ready for that burger."

Cassel didn't move, but his face got redder. "Have you been telling people Tim's involved in this?" He asked that in a soft voice, but he looked angry enough to snap Mick's neck.

"No, sir. I don't know Tim."

"Tim says you do."

"I mean yeah, I know who he is. That he's your son. I've never talked to him. He, uh . . . ." Mick had been going to say that Tim and his friend were here today threatening, but Gary's earlier warning stopped him. Did Cassel know that? Could you get in trouble for carrying a concealed putter? Did Tim tell about Mick hitting him at school? "Tim is in the class ahead of me."

Gary, outside, broke in again. "Well, take your time. Grace and I'll just wait on your porch. No hurry." You could hear wood scraping as Gary moved something near the door, probably a box to sit on.

Cassel's eyes looked narrower for a second and then he seemed to ease up. He pulled a pen out of his shirt pocket and flipped to a new page in his notebook. "Mickey Fitzhugh," he said, writing carefully on the lined pages like it was some kind of legal document. "Phone?"

"Don't have a phone, sir," Mick said.

Cassel's eyes shot up again, assessing if the boy was fooling with him. He looked around the room. Shook his head. He walked to the side area past the beds and pulled back the curtain, exposing the toilet cubicle. Shook his head again. His eyes traced the perimeter of the room. Looking for a phone line? He saw the cooler by the kitchen table. Opened it. Lifted out a soggy package of bologna.

"Nice," he said, dropping it back in, leaving the lid on the floor. "Father's name?" He was moving slowly toward the door, looking at the walls and furnishings like he was memorizing the place.

"Fitz Fitzhugh," Mick said.

"First name!" Irritated.

"Tighe," Mick said.

Cassel gave him a long look. He didn't write down what Mick had said. "We need to have a talk at my office, son, sometime soon. A little more privacy. Sort out some of these details. Tell your father to come find me."

Mick expected Cassel to slam the door, but he didn't. He left quietly. The next sound Mick heard was the cruiser starting. Mick took a deep breath but it didn't do any good.

Gary and Grace came in and sat on the bed while Mick replaced the cooler lid.

"Sweet man," Gary said.

Grace was pulling at a strand of hair. Her foot was tapping. Second time in two days Mick had seen her shook-up.

"Think it might be a good idea for you all to take a little summer trip for a few weeks before school starts," Gary said, staring out the window at the dark parking area. "Tina's got a half sister in Spokane. I got family in Boise." He sighed. "We need a car."

Grace closed her eyes. Mick thought he knew what she was thinking: have to leave to save herself. Dollars to doughnuts she got here by running away from home.

Gary noticed. "You don't have to go," he said, turning toward her. "We just got to keep JJ and Jon away from Cassel and his spawn. Mick can drive them."

Grace raised her head and gave him a look. "Right. And who's going to take care of Jon? He'll leave JJ at the gate and Mick would have to kill him to get him to mind."

Mick wanted to say that she wasn't doing too well with Jon, as far as he could see, unless fighting and losing was what she considered getting him to mind.

"I bet JJ and Mick could handle him," Gary said. "Send the

meds along, and I got a little mad money stashed to keep them in food and a motel once in a while."

"That's the sad part," Grace said, holding Gary's eyes. "Jon's your kid and you don't even get him. He's so out of control. If Mick's dad hadn't grabbed him this afternoon, Jon'd be up in town right now telling more people that JJ said Cassel did the girl. He'll trash anybody, Gary. He doesn't care."

"Ah, hell, he's mostly mad at his mom. If he was away from her he'd settle down. Let's see what Fitz says when he gets back." Gary got up. "Come on, we'll go get that double-cheese just in case whatsit is parked up there to check out my story."

Grace stayed put. "You go," she said. "I want time by myself."

Mick didn't think Grace'd be there when they got back. He figured she was getting ready to find a new town.

MICK AND GARY got back from Skinny's long before his dad came back with JJ and Jon. The first thing Mick did was look for Grace. Gary opened the trailer door and Mick barged in, pinching his nose against the stink. He didn't see her. Not back in her bedroom or in Gary's, where Tina was snoring. He was down the steps running too fast to catch whatever Gary said. Checked his own place. Not there either. Outside again, Mick hustled to the Chevy. Walked around it. Gave up. She was already gone.

Gary was leaning on the railing of his small wood porch. "I said her clothes are still here."

That clicked something. Pretty sure she wouldn't leave without them. They'd just been up on Main Street, so she wasn't up there. Starlight let him see most of the crannies in the parking area. Scanning east, Dovey's trailer. To the south, he could make out the sage, scrub, the willows . . . he started running again. Found her sitting at the edge of the river. Crying.

She stopped when Mick knelt beside her. There didn't seem to be anything to say. The water filled the silence, the fast rush of current in the middle, the trickle over shallows by the bank. Across the river he could see bats darting and skimming, harvesting insects. Above them, torn clouds hesitated near a glob of moon while a jetliner glided west, barely more than a flashing dot.

Mick knew what he wanted to say. *"I love you. I'll protect you."* But he'd be the first to admit he didn't know what those words meant. Though she was only a grade above him, somehow she was years older than he was. She knew it, and he knew it, and love like he yearned for was out of the question. And if he ever said such a thing she'd split him open with a laugh or hit him. So what was there to say? *"I won't let Cassel hurt you"*? She'd been hurt before. Mick would bet on it. And Putter Boy was going to defend her? Not very damn likely. And just like that, Mick had a plan.

"You know how Dad took JJ and Jon for a ride tonight to keep them away from Cassel and his questions? Listen. Dad and I move all the time."

He thought she was hearing him but he wasn't sure. She didn't stir or acknowledge his words.

"Hey. We could take them and just move again. Go someplace else. Denver, or Salt Lake. Big towns where no one knows anybody. Dad can get work and school hasn't even started. They can stay with us and then, when things settle down, they can come back home."

At the word "home," Grace shot a look at him. Okay. He had her attention.

"Dad can handle Jon. Fitz can be a scary guy when he wants to be. And JJ'd be okay. She'd probably be okay anywhere. You know. It'd probably even be good for them to be away from that trailer for a while. Away from Tina. And Jon and I could do things together like brothers."

Mick heard himself. Heard himself give away everything he'd wanted about staying here and settling. Wasn't this real love? And he would do it. Do it for Grace.

He waited, but she didn't speak or look at him again. "We could even go tonight, I'll bet, tomorrow at the latest. Hit the road. Make it safe for everybody else."

Grace stood so quickly, she startled him.

"Mickey." She was breathing hard like she'd left off crying and gotten angry sometime in the last couple of minutes. "Don't you get it? We may all have to leave!" She ran her fingers through her hair. Exasperated. "Damn it!" she groaned, and pounded her fists against her legs. "Cassel will bust Gary for dope, take the kids away from Tina. He could send me . . . He could pin the Evelyn thing on you. We're screwed. The asswipe universe screwed us and we have to get out of here. I have to. Probably all of us!"

She left him standing there. Wondering. "The Evelyn thing." Could they pin it on him? Was that even possible?

34

JJ HATED BEING TRAPPED in the car with Mick's dad. She saw him pop a couple of pills as they drove off. More, she could tell he had badly frightened Jon and that wasn't easy to do. The man seemed so hair-trigger. Best JJ could do was keep her mouth shut and watch, wait for this trip to be over.

Mr. Fitzhugh made a big circle: Noxon to Troy, where they ate some bad pizza, then east through Libby to Logan State Park before finally turning south to follow Salish River Road home. He'd told her that route would take several hours, keep them out of Cassel's path. He traveled the speed limit, kept the windows down, and listened to country music on the radio.

JJ wondered if Gary or Tina had given Jon something so strong it kept him nearly comatose. He'd hardly eaten any pizza and slept the whole time in the car. A couple of years ago they'd done that same kind of thing with her until they got in trouble when JJ developed double pneumonia after a week of being given doses of Tina's vodka to "fight her cold." The hospital initiated an abuse investigation but found no other specific evidence that would remove JJ from her aunt's custody. Since then, JJ wouldn't let Gary or Tina give her any drink or medicine that didn't come from a pharmacy. But Jon? They could have slipped him anything. Come to think of it, JJ wondered if Mick's dad had given Jon something. Besides a heavy dose of fear.

She didn't intend to sleep, but the motion of the car and the occasional oncoming headlights were almost hypnotizing. She woke late that night to the rough sound of tires on hardpan and loose gravel. The kind of road where they'd gone swimming. Salish River Road. Mr. Fitzhugh had been driving slowly, keeping the dust down. From the backseat JJ could see silhouettes of trees and boulders along the roadside, hatches of white moths swirling in the headlights.

It looked to her like they were getting near the area where they'd gone swimming, where Jon had found the girl. Just above the area where she had walked, detoured around the big rocks. Mr. Fitzhugh slowed because the road ahead was starting to glow near the bend.

Closer, there was a barricade in the headlights, two uniformed men standing in front of it. One man pointed a long flashlight, the other had a rifle down at his side. Mr. Fitzhugh stopped and the man with the flashlight came to his window.

"Pretty late for a drive on a road like this," the man said. He leaned down and looked inside the car.

Mick's dad played the guy off. "Well, hell, we day-camped at

Logan Park up on the lake and lost track of time. Figured this was the closest way home."

The officer didn't react, may not have believed him.

Mick's dad asked the officer what was going on.

The guy didn't say. Instead he asked for Mr. Fitzhugh's license and registration. His partner, the other uniform, came over and peered in the passenger side and then walked to the back of the car, maybe, JJ thought, to copy the license plate number.

Mick's dad asked if they were having trouble with an accident or a landslide.

The officer ignored the question. Just handed the papers back and told Mick's dad to turn around. Said the road was closed.

Mick's dad argued but it didn't do any good.

He was muttering and irritable the rest of the trip. They had to go all the way to Kalispell and then down to home.

"People wonder why I hate the law," he griped. After a while he said, "Must be about that girl."

Mick's dad grew increasingly angry, practically radiating. Scary. At the edge of town he looked at JJ in the mirror. "Know anything about this?" he asked.

JJ shot a look at Jon. The boy was just starting to wake up. He began kicking at her and she couldn't keep him from blurting out what he thought he knew.

35

THE SHOT MICK HEARD in his dream was the front door slamming.

His dad threw the covers off him and kicked the foot of the cot.

"You nailed me to the goddamn wall!"

What wall? It was still dark. Middle of the night? Mick struggled to wake.

"Sit up, damn it! We're talking!"

His father sounded as mad as he'd ever heard him and Mick had been through his mad plenty of times, drunk or high or sober. Mick couldn't think what had set his dad off.

"Never lie to me! You don't know what the hell you're doing!"

Mick stood and watched his dad pace to the front door, look out, and come back.

"I hit a roadblock tonight and now we can't run and we can't stay." He had come up on Mick, both hands fists, breathing like a locomotive.

Mick was still trying to catch up. What had happened? Dad took JJ and Jon for a drive to keep them from being questioned. Oh . . . he got it. "Salish River Road?"

"Damn straight, River Road. Sheriff's blockade. Thought you found the body south of town. Under the highway bridge, you told me."

"Yeah. Uh, yeah. That was our story. We didn't want anybody to get in trouble."

"Trouble! You didn't tell me what I needed to stay *out* of trouble!" His saliva hit Mick in the face. "Screwed both of us. Don't you learn anything?"

There was nothing Mick could say. His dad was right.

"They got my license, the car plate. If they're any good they'll backtrack us to McCall. They'll search this place and the Conoco. They won't find anything but I'll still lose my job. Could get extradited. You could wind up on the spot for this floater. Numbered hell! Don't you ever think?"

Mick thought plenty. He didn't ask his dad to steal the generator off that highway construction in McCall. He didn't ask him to sell it to some dickwad that turned him in. He didn't ask his dad to pull bonehead stuff like that all over the western states for the last how many years, always a half step ahead of arrest. He didn't ask him to spend his money on cars and drugs and beer. He didn't ask him to live like a petty-crap outlaw and carry Mick around like a saddle blanket.

"Hey," Mick said, his own anger rising, "I made a mistake! I didn't—"

"You sure did, Bucky Boy, you sure did. Now maybe you can get up and help me and Gary figure out what to do next!" He stormed out, heading for the Stovalls'.

Mick pulled his jeans on and looked for a weapon. His father was about five ten, maybe a hundred and eighty, most of it muscle.

Mick wasn't going to let the man beat him again. Not for this. Not for anything anymore. His souvenir bat . . . no idea if he'd even brought it home from school for the summer. The putter? His dad wouldn't feel it. Mick found a foot-long section of pipe, the cheater bar his dad used for leverage on stuck bolts. Mick put it on his bed within easy reach, covered it with a T-shirt.

Fitz rammed back in, still in a huff. Gary came behind, wearing sweatpants, his hair mashed to the side of his head. His father clattered a wooden chair for Gary beside Mick's cot and pulled the cooler over for himself.

Gary was shaking his head. "Shit luck," he said, to no one in particular.

Fitz started. "I can get my stuff out of the Conoco when it opens at seven. Hide it. Keep working like nothing's happened. No way I can be connected to the girl. Mick, though, he's got to get out of here and he can't take the Bonnie."

"Maybe the Chevy?" Gary offered.

"Fort Knox don't have enough money to get that pile running." Mick's dad ran his fingers through his hair. "I'll buy a cheap ride. Get Mick and your kids on the road."

"We didn't do anything, we just tried—"

"Shut up!" Fitz barked. "You did enough."

"Me and Mick already been working on this," Gary said. "He'll take JJ and Jon, go visit Tina's family in Spokane or mine in Boise. Out of here for a few weeks and back in time for school."

Fitz shook his head. "The way this thing moves . . . could be next week, could be never."

It sounded to Mick like he was getting divorced. He'd become a liability and his dad was cutting him loose.

"Well, I'm not giving away my kids," Gary said, sitting a little straighter.

"Join 'em in a few months," Fitz said.

"Hell, I got a business here," Gary getting louder.

Fitz snorted.

"You're scared, you go," Gary said.

Mick's dad brought a small pistol out from under his shirt. "You're not giving me orders, pothead."

Mick had seen his father like this once before with a guy he said was trying to stiff him.

"Whoa, whoa!" Mick was standing now. "Cool down. We'll figure this out. Gary's right. We were already working on it earlier tonight."

His father towered over Gary. "I'm getting you a clean car by tonight. You two figure out who's going where." He turned and was out the door.

It was so quiet all of a sudden, Mick could hear the river.

36

MICK WOKE TO KNOCKING. Morning sun hurt his eyes. Another knock shook the whole room. His first thought was Tim and his buddy. Going to finish what they started yesterday. He was up in his underwear looking for a weapon. Where had he put that cheater bar?

"Open up! Sheriff."

Oh . . . his dad was going to kill him for sure.

He pulled on his jeans and opened the door to a stocky old man with a small dab of jelly in his mustache.

"Mickey Fitzhugh?" His voice sounded like a road grader.

"Yes, sir."

"You make a phone call a couple of days ago? 911?"

What the hell?

"Booth at the river park east of town?"

Could somebody have seen me?

"Afternoon. About three?"

"No. Uh, no, sir. I might have been working. Hardware store."

"You weren't. Witness says a kid matching your description made a phone call from River Park. Right about the same time dispatch got a 911. From the same phone."

"Huh. Well, there were some people just leaving the park when I pulled in."

"Pulled in?"

Crap! Mick needed to wake up. "Earlier this week I was down there swimming. I don't remember which day."

"Who were you calling?" The man hitched his belt, but it still didn't get up over his belly. He usually looked off to the side as if he were picturing what Mick was saying, but at the end of each question his eyes went up to Mick's and held them.

"I don't remember calling anybody."

The sheriff sighed. "Son, based on the lies you're telling me, I'm going to need fingerprints and a recording of your voice. May even need a tissue sample. Finish getting dressed and we'll go to my office."

"Sir, you can't arrest me. I haven't done anything. I have to go to work."

"Look at me." The man paused, letting it sink in. "You think I been doing this job long enough to know what I can and can't do? I got something I'm working on a bit more important than your convenience." He took his hat off and ran his hand over his hair like it was bothering him.

"I apologize. I didn't mean any disrespect. Really I was just . . . begging. I can't afford to lose my job. I, uh, I'm raising money for my cleats and uniform. Play ball for the Trappers this year." Mick could feel sweat rolling out of his hair and down the back of his neck, and he knew the man could see it beading on his lip.

"Uh-huh. Well, I don't mean any disrespect either. You're lying to a law officer investigating a murder. How serious you think that is?"

"Uh, I know that's really serious . . . I'm just scared. To be involved."

"You want to quit lying and tell me about that call?"

"I thought she deserved to be found." A part of Mick stood back watching, knowing he was going down the tubes, but for the life of him, he couldn't think what else to do. Wasn't talking to this guy better than talking to Cassel?

"I was swimming. I—"

"Alone?"

"Alone. I saw this thing across the river. I thought it was a log or something at first and then I realized it was a body. I ran. When I got back to town I called 911 because I didn't want the animals to get her. I didn't want her parents to keep worrying."

"You knew her parents."

"No. I hadn't ever seen her before. Didn't know her from nobody."

"How come you're lying about making the call?"

"I'm not! I did at first because I thought you'd think I did it."

"Why?"

" 'Cause I'm young and you'd have me . . . and you wouldn't have to keep looking."

"You don't have a very high opinion of law enforcement." The man made another try at his belt.

Mick didn't say anything to that. He knew his dad had never been caught.

"That your vehicle out front?"

"Yes. My dad's."

"A Pontiac with that license number was stopped at a road-block on River Road last night. Right where the body was found. Kind of a coincidence, huh?"

Mick knew the man could see him react. Mick didn't think he grimaced but he could feel his skin flushing, hear his breathing getting louder. Worst of all, he couldn't think what to say.

The sheriff waited Mick out.

"That might have been my dad. He took our neighbors for a drive last night. I don't know where they went. Dad didn't know where I saw the body. I never told him."

"Never told him anything."

"No."

"Why not?"

"When you were a kid did you tell your folks everything that happened when you borrowed their car and they didn't know it?"

He considered that. "Give me your driver's license," he said.

"I don't have one."

The sheriff looked away and nodded. He hadn't thought Mick did. He had Mick going and coming. Grace and Mick's dad had both been right. Before this was over Mick could see that he might be charged with murder. Might wind up in prison if they found traces of him at the beach. Did he touch the body? He couldn't remember.

37

MICK TOLD THE SHERIFF that he had to go to work, that his dad worked in town, that they weren't going anywhere, and that he'd come in after work and do a voice recording if the man still needed one.

The sheriff looked at Mick for a long time. Assessing.

Mick rubbed his hair back, trying for a little grooming. His T-shirt smelled like sweat, his jeans were grubby, and he looked like a bum. Could the man trust him? Mick had to admit he himself wouldn't. But maybe Mick reminded the old man of somebody. Because he left.

Mick pulled on fresher clothes. He'd go to the Stovalls', talk with Grace. Find out if she was still planning to get out of here like she'd said last night. Tell Gary about the sheriff. As he left the studio he saw Dovey watching him from her front porch. Mick stopped and walked to her.

"Looks like you're starting to do a lot of business with the law." She put her hands on her porch railing and leaned into a stretch.

"I made the 911 call on the dead girl," Mick told her. She'd know soon enough anyway, and you had to give something to get something. "Who was that?" he asked, cutting his eyes toward the dirt road the sheriff had left on.

"Cardwell. Cardwell Paint. He's the county sheriff. Office

near mine. Good man. Lot to him." She straightened and looked out to the river. "In some trouble?"

"Yeah. I told some lies and they bit me."

"You hurt that girl?" Her eyes returned to Mick's.

"No. Just found her. Never seen her before."

"Beat to death," she said. "Found her car halfway to Plains. Think she was probably killed there. Dumped up on the Salish."

The Clark Fork River ran through the town of Portage, northwest all the way to Bonners Ferry in Idaho, and southeast through Missoula and beyond. The Salish River, the place where they'd gone swimming, ran north-south and poured into the Clark Fork just south of the town limits.

"Yeah, I know. That's where I found her. But I said I found her at the south bridge around River Park. I thought I wouldn't get anybody else in trouble."

"Anybody else?"

Mick didn't answer that. He was realizing Dovey could be an ally. She had the unofficial ear of the law. And she'd always been nice enough to the kids in the compound. Didn't seem too judgmental.

"Instead I messed things up. Now they might even think I did it."

"They?"

"Yeah. What's his name, Sheriff Paint, and the Highway Patrol guy, Scott Cassel, too. I had a run-in with his son and his son's goon yesterday."

"Stay out of their way."

"Yeah. I know."

Mick wanted her to put in a good word for him, but he didn't want to seem too obvious. Wanted her to think it was her idea.

"I can't afford to get in trouble," he told her. "I got a job stocking for the hardware and the feedstore. Want to play school football this year."

"Been here about five months?" she asked.

"Yeah. Yes." *Manners, idiot!* "Moved here from McCall, Idaho." Was that right? Mick couldn't keep it straight. Maybe he shouldn't tell her anything about where they'd been before. What if, in her job, she'd seen a warrant? "My dad works at the Conoco."

She didn't say anything. Gut level, Mick didn't see she thought much of his dad by the look on her face.

"Cardwell thinks she was killed Monday," she said, watching Mick's eyes.

Does she think I've been lying to her?

"Monday night, out 200 on the highway to Plains. Whoever it was had to have had a car to put her up on the Salish."

Where was he Monday night? Mick couldn't remember.

"Well," she said, turning to her door, "I have to get to work. Take care of yourself." She paused at the door. "Tell JJ to come see me one of these days. And watch out. I mean it."

Mick stood in front of her trailer for another minute wondering what it was like to be old. What was it like to lose a husband? What if it tore your insides out but you had to keep living?

Would he feel that way if his dad died? Mick probably loved him. At least he was grateful that his father kept him, raised him, such as it was. His dad didn't have to, but he did the duty. Been easier to put Mick in foster care. More and more though, his father was blaming Mick for his own problems. Whenever his dad got in a jam, Mick was a handy goat. Mick knew he'd miss him sometimes, but when he thought of working, going to school, taking care of himself without having to keep covering things up? Mick would be a million pounds lighter. He was getting clear on that.

Grace came out on their porch when Mick walked up their steps.

"Things don't seem to be getting any better," she said, hands in her hip pockets.

"What?"

"Cop car?"

"Sheriff. I called 911 that day."

"You're a . . ." Grace took a deep breath and looked away. "Guess that was the right thing to do," she said, turning back. "You tell him I was there?" Her eyes were bloodshot. Lack of sleep? She had on the same clothes as yesterday.

"No. I said just me," Mick told her, glancing at the alley, nervous that Paint might change his mind and come back. "I, uh, told Dovey the same thing. She might help us."

Grace muffled a smirk. "Right. County clerk. People like her don't help. Not their job."

Mick didn't want to argue. Couldn't remember why he'd wanted to talk with her in the first place. "I got to go to the hardware in an hour or so," Mick said. "Why aren't you at work?"

She looked away again. Decided to tell him. "I don't go in till one, but I already called in sick."

"Gary tell you Dad might make JJ and Jon and me leave?"

She cut her eyes at him. Pissed. "Right! JJ will be in la-la land in the backseat and Jon will chew your arm off while you drive. There's a plan. You won't get fifty miles."

"Tina's got relatives in Spokane."

Rolled her eyes. "Sure. You think they want anything to do with her or hers?"

Good point. "Gary's got family in Boise."

"I was there when he said it." She rubbed at the end of her nose like it was bothering her. "I could see you and JJ bunking with them for a week or two, but Jon? He'll bring everybody down. Bound and determined. Right now Gary's got him hand-cuffed to the bed. Gave him something to knock him out."

"He can't keep doing that." Imagining the scene made Mick's stomach churn. "Somebody'll come over to get something fixed, see that, and report him. Or Dovey'll find out and tell Paint. They jail people for stuff like that."

"Tell me." Grace crossed her arms as if she could wall off this reality. "This whole scene is nitro."

"Let's you and me go!" Mick's new idea. Out of nowhere. "Right now! I got car keys and cash in my pillow." He winced. That sounded dumb.

She looked at him like he was from outer space. "I can't leave!"

Mick thought for sure she was going to take a swing at him. Handy again. Rent-a-punch. "Last night you said you have to leave!" Mick, talking faster than he could think. "You can't save the Stovalls."

Grace cut him off. "I remembered. I can't run. If the cops catch on, they could send me back."

Back? To what? Runaway in the first place like Mick thought. But he was puzzled. What had changed so much since last night?

She was twisting her hair, pulling hard enough to rip it. "I'm trapped. Can't go, can't stay."

"I don't get it."

Grace gave him the look. Of course he didn't get it, because he was an idiot. "One, Jon's ballistic and the only thing Gary knows to do is drug him. Sooner or later Jon'll get away and spill everything. Cassel or the sheriff or both'll come after us. And how can we leave JJ with Cunneen or Tim out to hurt her? She can't . . . she's not . . ." Grace looked annoyed by her surge of tenderness and the responsibility it evoked.

Mick thought she had been going to say JJ wasn't a street rat like him and Grace.

"Yeah," he said, "but let's go anyway." He couldn't seem to give up on the idea of driving off alone with Grace and where that might eventually lead. Bonnie and Clyde. Fugitives, then lovers.

Her look withered him. "Get away! I mean it!" She was yelling and crying at the same time, tears, snot, everything. "Get out of here!" Even louder. And then the bang of the trailer door slamming.

Mick backed off the porch. Did Dovey see this? Her car was still there. Did she hear Grace?

He was ready to jump in the Bonnie and drive it into the river.

38

MICK COULDN'T KNOCK on the Stovalls' door and talk to Gary about the sheriff's visit right now. Grace needed to cool off. He went to his place instead, washed his face, drank some water, left for Main Street and work. Turning the corner, he saw the Highway Patrol cruiser sitting in front of the hardware. He didn't know what the man had in mind, but he didn't think Cassel was buying fencing.

When he got back to the compound, JJ and Grace were standing on his porch, holding duffels.

Grace wouldn't meet his look.

"We're going!" JJ, afraid but excited.

"JJ's my girl. I don't leave without her," Grace said, still not meeting his eyes.

She's embarrassed, Mick thought, by her quick change of mind.

"Hammond called Gary looking for me," Grace explained. "Not my boss about why I was sick. Hammond. Like all of a sudden he wants to keep track of me?" She shook her head. "Let's get moving."

Suddenly Mick wanted to reason. To figure things out. To have a plan. To be a man. To be in charge. He wanted this action to make sense, to fit into other things. School. Football. His dad. The Stovalls. His thing with Grace. He wanted to know what the bloody hell he was doing. But he couldn't make it compute. Couldn't come up with anything to say.

Autopilot. Mick stuffed an empty grocery sack with another shirt and underwear, grabbed his folding money, threw all their stuff in the Bonneville, and they eased out of the alley, turning right on the highway, heading away from the main part of town.

JJ kept watch out the rear window. After a moment said, "We're clear."

Mick set the cruise control on the speed limit, recalling the many times he'd fled. Heart racing, mind spinning, eyes locked on the road. One difference. No Dad.

Mick had said he'd never do this again. Portage would be different. The place he settled. A while ago he'd seen a movie about a gunfighter. The man had wanted to start over, start living a peaceful life, but trouble kept finding him. He got killed before he could change.

39

GRACE KNEW SHE WAS OUT OF CONTROL, hyper. It was nerve-racking, watching out for the next attack. JJ had upped the tension running home this morning after seeing Tim Cassel waiting at her work. And Mick's visit from the sheriff felt like a noose tightening. She might be questioned as a suspect . . . could they match her description to the California runaway report? She didn't think so but she didn't know. And Hammond's call to the trailer? Like all of a sudden he needed to know right where she was and what she was doing. Why? So he could get rid of her quickly if he needed to?

Her thoughts were all over the place. Run? Stay? She was purely scared for the second time in her life. She seldom let herself remember that first night when her two brothers came into her room and held her down. She'd been so terrified she couldn't even breathe. After a couple of months that fear boiled into hate. But this? Killing Ev? What if it was someone she knew? And what if she was next? She'd never pictured her own death before. Scream! Run! All she could imagine.

So she ran. Told Mick she was backing her girl, JJ, but, no, it was fear and instinct. Grace didn't feel safe. She wanted some distance from the mess so she could figure her next move.

Hammond or one of his bunch could have eliminated Evelyn to send a message: Compete with us and you're history. Or maybe Evelyn learned something from one of her customers and Hammond had her disappeared because she knew something that threatened him. Was that what happened to Ramona? If Hammond thought Grace knew too much after finding the body, would he come after her as soon as the dust settled? Did he kill people himself or give the job to someone like Larry?

But what if those guys had nothing to do with it? What if Ev was killed by a customer? What if Ev tried to make more money by squeezing a local guy who was married? Money for the sex, then more money for silence? Evelyn might have tried that. Or, what if the guy was a tourist or a trucker just passing through and this was just a random one-time thing? Then Grace's running would make it seem like she actually knew something important when she didn't.

The bottom line? She needed Mick to get her out of town. She didn't need him or JJ in her business.

40

ROAD TRIP. They went east to Plains and made a right on the small two-lane toward St. Regis and the 90 freeway. From there they could go east to Missoula and beyond, or west to Idaho. Driving calmed Mick, focused him, and little by little, his brain came back. He'd left his checks under his mattress. Brilliant. Drove off with forty bucks. Like that would buy them gas, food, or a motel.

Gas? Mick looked at the gauge. Half full. He remembered his dad saying it worked but the damn thing was always optimistic. Okay, twenty-gallon tank, so seven or eight gallons left. Fourteen miles a gallon on the highway. A hundred, a hundred and ten miles. Ten bucks for food, the rest for gas. Another hundred miles. They would be somewhere within two hundred fifty miles of Portage before they stalled.

Grace was up front with him.

"Look for a map," he told her.

She rummaged through the glove compartment. Tire gauge, a ballpoint, shop rag, tattered receipts. She finally found an old one under her seat. Held it up.

"We need to get away from Sanders and Lincoln counties, out of state if we can." Mick talked loud enough for JJ to hear in back. "The bigger the town, the easier we disappear." Mick realized his dad had rubbed off on him a little more than he'd thought. Mick seemed to be better at running from the law than he was at most schoolwork.

"You got any money?" he asked Grace.

She shook her head. Mick didn't believe her. She made some kind of wage at the restaurant, plus her tips. She could be sending her money somewhere, to a sister or mother, but he didn't think so. He couldn't picture her with a bank account, never seen her use a card or anything like it. Come to think of it, Mick'd never seen her pay for anything, period. So he bet she had a stash and she was carrying it. He glanced at her purse. She caught him looking and used her heels to push the purse farther under the car seat. Point made. Whatever she had, she wasn't going to share it.

He glanced at her face. Grace looked like she was in pain. She'd begun hitting her legs with her fists again, grimacing. Mick thought he knew what she was feeling. She wished she'd ditched them, hitched a ride and gone away on her own. Then she wouldn't be stuck messing with him and JJ and having to deal with what they needed or wanted.

Out of the corner of his eye, Mick saw JJ reach up and touch Grace's forehead like she was checking for a fever. She kept her hand there and Grace quieted. After a minute or so, Grace covered JJ's hand with her own and a bit later JJ withdrew and sat back.

Grace took a deep breath. "Okay," she said, and handed JJ the map.

Mick heard the paper rustling as JJ unfolded the thing and studied it.

"Are you still mad at me?" Mick asked Grace. He didn't think he deserved it.

Grace looked at him and then out her window at the mountains, rugged and wooded to the west of the highway.

Mick gave up and tried JJ. "What about it?" he asked, watching her in the rearview mirror. "We got to make an east-west decision at St. Regis. Maybe fifteen minutes or so."

"West," JJ said.

"Forget about it," Grace said. "It's not you . . ."

Grace went on talking, seemed like more to herself than to them, voice sounding flat, distracted. "I called in sick because I didn't want to hear about the dead girl all day at work. A few minutes later, Hammond phones like he needs to find out what I know. He's never called me at home before. Jon must have spread the whole story, us on the river."

She hooked her thumb back at JJ. "Eight o'clock this morning. Tim's Mustang at the recycling center. Him standing out front, waiting. Just luck my girl saw him first."

Mick nodded. Okay, seemed like running was the right option before anybody got hurt. Had Scott Cassel noticed they were gone? Had he put out a bulletin? Guess they'd find out soon enough.

Still looking out the window, Grace went on. "I'm . . . not

mad." She distracted herself scratching her knee. Gave up, took a breath. "I'm sick of *guys!*"

Mick kept his eyes on the road ahead. Kept his mouth shut and tried to ease his grip on the steering wheel. He could feel JJ's attention behind him.

Grace made a rattling sound. Mick couldn't tell if she was growling or clearing her throat.

"You're never safe," Grace said, shaking her head. "Some hard-on wants to do you and then he kills you or you kill him and you run. What kind of life is that?"

Mick didn't think she was looking for an answer. JJ didn't reach over to soothe her.

"It never stops. You never get free. Go swimming? There's a girl's body . . ." Grace seemed to run out of energy, leaned her head against her window, put her hand to her mouth, covered it as if that would make her thoughts go away.

Two hours later Mick exited the freeway at Wallace, Idaho, breathing easier since they'd crossed the state line. At a busy service station, JJ bought gas and snacks with Mick's money. He and Grace thought JJ might be harder for clerks to remember with her hair up under the ball cap she'd found on the back floor.

Afterward, they took streets that skirted the edge of town where it abutted the mountains and drove north on a dirt road along a creek until they saw ruts leading toward a shady spot to pull off out of sight. JJ and Grace went to a flat clearing between the creek and the car, used their jackets for pillows and slept.

Mick continued to sit behind the steering wheel, listening to the engine slowly cool. Threats behind him, he considered what he was about to do. Give up the dream he'd had for years. Act like his dad.

Mick had found a town he liked, made a good friend, got a job. Even the football was going to happen. But he was going to trash all that and run. Why? He didn't like what he was thinking. Because he liked Grace and he wanted to save her? From what exactly? He couldn't actually say. Never mind what. He wanted to save her so she'd like him enough to be his girl. How feeble was that? She'd had plenty of chances to like him. But she didn't. Not in the way he was hoping. She was hard as metal, always several steps ahead of him, did what she wanted, kept her own counsel. Truth, he probably couldn't save her from anything. And there was nothing he could do to *make* her like him. She would or she wouldn't, not the type to swoon with gratitude. He banged his head on the steering wheel as if that could knock out the stupid notions.

What about JJ? Mick needed to understand the backdrop for Evelyn's killing. Who did what with whom and how were they connected? Would JJ know that? Some of it. She'd recognized Cassel's girlfriend. In spite of her spaciness, she picked up on things. And Mick? He had one advantage. He knew how to think like a crook.

So why was Evelyn Edmonds's car down on Highway 200 when her body was in a river fifteen miles away?

41

GRACE GAVE HER SPEECH about Hammond being after her. Thought she'd toss Mick and JJ a bone to knock them off the scent of her money. She needed every bit of it. The more scared they thought she was, the more slack they'd give her. But she'd gotten a little close to the truth with that stuff about men. So close she felt her stomach roll.

The confusion, the frustration she'd been feeling was real, but the farther they got from Portage, the more she worried she'd screwed up big-time. She shouldn't have run. Should have talked to Hammond when he called. Fed him a story. Said she was there when Jon found the body but of course she didn't report the death because she was afraid she'd lose her job and her placement.

Hammond would believe her, trust her, if she gave him time to cool down. He'd realize she'd just been afraid and he'd want her close by to find out if she knew more than she was telling about Ev. If he and his guys thought she'd run because she knew something damaging . . . now *that* was scary.

So if Hammond thought she was safe, he wouldn't bother her, but Mr. Highway Patrol or the sheriff? Not so sure. Would one of them pick her up for questioning? What Grace didn't want was either one going national on her. Putting a search on the runaway database. She'd kill herself before she'd go back to San Rafael. The courier envelopes and her referrals, sending truckers and tourists to Hammond's gambling houses, brought in twenty a pop. Three hundred for the sex sting. In a few more months she would have had five thousand saved. She could've moved on then if she needed to, eighteen or not.

In the last few weeks she'd been seeing Larry Cassel more often than anyone else. Publicly, in the restaurant, she ignored him. People talk. But he found lots of ways to run into her from time to time, offering a cold beer or a tiny bottle of liquor on her way home from work. Earrings. Little treats. The out-there casino trips. He was sort of intriguing, sort of attractive, and he had mega-power. She'd probably call him when they got wherever they were going. Maybe he could smooth things over with Hammond.

So running was probably a mistake and now she had to deal with it, needed to recalculate. Maybe she better go all the way. Go to another city. Set up shop. Use what she'd learned from Ev and Hammond. Pick up where Ev left off but be more careful.

Her neck and shoulders ached. Was she overlooking something? Probably just paranoid.

42

MICK FOUND THE GIRLS several yards away wading in the creek. "Hey," he yelled over the noise of the water. "This won't work. We have to talk."

They dipped hands in the stream, rubbed their faces, and came back to the clearing to dry.

". . . think we know something," JJ was saying as she sat, nodding to her side to include Mick.

"Hammond's call just freaked me," Grace said. "Like he thought I was involved."

"Like what?" Mick asked. "What do we know?" Mick could easily imagine Grace holding things back.

"What about this?" JJ took the jewel from her pocket and showed them.

Mick didn't know what it was, but Grace seemed hypnotized by it.

"I found it at the river. When I went for a walk. It was near the ban—"

"Did you show that to anybody?" Grace's voice was shrill.

"No. I meant to tell you before but—"

"It's Hammond's. His ring," Grace said, closing her eyes, picturing. "Or Mackler's? Or Larry? I think he had one like it."

Mick put it together. "Hammond, where we found the body?"

"Upriver where I walked . . ." JJ said.

"You didn't tell us?" Mick, disbelieving, then angry.

"I didn't know what it was," JJ, her own voice rising. "I'd never seen . . . there were, uh, it looked like somebody, looked like a spot where somebody put a boat in the water. It could have—"

Grace's cursing cut her off. The girl stood, turned around a couple of times like she was looking for a way out, seemed to give up and sat again. Put her head in her hands.

JJ kept talking, defending her reasoning. "I was going to ask

Gary but everything happened so fast I never got a chance. And this morning . . . it never seemed like the right time. It's just been in my pocket."

Mick cut his eyes toward JJ. Saw the pain on her face. Kept from saying he thought she was a dunce.

JJ shook her head and looked up at the sky as if a ghost moon might be out there to help her.

Mick was trying to digest what this ring meant. He'd never seen one before. Who had that kind of ring? Several people, or just Hammond? "This is what I mean," he said. "Running's going to make things worse. We need to figure out who did it, get ourselves off the hook."

Neither Grace nor JJ looked at him.

"I screwed up," JJ said, "but we never really talked about this till today."

Grace shrugged. Mick nodded. It was true. Jon telling other people about finding the body had started a gas fire.

Mick tried again. "We could start simple. We tell Hammond we have this jewel from his ring that puts him at the murder and we tell him to leave us alone. Like a standoff." Mick glanced at Grace to see her frowning. Went on. "I go to the sheriff and tell him I'm innocent and let him fingerprint, make a recording, whatever. Doesn't matter because I didn't do it. I never even saw the girl until we found her."

"You wouldn't tell him about the ring part?" JJ asked.

"The sheriff? Paint? No. We hide that . . . No, we put it in an envelope and give it . . . to Dovey. Like for insurance. She'd keep it and we'd tell her if anything happens to us, give the envelope to Paint."

"You guys have no idea how much is going on," Grace said, disdainful. "Hammond and Bolton? The banker Greer? Mackler at Social Services? There's big money. Lots of deals. Larry Cassel, too. If they're messed up with Evelyn at all and they know one of us has major evidence? They'll get it from us, one way or another."

"No way, the sheriff—"

Grace interrupted him. "The sheriff? Dovey? They're fossils. They're a joke."

"What deals?" Mick asked.

"Hammond's a county supervisor?" Grace, tone of voice like teaching a dull pupil.

"Yeah." Mick was guessing. He didn't know anything about a supervisor or that Hammond was one.

"That's how he found out there was going to be new construction on the dam and bought all that property so he could fleece the Army Corps when they had to buy that same land for the staging area."

Mick looked at JJ. He could see that she didn't know what Grace was talking about either.

"Hammond and the banker are partners in the card rooms. Have private gambling in Belknap and Plains. Make all kinds of under-the-table money. Sports bets, loans, you name it. Maybe girls, too. Evelyn's small-time tricking might have been cutting

into their business. Hammond got Larry hired as building inspector so he could rake money from construction. They all get
kickbacks from local businesses . . . insurance or something. Patrol
guy probably hassles people that get in their way. They got me to—"

Mick interrupted to slow her down. "Evelyn . . . the girl we
found was a prostitute? I thought she worked at the café." He
turned to JJ. "Er, how . . . ? Uh, did you know about any of this?"

JJ shook her head.

Mick, back to Grace, "How do you know this stuff?" He wasn't
sure these weren't just wild accusations.

"I listen. I hear conversations all the time in the café. And the
motel? I hear that trash, too. Who's sleeping with who."

"People wouldn't talk about *that* kind of stuff in a public
restaurant." Mick could hardly believe it. Portage? She made it
sound like the Mafia.

"Everything I just told you?" Grace said. "Heard it all. And
Cookie. He's worked there for years. He's like the town wiki. I
want to know something, I ask him.

"I didn't show for work and ran. Hammond's thinking I have
something. Like maybe Evelyn told me something. Him and the
judge, him and Larry, even the doof at Social Services. Any of
them might be doing something that Evelyn found out about. Or,
it could be the escort thing."

"Are you making this up?" JJ asked. "Anybody in western
Montana could have killed Evelyn."

"So why was Hammond calling as soon as he learned I was
there when we found the body?"

"Uh, he was worried about you?" JJ offered.

"No way. He knows my name. Flirts. I've done a couple of things for him outside work. But he collects lots of girls like me and he doesn't call to see how they are. We're just the help, just advertising. End of story. Until Evelyn was killed."

"You did things for Hammond?" Mick remembered. "Like what?"

Grace shook her head.

Mick would go after that later. Maybe when JJ wasn't around in case Grace was embarrassed to tell in front of her. Right now he was thinking about men he'd met that were like his dad. "I don't see a guy like Hammond killing Evelyn. I don't see him needing to. It'd have to have been an accident."

"Maybe," Grace said, "but Bolton? He's like the whole law. A judge. He can do whatever he wants and no one can touch him."

"Yeah, but same deal," Mick argued. "Why? Why would he put himself in that position? Risk everything?"

"Okay, Scott Cassel," Grace said.

"What about Larry?" JJ asked. "You think he couldn't kill a girl if she said no to him? Or how about Tim? Tim and his buddy sure want us to shut up and I wasn't even thinking of him and Evelyn."

That statement stopped the conversation.

"You weren't?" Mick, incredulous. "Who did you mean when you asked if the body was Cassel's girl?"

"Larry," JJ answered.

Mick and Grace looked at each other openmouthed.

"You couldn't have said this earlier?" Mick asked, sarcastic.

"Cassel's girlfriend?" JJ held her hands up like stop, let me explain. "I'd seen her talk to Larry a few times and I wondered. That's all."

Grace was leaning forward. "Larry Cassel? Evelyn? She wouldn't give him the time of day. Not even for money. She was afraid of him."

"I don't know about that. I just saw them together . . . or maybe not exactly together, uh, with each other. On the street, in a store, I just assumed—"

"You're wrong," Grace interrupted.

Mick was surprised by Grace's energy on this subject. She couldn't have a thing for Larry Cassel. Not him. Just the edge of the idea made his heart sink.

"It was just a thought. I reacted," JJ said, defending herself. "It's not like I knew anything. I didn't even know the girl's name."

Nobody spoke for a minute or two.

Finally, JJ. "Okay, Mick's right. Doesn't seem like the killing is something a person like Hammond or Bolton would do. It could have been somebody passing through, somebody none of us will ever meet. So, what's next?"

"Dovey told me the girl was killed Monday night," Mick said, eager to keep figuring it out. "She said whoever did it had to have a car, 'cause her car was left east of town on the highway to Plains. So she was probably killed there. Right? And then taken to the river."

"That's dumb." This from Grace, while she tried to remember

if anybody had been waiting for Evelyn in the restaurant parking lot that Monday night. "That would put the car right near the Clark Fork. Easier to dump her there."

"Yeah, but more river traffic. The guy probably thought nobody would find the body for weeks up on the Salish. It was just luck we did," JJ said.

"Maybe whoever killed her freaked, grabbed the body, and drove away to hide it. He probably never gave her car a thought," Mick said, imagining what he might feel like if he killed somebody. "If I did it, I'd run as fast and as far as I could. I wouldn't be doing any great planning."

JJ could see the logic. Two people, in their own car, they would have hid the girl's car, too. One guy to drive it, the other guy to follow. One person, he'd have to leave Evelyn's car where it was. "But how did some guy stop her out on the highway?" JJ asked. "Would Evelyn arrange to meet the guy out of town, on the road?"

Grace was going to shake her head no but reconsidered. Ev might. For a quickie.

"Not in the middle of nowhere," Mick said. "There's twenty better spots: a bar, the river park, the overlook . . ." He caught Grace's eye. *Oh.* Okay. Maybe it was convenient. "So the guy didn't make her stop? She chose to?"

"How?" JJ couldn't picture it.

"She knew him. Or she set it up." Mick could see it now, could see how it probably happened. So it could be any of Evelyn's customers?

"Or somebody could have surprised her . . . or tricked her," JJ said, not liking the idea that Evelyn set herself up to be killed.

Another hour's talking left them with a lot of theories, no conclusions. Mick decided that Grace's revelation about Evelyn's hooking was the key. JJ disagreed. Grace was preoccupied and rarely offered any opinion about the murder itself. Afternoon moved into evening, time to decide. Grace was suddenly involved and adamant. Keep going to the next city. "Coeur d'Alene," she said. "Party town. Lots of tourists."

Mick was against it. Wanted to go home and face the music. By the time they got back, Dovey could give them some of the missing information, like where the girl was actually killed and what was found around the body, and then they might be very close to figuring out who could have done it.

JJ wanted more time away from Portage, stay out of town another day or two, let tempers cool. She made her case to Mick. "Think about it. There's possibilities we haven't even had a chance to talk about and we need to solve this thing before we go back."

"Coeur d'Alene's close," Grace chipped in with JJ. "Good place to wait while Portage calms down."

Majority rule. They decided to drive back into Wallace for food and cell phone reception, each call their work with an excuse, and head back to the creekside for the night. In the morning, farther west to the edge of the Idaho panhandle and Coeur d'Alene.

43

JUST AFTER DARK, back in Portage, Mick's dad kicked in the door of the Stovalls' trailer. His pistol was in his hand and he demanded they tell him where Mick went. Tina couldn't get herself organized and Jon, still handcuffed, started crying.

Gary saw Fitz's pupils were pinpoints, thought Mick's dad looked tweaky and lethal.

"They didn't say. Didn't tell anybody. I wasn't here when they left," Gary said, remaining seated, trying not to escalate the situation.

Fitz poked Tina with the gun. "How about you?"

"Dunno," she said.

He pointed the automatic at Jon and Jon went crazy, screaming, crying, jerking at the cuff so hard his wrist started bleeding.

"I'm going to hold him, okay?" Gary said, looking for permission.

Fitz nodded.

Gary moved to the floor and wrapped his arms around Jon. Held him like you would a baby so the boy couldn't hurt himself further. "They just left," he said. "Took clothes. I checked after I saw your car was gone."

Fitz glanced out the open door and back, shook his head.

"Must have split this morning, nine or ten," Gary said. "One of 'em, Grace probably, got my cell phone. Why are you . . . What's going on?"

"Cassel. At the Conoco. He'll be back. I'm not taking Mick's fall."

Gary flinched as he watched Fitz's hand tighten on the pistol.

"Let the boy go," Fitz said.

"I can't," Gary told him. "I don't know what he'll do. Run off. Talk. Make a shitstorm."

"You should shoot him," Fitz said.

"That's the drugs talking," Gary told him. "You love Mick. You been taking care of him. Jon here's like that. I just don't know how to help him. If I did, I'd do it."

"Let him go," Fitz repeated.

Gary looked at the man. Pleaded. "You've seen him," Gary said. "Words don't work. What . . . You got a better idea?"

"Put a gun in his mouth, like I did," Mick's dad said. "He don't mind you, pull the trigger."

"You've done that to Mick?" Gary asked him.

"Discipline," Fitz said.

Gary swallowed. Looked at the man.

Fitz gestured with the pistol. "It's loaded."

Gary reached in his pocket, took out a small key, and opened the cuff.

Jon was up and out the door in a blur. Before anybody could move.

Gary kept looking at Fitz.

"Shoot you?" Fitz asked, belligerent.

Gary shook his head.

"Looks like you better git while the gettin's good."

"Can't," Gary said. "I live here."

Fitz shook his head. "Mistake," he said. "Don't be coming outside."

In a minute or so Gary heard a car start. Looked out the window, saw taillights turning up toward the highway. Hoped it was Mick's dad, leaving for good.

44

THEY MADE THEIR PHONE CALLS at the gas station complex and drove north out of Wallace on the creekside road past the twinkle of homesteads in the hills bordering the wide canyon. Soon found their same spot from the afternoon and began discussing sleeping arrangements. Grace wanted to be by herself, but they had nothing that would make decent bedding in the flat area nearer the creek. JJ told her that in this mountainy area you couldn't guarantee what kind of animal would come to the water at night. Could even be a bear. Grace took in the information. Said, "Open the trunk."

Mick didn't think the trunk would make a tolerable bed, but maybe Grace was thinking about finding a weapon or a blanket. No one had a light. Luckily the trunk itself had a small bulb at the back that showed a burlap bag of tire chains, an oily towel, a folded tarp, and a sweatshirt that might serve as a blanket.

"It'll do," Grace said. She got her duffel from the rear seat and tossed it in the back, on top of the chains, while JJ got in front with Mick. Grace stepped high, putting one foot over the bumper, and started to lever herself in when something stopped her: the distant sound of an engine or, more likely, the flick of headlights between trees. Within seconds they all realized a car was coming. *What the . . .*

Grace pulled her leg out, slammed the trunk, and ran for the trees. JJ had both hands on her door leaning out the open passenger window to see better. Mick was frozen behind the steering wheel trying to decide if this posed a danger. Just a rancher driving to a home farther out? A landowner who'd spotted them parking, coming to tell them to move on? Or . . . a sheriff checking make-out spots and flushing kids home.

JJ called it. "It's got a light bar!"

Okay, Mick had seen Grace run but what should he do? What would look less suspicious? He didn't want to give a cop any reason to check out the car. They'd all be screwed. His dad had stolen plates from a wrecked Dodge near Plains months ago. Mick knew that when Fitz had been stopped at the river barricade the night before, the cops there had gotten his plate numbers. If this sheriff or whoever it was checked these plates now on his in-car computer, they were busted. But maybe he wouldn't. If they ran . . . could they pull any farther out of sight?

JJ slid across the seat and crawled on top of him.

"Hey!" Mick tried to push her away but she had her arms around his neck. "Damn it, we have to run," he said, his words mashing into her hair.

"Shut up."

"JJ—" The headlights pulled into the clearing. *Trapped.* "Let go, damn it!"

"Shut! Up!" she hissed in his ear. She brought her face around and kissed him just as the headlights swung in behind and illuminated them through the rear window.

Oh.

She jerked her head away, pulled her hands up over his head messing up his hair, and slid to the seat beside him.

Mick was breathing hard. From fear? From wrestling? From the kiss? He put his hands on the steering wheel to steady himself as he heard a car door opening and steps coming his way. The beam from a flashlight lit the back of his head, moved to the wheel and across the dash. A uniformed man stepped up to the window.

"What's going on?"

"Uh, we . . . we were just talking." JJ, sounding breathy.

The man snorted. "Yeah, I could see that."

"No, I mean, we didn't have, er, we wanted some pri—" Mick, getting into it.

"My mom doesn't like him," JJ interrupted. "She's super strict and I have to be home prettty soon." She smoothed Mick's hair back. "We just wanted a little time together. We weren't going to do anything."

The man leaned over and shone the light into Mick's eyes, then JJ's. "Been drinking?"

"No, sir," Mick said.

The man shone the light on their feet, the backseat, the back floor. "Duffel?" he asked.

"My things," JJ said, "laundry."

"Fool her?" he said.

"Yeah," JJ said, giving an embarrassed smile, "so she'd let me out tonight."

"I used to do something like that," he said.

Mick breathed. First time in a while.

"Sack?" the man asked.

JJ dug her fingernails into Mick's leg.

"My gym stuff," Mick said.

The man nodded. "I'll be driving back this way in twenty minutes. Be gone." He returned to the cruiser, made a K-turn, and regained the road to go farther out on his patrol.

Mick wiped his face on the bottom of his shirt. Wanted to look at JJ. Didn't. Started the car instead. In a few seconds Grace popped in the backseat.

"Nice," she said. "What'd he say?" When neither Mick nor JJ spoke, Grace lay down and used JJ's duffel for a pillow. "Coeur d'Alene's not that far."

Mick backed to the county road and they were on their way. Thing is, by the time he reached the freeway, both Grace and JJ were sleeping. Time to use his own judgment. If he took the left, back toward Montana, he'd seen several places including the out-skirts of St. Regis where they could pull over and sleep the rest of the night. Mick parked across from the on-ramp. East or west? Two hours back to Dad and interrogations, or one hour forward with the girls to a new town? Put it that way, it wasn't so hard. He swung the car toward Coeur d'Alene.

45

IN SANDERS COUNTY, law officers continued to investigate the murder. The jurisdiction was split as it often was in rural areas, and collaboration was weak as neither Cassel nor Paint had any use for each other.

The same day the body was discovered the Montana Highway Patrol began advertising on radio and TV, searching for drivers that regularly traveled Highway 200 at night. They began tracking down commuters between Portage and Plains and sales vans or semis with regular routes between Missoula and Sandpoint. They also reviewed trucking company logs and traffic citations for the afternoon and evening of the murder.

The Sheriff's Department started a similar and parallel investigation, posting pictures of the girl and her Subaru on bulletin boards at convenience marts and community business windows in a thirty-mile radius asking anyone who had seen Evelyn Edmonds talking with male friends or strangers to contact officials.

By Thursday deputies had canvassed the restaurant staff and interviewed local girls between the ages of sixteen and twenty-five. Because Evelyn was a waitress and a friendly one at that, the compiled list of male acquaintances was a long one, well over a hundred, many with no alibis.

Evelyn's father and mother believed that she currently had no regular boyfriend, an assumption that was confirmed by the girl's friends from Plains. At that point Patrol investigators learned Evelyn had lately been receiving a number of gifts and selling them. Conjecture began concerning her extracurricular work activities.

Paint had arrived at a similar assumption about Evelyn's additional employment after examining her frequent male contact survey. The results suggested something other than plain affability was at work. It reminded Paint of a stakeout he'd done a few years before on a meth house where, in the course of a week, the place had fifteen to forty different nightly visitors. A phone call to the investigating deputy in Plains confirmed his suspicions. Girlfriends reported Evelyn was dating a "whole lot of guys" and had "big plans" involving Seattle or L.A., but none knew any specifics.

46

NEAR MIDNIGHT, the city of Coeur d'Alene was lit up like an amusement park. Knots of tourists still walking the main streets near the wharf, restaurants and bars still open. They didn't have motel money, so where? They drove the lakeshore hoping to car-camp near water, but everything was built up, marinas, condos. On the southeast shore, just before the street reached water's edge, finally, a cheap-looking motel that had parking in back near a poplar grove. Figured they could sleep till dawn or maybe even later, then go find a public park and clean up.

• • •

Mick woke agitated. He'd been dreaming about kissing. Who? He couldn't remember. Fugitive, car thief, stud wannabe. Pretty feeble. He needed to get his mind off sex. First priority, food, and they'd been wasting their money on junk. Right. Like Mick was an expert. He and his dad, salami and Fritos. They had enough money left for block cheese, apples, maybe enough for bread and peanut butter. Before he could share his insight, everybody had to pee. They used the poplar grove.

The wharf area by the fancy hotel was clean, well kept, bordered everywhere with blooming flowers and expensive landscaping. Ferries? Lake tours? They parked in a free lot near some big boats and explored the docks that weren't gated, continued following sidewalks a few hundred yards into town. After an hour or so they returned to sit on the hood of the car and survey the lake. Watched gulls, and some graceful black-and-white birds that no one could name. An osprey circled farther from shore.

"We should hide the car," Grace said, looking west toward the Spokane River in the distance.

"How would we get around?" Mick asked.

"They'll be looking for the three of us so we should split up," Grace said. "Me and JJ team, you on your own."

JJ turned to look at her. "What's Mick gonna do?"

Mick knew he didn't like this idea. "That's crazy. You wouldn't be safe. You got no place to stay."

"Women's shelter," Grace said.

JJ had misgivings. Mick could see it. As close as she and Grace were, living together, JJ and Mick were probably closer. They trusted each other.

"That's just what you can't do," Mick argued. "Go to a government place. Get your descriptions on their computers. That's the first place the law would look, missions, shelters, places for runaways."

Grace ran her fingers through her hair, seeming to think about what he said.

JJ pointed. She'd seen a police car pull into the public parking area and begin a row-by-row cruise.

They were off the hood, into the car, and rolling within seconds. Couldn't tell if the patrol car was following.

Mick headed north on Lincoln and west on Seltice Way toward the town of Post Falls. After a mile or two he pulled off the street into a stand of pines on the edge of a construction site and shut off the car. Turned, ready to argue. "That's stupid. We have to—"

"Separate," Grace interrupted. "Face it."

Mick, furious. "That's horseshit! I'm trying to be here for you. I got you out of town. I'm trying to protect you!"

Grace was ahead of him. "You're putting JJ and me in danger. The sheriff is looking for *you*. This car."

Mick waved her off. "Do you hate all us guys so much you can't think straight?"

A moan from the backseat. Mick glanced back. JJ had folded her knees to her chest, holding her ears. He could guess what she was thinking. JJ had left one hell and he and Grace were creating a new one.

"I'm thinking good," Grace said. "You're a little fuzzy 'cause you're scared."

That hurt. "Of course I'm scared. I don't want anything to happen to you or JJ."

"I mean scared to be on your own." She paused, reached out to touch his shoulder.

Mick shrugged off her hand. This was the thanks he got.

"You're right to be scared," Grace said, her voice softer.

Mick thought she was manipulating him, but her words were stinging.

"It's horrible to be totally cut loose. Imagine what it's like for a girl." Grace glanced back at JJ. "When I was on the road, everything was out of control. Anything could have happened anytime."

Mick looked away at nearby trees and the flock of small gray birds that were gathering on branches. An empty six-pack hung in a bush. Around the small clearing: white paper fast-food bags, wadded plastic diapers, a soiled blanket. Was this going to be his life from now on?

"Listen." Grace had dropped the angry tone. "Think. You're the target. You're the one that's tangled."

She reached out again and Mick stiffed her again.

"The only ones laying for us is the Cassels. You split after talking to that old guy, that sheriff. He's probably got a wanted out for you and the car by now. He doesn't care about JJ and me."

Mick wanted to disagree, wanted to show Grace he was on top of things. But beneath that, he *was* scared. Leaving his dad. Now leaving JJ and Grace? He couldn't get his mind around it.

"Let us go, Mick. At least for today and tonight. Let's take a break. We can think about it again tomorrow."

Mick heard a muted sob from the backseat, but neither he nor Grace turned around.

Mick hadn't considered things from Grace's point of view. She was probably right. And he saw something else. Grace had just used him to get out of town. He wasn't like a boyfriend. He was transportation, convenience, pure and simple.

"Let's find the bus station," Grace suggested. "They're usually downtown. JJ and I can stash our bags and make that our base. Meet there tomorrow."

Mick shook his head not wanting to hear, but, inside, he wasn't really resisting.

"Before we go, we search the car, scrounge under the seats, see if there's any money, anything we can use." Grace was really talking to herself. "We go to a market, get food, split it. After that, we break up and hide for a bit."

Mick had stopped shaking his head. Stopped denying. He wasn't going to talk her out of this. Case closed.

"You ditch the car and we hook up tomorrow morning at the bus station and decide what's next." Grace was on a roll. "We'll call Gary and see what's happened."

Mick wanted to know what JJ thought of this plan but he was stuck giving Grace the silent treatment. Strong silent type? Pouting? He should front Grace for some money but he didn't want to risk it. Didn't want her to blow up and ditch him altogether. He got out of the car and emptied his pockets on the hood. Took the folding money out of his wallet. Went to the trunk and got their duffels. He opened the back door and got his things. Glanced at JJ. She was staring off in the direction of a thick line of cottonwoods. Avoiding.

Mick dumped his sack beside his money and leaned against the fender, hands in pockets, waiting for them to follow suit.

Grace fished out nearly three dollars in change from the car floor and the backseat crease. The big surprise was JJ. She had a twenty tucked in her overalls' chest pocket.

"Where did that come from?" Grace asked.

"Birthday," JJ said.

Grace rummaged in her purse and came out with another twenty. All pooled they had fifty-four dollars and change. They spent twenty for food. By Mick's calculation, they might be able to buy enough gas to get back home.

THEY DIDN'T FIND A BUS STATION. They didn't find a train station. The nearest were miles away in Spokane. They did find the public library. The entrance foyer had vending machines, large bathrooms, and a short wall of lockers where students from the local college could store books and laptops when they took study breaks. Fifty cents got you unlimited time and a key.

"Take what you need overnight," Grace told JJ, while she

herself pulled a small green leather purse out of her tote bag and stuffed it with a top and underwear, pitched in some lipstick.

JJ jammed an extra pair of panties in her pocket.

"Hey, take care." Grace punched two quarters in the slot, pocketed the key. Gave Mick a quick hug.

He didn't return it.

JJ held him by the shoulders. Her look carried a stew of feelings. "Luck," she said.

He nodded, muted by the flood of his own emotions.

Mick sat in the car and watched them walk together toward the downtown resort area and hotel marina. His eyes got wet and then he was crying. Hands over his face, muffling his noise. At first, because he wanted Grace to want him and she didn't. And then because he was alone. Really alone. He knew he was going to miss JJ. Her solidity. Her friendship or affection or whatever it was. And then, tears because he missed his father. Go figure! And finally he cried for his mother and her leaving and her not loving him enough to stay or take him with her.

He sat struggling with his thoughts until he feared he might be attracting attention. Okay, what now? Work? He might find a quick job, make a little gas money. Later he could look for a place to stow the car.

The work part came much easier than he'd imagined. He drove south on Third and east on Sherman. In ten blocks or less he passed a corner storefront being gutted. A bright red GMC pickup was parked at an angle by a dumpster at the side door. A hastily painted sign on the edge of the building said *Future home of Fly By Day Fishing Outfitters.* From the curb he could see two guys tearing off sheetrock, pulling old wiring out of exposed studs.

He parked, walked around to look in the pickup bed, went in the side door and stood near the two men. The smaller one noticed.

"Help you?"

"Yes, sir. I need a little work. Fifteen dollars the rest of the day, I'd haul crap to the dumpster so you can finish your clean-out twice as fast. Hold rock or fiberboard so you can nail straight. I've been working at a hardware. I can do things."

The bigger guy had stopped prying the sheetrock while Mick was talking. Looked him over. Suspicious.

"I mean it," Mick said. "I need gas money. I'm used to stacking, lifting. I'd have wanted to steal something I'd taken that Milwaukee Power Set sitting in your pickup bed. You'd never seen or heard me. I just want to work and get paid a little cash for it."

Neither guy said anything.

"I don't do drugs," Mick said. "My dad does. I don't."

The men glanced at each other. Looked away for a few seconds.

"Miles." The smaller guy stuck out his hand. "Jimbo." He pointed to the other guy. "Start trucking and keep trucking and you got your fifteen. Begin by getting this shit off the floor and into the dumpster." Both of them turned back to the wall and recommenced ripping.

• • •

When they stopped for the day, Mick got his money, fifteen and a five-dollar tip. He'd known it wouldn't get a motel, but it was a meal or more gas if they needed it on the way home. He hadn't wanted the demo guys to have any reason to turn him down. Now, the second order of business, keep the Pontiac out of trouble.

Big Bonnie hardtops were scarce, either a collector's car or a wife-beater ride. His dad's looked like it was in the second category and it helped that a lot of other cars from that time looked pretty close to it. If you were searching hard, you'd spot it, otherwise you wouldn't. Mick intended to sleep in it that night, so where would it be inconspicuous?

Cheap motels might work if Mick could find another one. Not easy in a fancy tourist city. Should be a different one from last night so nobody gets suspicious. The neighborhoods around his job site seemed too upscale. People might notice a strange car. But Junkville? That's what his dad called poor neighborhoods that had appliances on the porches and ratty vehicles on blocks in the yard. His father didn't seem to realize that's exactly where he and Mick always wound up when they weren't in a motel. The one in Portage, Mick guessed, would be Shackville. Within twenty minutes he'd found a suitable area on the edge of town, near a run-down trailer park surrounded by shabby homes that had once been in the countryside before the city grew around.

Mick arranged his clothes to minimize the driveshaft hump and used the tarp from the trunk for a pillow. The Bonnie's back windows were tinted. He didn't think anyone would see him unless they made a real effort with a flashlight. Mick had trouble sleeping that night, but it wasn't because the back floor of the Poncho was too uncomfortable. Though he was safe and warm, feelings of loss and loneliness weighed on him like heavy blankets. Feeling sorry for himself took him into a troubled sleep with nightmares and thrashing that left him more tired in the morning than he had been when he bedded down.

48

FROM THE LIBRARY Grace and JJ walked west on Front Street, soon reaching the parking lot they'd visited earlier in the morning. A good-looking blond attendant at the boat docks told Grace about the local college, told her Macaroni's restaurant was the town hot spot for drinks and conversation.

At the thoroughfare that appeared to be the tourist mecca, JJ marveled at the way Grace easily met different people and asked questions about the city. A taxi driver, parked and eating his sack lunch, told them they could go a few blocks farther north to St. Vincent's shelter if they were low on cash. Get a meal and spend the night. Grace took her time bending over to adjust her sandals before asking him if he'd give them a ride to the place. When he put his food away and ushered them into the backseat, JJ rolled her eyes.

On the way, the man offered to show them the town at the end of his shift.

"That might work," Grace said. Asked him for his number and wrote it down. "We'll call if we can meet you."

"So what's your phone?"

"My friend doesn't give out her cell," Grace told him, sounding disappointed but resigned. When he pulled up in front of the H.E.L.P. Center, they were out and down the sidewalk before he could open his door.

Inside the women's shelter they were told they'd have to register for a bed. The whole process took less than a half hour, meal ticket and everything. The staff directed them to a dayroom where they could read, watch TV, or rest until dinner. JJ lounged on a couch facing away from the television and was shortly asleep. Grace sat near her in a threadbare overstuffed chair and made plans.

This town was hopping, just like they told her months ago when she was ten or twenty miles west in Spokane. It might be too small for settling down but it was definitely the right spot for the rest of the summer. The best part? Full of tourists. Men who would do things here and go home. Big enough so locals wouldn't see her as anything but another visitor. An ideal place to make some money.

Her brothers had taught her a graduate seminar in coercion. In the past few months she'd learned a bit from Cookie and watched or played a part in some of the ways Hammond put pressure on people and used their weaknesses. And Evelyn, poor dear Evelyn, that girl was literally money in the bank. Grace just needed a little more information, the lay of the land here in Coeur d'Alene, and she could begin putting this education into practice.

49

AS THE INVESTIGATION PROCEEDED, restaurant employees named a total of twenty-four men, including eight high school students, who had visited Evelyn at work more than once over the last ten days. Eventually the sheriff's list reached Scott Cassel's desk at the Highway Patrol office. He was discomfited to see his older son, Larry, among those identified, as well as his younger boy, Tim, and Tim's best friend, Dave Cunneen.

Cassel had no idea where either of his sons were on the Monday evening Evelyn was killed. Larry lived north of town and kept a very irregular work schedule. Tim lived at home with Scott but he had a separate entrance. Cassel didn't think Tim had come home that Monday evening before he himself went to bed at ten-thirty. That wasn't unusual. Tim partied hard most nights during the summer months.

For the first time in years Officer Cassel found himself reluctant to interview a possible suspect. When he tried, Larry brushed him off, saying he had been with a woman on that night and it was none of his dad's business. The interview was not only brief but hostile. Scott and his older son hadn't been close for the last few years since Larry had been asked to leave the Highway Patrol Training Academy after an altercation with one of his instructors.

When Cassel asked Tim, the boy told him he'd been with Cunneen earlier that Monday night, visited a few places, and, since he was taking a road trip to see a buddy in Whitefish the next morning, he'd come home early and gone to bed. For the life of him, Scott Cassel couldn't remember if he'd heard the Mustang's throaty rumble in the driveway on that particular night.

None of the bulletins or interviews produced a particularly viable suspect. The coroner's report revealed that the puncture wound came from a rounded half-inch-in-diameter metal rod with rust and bits of black paint on its surface: a rebar, a tire iron, or a large blunted Phillips screwdriver were named as possible weapons. Most likely? A tire iron. The girl did not die of the puncture, however, but from a brain injury caused when the back of her head was smashed against the top point of the open car door, creating a fatal wound to her medulla and stopping her breathing.

Cassel was troubled by his missing witness, the Fitzhugh boy, who apparently fled the morning following their conversation, three days after the murder, stealing his father's car for a getaway. Sheriff Paint, who had already formed an opinion about the boy's innocence, was more concerned about another missing witness, Grace Herick, who, after having worked with Evelyn, also fled, possibly holding some key pieces of information. JJ's fears about invisibility would have been confirmed, as neither department gave her a thought or even realized she was gone.

In the course of his broader investigation, Cassel learned that his missing witness's father, Tighe Fitzhugh, was relatively new in town. Searching the Western States database, Cassel discovered a possible connection to theft and crimes against property in Idaho and Washington. Paint, similarly researching the name Grace Herick, found a remarkable coincidence. A Grace Herrick, one letter difference in the last name, had been killed in a vehicle accident in Spokane a few days before Grace Herick, one "r," arrived in Portage. The hunt for both missing witnesses stepped up.

Friday afternoon, an anonymous phone tip changed everything. A muffled voice suggested officers search the small wooden porch of the Fitzhugh studio. Doing so, Paint discovered a souvenir baseball bat, Boise Hawks, wrapped in a pile of rags that turned out to be Evelyn Edmonds's underwear. A stain on the handle appeared to be blood. Scott Cassel, having received the same tip, picked up Tighe Fitzhugh for questioning.

Paint issued a murder warrant for Mick's arrest.

50

EARLY THE NEXT MORNING Mick drove to a nearby city park and used the restroom, brushed his teeth with a finger. A maintenance truck was parked next to the Pontiac when he came out of the building. On the other side of it, a police car. The officer behind the wheel was talking to the city guy in the green coveralls. Mick left as unobtrusively as he could and the police car stayed parked.

Wise up! Mick needed to get this outlaw thing down better. Early morning, police patrol the parks looking for vagrants, druggies asleep in their vehicles. Safest place to clean up is a big gas station, a convenience mart thing with a lot of commercial traffic. Live and learn.

Just before noon Mick parked the car around the corner from the library and sat on a bench inside where he could watch the locker. They'd agreed: "Tomorrow, noon, the library." One o'clock. Two o'clock. Three . . . Mother of Mercy, he'd never really let himself consider the possibility. *They're not coming.*

He went to the locker and shook the door. It was still locked. They hadn't come back.

"You need something there?" Some man with a plastic name badge.

"I was just seeing if my sisters are still in town," Mick said, rubbing his nose to mask his face and keeping his eyes on the floor like he was embarrassed. "Uh, thanks, I'll check back." He was moving toward the glass exit doors. Could the sheriff have circulated his photo to public buildings in neighboring states? He thought they shared the same government Internet system. Did Portage High have a picture officers could have used? Mick didn't believe so.

"What they look like?" This from behind him, a female voice.

When he turned, a woman janitor was facing him, hand on the mop sticking out of her rolling water pail.

"At the lockers? Pretty? Kinda slim?" she asked.

Mick stopped and walked back. What the hell? Nearly everything he'd been doing lately was a risk.

"Dropped my broom," the woman said. "She bent right over and got it up. Nadine don't meet many like that anymore," she said, shaking her head.

Mick saw "Nadine" stitched in red on the woman's uniform.

"Yeah, yes," he said, "that's her. One of them. Uh, I've been working . . . I told them I'd give them a ride back—"

"Them girls should be with they folks! Too young to be out travlin'." The woman frowned at him like it was his fault.

"Yeah, you're right." Mick looked around to see if anyone was paying attention to the conversation. Didn't seem like it. "So"—he faced her again—"you see what she did? Get bags and take off?"

"Well, got more clothes is alls. Early. I just come on. They probly still around. I see 'em I tell 'em you're looking."

Mick sat in the car near the building until four, then drove downtown. Party town. Wouldn't Grace be right in the thick of it?

He went to the boulevard that ended at the big hotel on the lake and rolled slowly down the street that seemed like the town promenade. In this area, the sidewalks were crowded: khaki shorts, bright T-shirts, fathers with smiling families, jocks and fraternity guys cruising, girls with arms around each other, couples

chatting in convertibles. *There!* Grace standing by the rail at
Macaroni's sidewalk café. Good place to panhandle. He didn't see
JJ. Where were they staying? He honked, waved. Grace didn't pay
any attention. Mick found a place to pull over in the next block,
but when he ran back she was gone.

He cruised the area for the next hour until he began to feel
guilty about the gas he was wasting and put the car in a mall's
nearly full parking garage. Inside, he found a bench in front of
a fancy store and watched crowds of shoppers. What should he
do? Try to find permanent work here? Go back to Portage and
face . . . his dad, the sheriff, the Cassels? Not without the girls.
That made him think about the Stovalls' trailer and Gary.

Over the past months JJ had told Mick a lot about Gary that he
wouldn't have guessed. One, Gary had spent three years in prison
for growing dope. Gary and Tina had been caretakers of some
old vineyard property north of Napa. Planted bud at the remote
edges. Did okay for a couple of years and then, federal bust. Tina
was pregnant and had a kid two weeks before she went to a locked
women's facility. The kid died. Gary said Tina had a breakdown
and they released her to the state psych hospital. After discharge
she stayed with her sister, JJ's mom, until Gary got paroled. She'd
never been the same since.

He moved the family to Portage around ten years ago. Tina
had Jon. Gary started an electronics repair business, something
he'd learned in the Navy. Hardware store was his collection point
for the TVs, radios, DVD players. Pick up the broken, bring back
the fixed a couple of times a week. Gave Hammond a cut for a

handling fee. That and the dope sales and Grace's foster care money made a pretty good living.

JJ liked that Gary was kind. Decent to Tina, who's basically a lump. But JJ hated the drugging and cuffing that Gary did with Jon. "The man's just ignorant," JJ told Mick. "Doesn't know what to do. Those two should never have had kids."

Not long ago on one of those river nights, Mick had finally opened up a little more to JJ. Told her he thought Gary was a little like his dad. Both men learned their trades in the service. Both did things against the law. He told JJ that he thought his dad loved him. Or maybe not loved him but felt responsible for him. Mick told her that for his part, he didn't particularly like his father, he didn't respect him, and that he sure didn't want to grow up like him.

The problem was, when Mick thought about it, he didn't know any older man that he wanted to grow up like. Being an adult seemed impossible. Like he had a lid on his future. And Grace? What was her future? Whatever it was, Mick imagined she'd fend for herself, do whatever she needed to. He was surprised to realize he couldn't picture her being happy.

What about JJ? Who could even appreciate her besides him? Who would know she was full of dreams? Who would listen to her moon stories? Those thoughts stung. Mick knew he only spent time with her because she was there. Handy. His mind was always on Grace. JJ deserved better than that. She deserved better than him. But how would she find it in Portage?

Watching families go store to store wasn't making him less lonely, it was making him feel worse. Depressed. Envious. Not because he wanted to be buying things, but because he wanted to belong to this ordinary world. Have a real family, a girlfriend, pick a college. Just be regular. Not very damn likely! Though he couldn't remember doing it before, he thought of praying. *Let there be something for me that I'm not seeing right now.* His father laughed at prayer, but lots of times his father was wrong.

51

THE NEXT MORNING, Sunday, shortly after daylight, Mick was back at the library. His neck was stiff and his shoulder ached. Sleeping in the Bonnie was getting old. Sign on the front door said the building didn't open until noon. He went around the block and parked across the street down a ways, the opposite direction from downtown. Waited.

Grace appeared a little after noon, walked up the steps, through the glass doors. Mick was on her heels, didn't think she even saw him as she went to the locker.

"Forget something?" He could hear the sarcasm in his voice.

She didn't look good. Pasty. Tired.

"Hi, Mick," she said, not much energy. "Sorry about yesterday. JJ's sick."

Mick already had a speech practiced about giving your word

and letting people down, but now no longer seemed the time to give it. He'd been imagining, hoping for a confrontation if he saw her at all, but Grace didn't seem to have the juice for that.

"No way. She was fine."

"No. I mean . . . she's been crying a lot. Misses you. Doesn't like . . . she's not so good. After we saw you she sort of shut down. You know how Tina does? Wouldn't talk, hardly opened her eyes. I couldn't come down here because I couldn't leave her and I didn't want somebody else getting worried and questioning her. A lady at the shelter said she'd watch her this morning so I could get here."

"You couldn't come here yesterday? The janitor saw you!" Mick had never hit a girl. Was trying to hold his temper.

"Damn! What's with you, Mick? All about you? Something's the matter with JJ!"

"Yeah, and something's the matter with me. You use me! Pick me up whenever you need something." Mick could hear a whine in his voice and didn't like it. Went on. "I drove you here. You didn't contribute shit. Said I was a danger, and left me. Didn't show up when you said. Yeah, it's about me. You treat me like dirt. You would have split again today if I hadn't caught you."

"Hey! Simmer down! You got problems with the law, I don't!"

Too loud. Everybody in forty feet could hear her.

"Yeah, but I don't deserve it! You said to lie about it! I just reported it so the girl could get buried. I'm not the goddamn criminal!" Mick was starting to wonder why he didn't just rent a speaker truck and tell the entire city.

"Piss off, Mick! We all got problems! Me, I'm homeless, my friend won't speak, I'm stranded, selling my butt for chump change. That's just a little more than I want to handle! I got nothing."

She didn't say "for you" but it was there, loud and clear.

"Take me to her." JJ was the key to the next move.

"It's a women's shelter. They won't let you in."

"I'll say I'm her brother."

"I already told them you were chasing us. I didn't want you showing up and breaking my story."

"You . . ." Mick didn't know what to say. What could he say? The string of betrayals . . . "Well for starters, you tell them different. Put the three of us together again. I'm done running. We're going back to Portage and straighten things out." Mick noticed Grace looking at his hands. Fists now.

His fury kept him talking. "Fix things at that shelter or I'm going to the police as soon as I walk out this door. I'm telling them I ran away after finding a body and you and JJ are in it with me." *When did he decide this?*

"You can't do that!" Grace, wild-eyed, hawk in a snare. "You can't blow everybody up just because your feelings are hurt."

"Try me." He knew in that moment he would do it. Truth or consequences. Anything was better than more running. Except in this case, it was probably going to be truth and consequences.

Grace turned back to the locker.

Mick was wondering whether to stop a cop car or find the police station. When he looked up, Grace was standing in front of him with their bags.

"Okay," she said.

Selling her butt?

52

GRACE HADN'T PLANNED to tell Mick about her dating game. It slipped out when he pissed her off. It wasn't like shame. It just wasn't his business. He'd find out anyway. JJ would spill it, hoping Mick would see what kind of person Grace was and maybe want JJ more. Grace didn't think that would happen. Mick would keep nosing around, hoping. Grace could practically smell his hunger.

She hadn't given tricking much thought. It would be better than fighting off her brothers. It turned out to be more complicated than she'd imagined. In the café, Evelyn had flirted with certain customers, getting chummier throughout the meal, teasing, making a little suggestion when she brought their check. It had been friendly, smooth, and Evelyn had selected the partners herself.

The street was different. Grace discovered yesterday that she would have to stand someplace accessible, look sexy and interested to attract the right men. She couldn't be too obvious or she'd get arrested. Plus, she had to be careful, had to plan her strategy so she could stay safe.

The wrought-iron fence in front of Macaroni's restaurant on

Sherman looked like the best place to set up shop. She would be one of several people leaning against it and people-watching while tourists dined in the row of tables behind her. The sidewalk was a thoroughfare, always busy with sightseers walking from the waterfront to nearby shops and bistros. A girl casually waiting or resting there wouldn't attract special attention and she could use the restaurant bathroom to stay fresh. Okay, but where could she bring her customers? It took her a couple of hours to find secluded places close to the restaurant that offered privacy but were near enough foot and car traffic so someone could hear her scream if she needed.

The guy would have to approach her and make the first move. She would get in a car if it was expensive and clean and the guy was older, like fifty or sixty. If strong younger guys like her brothers were driving, they'd have to park their car and do business in the alley behind Macaroni's or the thick stand of trees a block away at the end of South Third. And JJ was going to be a problem. She had walked with Grace while she'd scouted hideaways.

"What are we doing?"

"Getting some exercise, finding some places we can rest without having to go back to the shelter." Grace casually checked JJ's reaction to her explanation. Her roomie didn't seem convinced. "You want to go back and take a nap? I have some things I have to get and I want to meet some people."

JJ shook her head. "What people?"

"Anybody that can help us," Grace said. "See if we can make some cash."

"How?"

Grace didn't answer. Talking about her plan would make JJ more upset.

The girls walked a few blocks south on Sherman to a convenience store. "Get us a soda, okay?" Grace nodded toward the machine in back with the cups and ice.

While JJ was busy Grace hurriedly bought a box of condoms, a package of tissues, and a small bottle of hand sanitizer. Tucked the sack under her arm as JJ reached the cashier.

"What'd you get?"

Grace thought JJ already knew. "I'm going to make us some spending money."

JJ's frown spoke volumes.

Back at Macaroni's, Grace asked JJ to stay across the street and sit on the outdoor bench next to the burger shop. JJ, flushed, hands clenching and unclenching, gave her a hard look, shook her head, started to say something but held back.

"You don't have to do anything except watch my back and let me do this thing. Okay?"

"No."

"Lady Jay, you know I'm going to do it anyway. Don't make it harder."

JJ stomped to the crosswalk. Didn't look back.

Grace took a deep breath, composed herself, looked to see if anyone had tracked their exchange. No. Crowds of strollers, chatting and laughing. She entered the café's front door on the corner, got shown to a window table, and ordered coffee. Wanted to establish herself as a customer. She'd do the same for the evening shift. Leave a good tip each time so the staff would be grateful. Before the coffee arrived she went to the bathroom, locked the door. She took out the condoms, threw the box away, jammed them in her purse along with the tissues and sanitizer. She checked her face in the mirror, added a touch of Tina's lipstick, tousled her hair to give it a little more body. She hesitated before opening the door, removed her underwear, stuffed it in her purse. Ready. Now, if JJ would cut her some slack.

Grace positioned herself in an open area between groups of loiterers. Leaned back, elbows on the top rail. It didn't take long. She gave a big smile to a heavyset older man in golf shorts and a polo shirt. Ruddy face. Probably had a few to celebrate his vacation. He couldn't believe his luck, then got suspicious. Grace practically told him the truth, that she'd run away from a sick home. Said she was getting money to take a bus. Go to her aunt in Tacoma, but she couldn't tell the woman what had been happening until she got there. The man understood. Enjoyed her company. Afterward gave her a large tip. Grace got it. If she chose the right people it was quick work, good pay. Would she recognize trouble coming? She hoped so. She was setting up to do this for a while.

The fourth guy, Grace made a mistake. The old man was harder than he looked.

Said, "Cops don't pay for it. Ex-cops, same deal." He slapped her. Hard. "That's so we understand each other."

She held her cheek where it burned. Leaned closer. Offered her cheek. Said, "Kiss it and make it well." When he leaned in she head-butted him in the nose as hard as she could. He went down spraying blood. She searched him for weapons. No. Kicked him in the nuts while he was holding his face. "Tell the other cops a sixteen-year-old girl did this to you while you were trying to hump her."

After that she chose men who seemed shy and even a little embarrassed. Lucky. There were lots of them.

Okay. So now Mick knew and he wanted to go home, but that didn't change anything.

53

THE SHELTER WAS ONLY EIGHT BLOCKS AWAY. Looked like a normal house. They parked down the block. Grace spoke as soon as Mick turned off the ignition.

"I'll try to get her out for a walk. You stay here."

"How did Gary and Tina ever get to be your foster parents?" Mick asked her, out of nowhere. "Nobody who ever made a home visit would put you there."

"You want to talk about this now?" Grace looked at him like he was a pervert. Get the upper hand and then totally invade her privacy.

"I'm trying to make sense of what we're going back to." Mick looked out the windshield. If she wanted to shine him on, she could just get out of the car.

"Short story. I got put off a Greyhound in Portage, broke, and wound up at County Services. Man there, Mackler, called Hammond. A couple of things happened and Gary came through the door, said he was my new foster parent. Under the table. Gary and Hammond have these arrangements. I'm one of them. One of the reasons I don't want to go back."

Greyhound? Mick watched her walk to a nondescript building, knock and be let in, while he tried to think if he'd ever seen a bus like that in Portage. And what do you say to her story? Get sold like livestock? No wonder Grace hated men. Gary. He seemed like a nice-enough guy. What was happening inside him? Where was his conscience? Had he lived in that toilet so long, he actually thought it was a home? Anything all right with him for a little extra income and babysitting?

Mick knew that he had given Grace room to ditch him once more. Well, hell. He was hurt and mad, but finally, at least, he knew what he was going to do. He wouldn't leave without JJ.

A tap on his window.

"See your license, registration, proof of insurance?"

His bowels nearly loosened. "Sure." He was amazed he could speak.

The policeman waited.

Mick fumbled around in the glove compartment. Thank god! The registration. "Uh, I slept in a rest stop last night and a guy mugged me. Took my wallet. My license. I'm just here to pick up my sister and her sick friend, take them back home. Kind of a mercy mission." Would the lying ever stop?

"Proof of insurance?"

"My dad carries that. He loaned me his car for the trip. Didn't give it to me. Forgot."

"Step out of the car please." The policeman moved back from the door and unbuttoned his holster.

"Everything okay, Mick?" Grace. Walking toward them. Towing JJ.

"Uh, yeah, I think so," Mick said getting out. "This officer's just checking to make sure I'm not—"

"Bothering anybody," the policeman finished for him.

"He's just picking us up," Grace said. "He's taking us . . . home."

"Which is?" the officer said, glancing at Grace but examining JJ more closely.

Grace looked at Mick.

He nodded his head, hoping she understood that he thought it was okay to tell the officer.

"Montana," she said. "Above St. Regis."

The officer looked at Grace. Gave JJ another once-over. Then at Mick, his scar, his clothes still dusty from the construction job. The man's patrol car radio squawked. He checked the phone on his belt. Then looked back at Grace. "You trust this boy?" he asked her.

Boy.

"Yes, sir," Grace said, without taking her eyes off the man. "He saved us from some guys. Brought us here."

The car radio squawked again. "Where you taking them?" He canted his head, directing this question Mick's way.

"Home," Mick said. "Just home." Couldn't think of anything else to say.

The officer dragged a card out of his shirt pocket. Walked over and handed it to Grace. "You have any trouble again, *any*, you call me. Davis. Dispatch can reach me." He looked at her hard to make sure she got it.

She nodded.

He looked at the Pontiac's Montana plate, wrote the number down on a folded file card, and was out of there before the three of them moved.

Water rimmed Grace's eyes. And then JJ was crying.

Pretty tense. All Mick felt right then was relief, but he wanted to get moving before the man came back or anything else happened. "Let's roll." He was thinking to go back the northern route, fewer cops than the freeway.

JJ started toward the car.

"You two go," Grace said.

JJ stopped in her tracks.

"You can't talk me out of it," Grace said. "There's nothing for me in Portage. I can't even hide there anymore." She fumbled in her jeans pocket and brought out two twenties. Handed it to JJ who was back at her side. "Buy some gas, food, get going. I'll be okay."

"No, you won't!" JJ blurted. "You can't. I won't let you."

Was this JJ? Grace had said the girl was depressed. Mick had never heard her speak so forcefully.

"Hey, Lady Jay, I love you. You're my girl. But it's *my* life."

Mick began to feel like a spectator at a tennis match. Didn't he figure into the equation at all? Guess not.

"You know I'm right," Grace said, nodding her head as if that little extra effort would convince her friend. "Uh oh, he's back!"

JJ and Mick wheeled to confront the policeman. But nobody was there. When they turned around, Grace was nearly to the front door of the shelter.

"Take care," she said over her shoulder. "Don't follow me. I'll get you arrested!" And then she was inside.

JJ and Mick looked at each other. They knew Grace could think up a quick story that would land both of them in more trouble. They knew she'd do it if it suited her.

54

THEY GOT A CHUNK past Sandpoint when JJ asked Mick to stop.

"You need something?" His shoulders were tight. "We could get gas at Bonners Ferry."

"Turn around."

Mick's first thought was that JJ forgot something. Then he got it.

"We can't," Mick said. "Grace is better at this than we are. She'll jam us up and she'll skate."

"Pull over! I mean it." This, the new JJ.

Mick made the next exit and stopped near a vacant storefront.

"I know what she's doing, where she got that money," JJ said. "The forty dollars she gave us? There's a lot more. She's prossing."

You don't say prossing. Hooking, tricking, even whoring would work.

"It was ugly. Gross . . . I couldn't watch it," JJ said. "On the street with her, see her get the guys. The way she talked and acted. It wasn't her but it was. She was good at it." JJ's eyes were wet again. "I didn't want to imagine the sex but I couldn't hardly keep from it. Mostly I stayed at the shelter." JJ closed her eyes, remembering. "She came home at curfew and cleaned up. Washed herself." JJ shuddered.

God help him. Mick was getting excited. He knew what JJ was saying. Understood how much it creeped her. And he felt bad for Grace doing something so vulnerable. He thought maybe it was different, like, in a way, her choice. She wasn't being raped. She was in control. Maybe. But imagining Grace doing it, even with someone else, was making him want her. Sick. But true.

"Are you her friend?" JJ asked Mick. "Really?"

Good question. This whole time, had he been Grace's friend or her dweeb? Eager. Looking for a crumb.

JJ's expression was changing, growing disgusted.

"I want to be her friend . . . I think." Mick knew there was way more to be said. His attraction to Grace. His desire, craving. How that wasn't the deeper kind of friendship he had with JJ.

Weird, because he felt so much closer to JJ. Easy. Connected . . . and what about that kiss? When he got right down to it, Mick wasn't exactly sure how he felt about JJ.

"Turn around," JJ said. "Before something happens to her."

Mick had wet his hair and slicked it down, turned his jacket inside out. JJ had on the ball cap, sideways, and wore a tight pair of slacks she had picked up earlier from the bin at the shelter. Had he ever seen her in anything but sweats or a ball uniform?

JJ was on a metro bench across the street from the lakeside luxury hotel, the busiest part of the promenade. Mick was on the same side of the street down two blocks in the doorway of a florist shop that had closed for the evening. They had a good chance to find her, if, god forbid, she hadn't moved on to Spokane. More street traffic here, full of tourists, party atmosphere. Grace would see it the same way. Money.

Around ten, Grace stepped out of a Seville, right in front of Macaroni's, waved, watched the car move away before she straightened up and brushed herself off. Could you brush tricking off?

She walked around the wrought-iron fence between the tables and street, talked to a waitress for a moment, then went inside the restaurant.

Mick didn't have to signal JJ. The girl was already moving.

Timing would be crucial. Mick headed for the car in the public lot at the wharf. He'd bring it to the restaurant, double-park if he had to. Risk a ticket. He knew JJ would need help.

Mick was right but not the way he expected. By the time he

stopped the car, JJ and Grace were already in a loud argument outside the restaurant's front door. He was out and running in time to see JJ smash Grace right in the face with a ferocious round-house. *What the?* Grace grabbed her nose. JJ grabbed Grace under the right arm and Mick got there to catch her under the left.

People outside dining were standing now.

"Don't worry," JJ said to the crowd. "Intervention. My sister. Crackhead! Going residential. Show's over."

The new JJ.

They moved Grace to the car and JJ pushed her into the back-seat. Slid in beside her.

Mick jumped in front and they were gone. Him and JJ. Hooker-jackers. North this time. Roundabout. Up 95 past Sandpoint to Highway 2 and then down through Troy to 56 and home. Small roads. Out of the way. Probably less risky.

JJ asked if there were any rags up front. Grace's nose was bleeding.

Grace was crying and cursing and every so often groaning when a new wave of pain would pass through. "Goddamn it! I'll kill you!" Paused to get her breath. "Kill you both."

Mick could hear JJ shushing her gently, not arguing. In the mirror he could see her holding Grace.

After maybe twenty miles, Grace sat up and JJ let go. Mick wondered if they were going to have another fight the next time they got gas.

"What's wrong with you guys?" Grace sounded like she had the flu.

"Couldn't let you keep doing that," JJ said. "You don't have to. We'll figure something else."

"You . . . basket case!" That burst seemed to take a lot out of Grace. She dropped her voice. "You want them to send me home. Back to California?"

"California?" JJ said. "No way."

Mick thought he'd heard Grace cry before, but he hadn't. Not like she started to then, sobbing that took her whole body, possessed it.

JJ sat beside her. Not touching. Letting her grieve.

They stopped on the outskirts of Sandpoint for gas. "We're not going to make it," Mick said, across from a Chevron. They'd spent the money Grace gave them in Coeur d'Alene. The food was already gone. Mick held up the remaining cash. "We'll wind up probably fifty miles short of Portage. And hungry."

JJ stared at Grace.

Grace took off her shoe. Removed a thin fold. Peeled off two bills and put the leftover in her jeans pocket. Poked the money at JJ and looked away, out her window.

There was a lot in those two twenties. Seemed like she was giving up on her plan to keep running, at least for now.

Mick pulled across the street and put gas in the car while Grace and JJ went in the mini-mart. They weren't running now. They were going home.

55

MICK PULLED OFF 2 just before Moyie Springs, took a small road south to the Kootenai River. A paved parking area had three or four RVs and a pickup camper. Mick figured it would be a safe place for a quick nap before they crossed into Montana.

"What are we going to do when we get back?" JJ, after Mick shut off the engine.

He'd been batting that same question back and forth. "I'll drop you guys off and go look for the sheriff, I guess."

"We should call Gary and see what's happened," JJ said. "Have you called him?" This to Grace.

No reply. Bitter look.

"Have you?" JJ asked Mick.

"Don't know a thing," he said.

"You trust the sheriff?"

"Dovey does."

"I like her," JJ said. "Maybe you should talk to her."

"Maybe you should. I think I have to go to the sheriff right away. First. If I don't, and he sees me, he'll think I'm still scamming."

"What about Tim Cassel and his dad?"

Mick was really struck by JJ. She hadn't mentioned the moon lately. She'd stepped up to the plate. Brainstorming, involved in a way he'd never seen before. Grace had told him JJ'd shut down, pulled a Tina, and Mick remembered the slump of JJ's shoulders earlier when she and Grace were walking toward the Coeur d'Alene policeman. Not now.

Mick wondered if JJ had ever been needed like this before. To keep a friend from self-destruction. But it wasn't just that. JJ had started thinking ahead, trying to take care of him.

Maybe the only sane response to having your mom die and being stuck with addicts for years in a rancid trailer was to numb out. Living right on top of people? Putting up with Tina and Jon and how he was treated? No options? Who wouldn't go inside, daydream? That or go crazy. And in Coeur d'Alene, when Grace started hooking, JJ numbed out. Made sense. She'd learned that from both moms in different ways.

Somehow though, JJ had picked up a new way. Like she'd brought her strength and confidence from sports into the rest of her life, and Mick bet she didn't even realize she was doing it. You could fold or fight. Grace had forced Mick to learn that. Made him be totally on his own. He thought he could do it again, if he had to, if he didn't have his dad anymore.

"Well?" JJ broke into Mick's thoughts. "You don't think the Cassels are a world-class problem?" Annoyed, as if Mick had been avoiding her earlier question.

Maybe he had. "No. I mean, I don't know. I was thinking about you. You've . . . you're different."

"Goddamn it!" She swatted at him from the backseat. "I'm not stupid! Neither of you knows shit about me. And you don't care. I'm just around. You ask me places because you want Grace to go. I'm convenient. Period."

Mick hadn't fooled her. JJ could see right through him.

She wasn't done. "I'm . . . too private . . . or too out of it. But that doesn't matter now. This is about you. You have to be ready. You can't just walk in there like a dummy and let things happen."

Grace wasn't reacting, turned away from both of them, sullen, hurting.

Mick was pinned by JJ's words. He wanted to reassure her. Wanted to deny the charges. But she was right. He'd gone off on Grace for using him but he'd done the same thing to JJ. Gotten to know her so maybe she could help find a place to live if his dad took off again. Invited her places so Grace would go. Was it true? Did he really not care?

Mick clicked the car's electrics on for a moment and lowered the windows. A breeze came in off the water, the river moving so massively it was barely audible.

Mick did care. He could feel it but he couldn't explain it. Just as well. If he tried right now, JJ'd think he was lying. And, JJ was right. He couldn't just walk into the sheriff's office and expect things to go well. He had been wanted for questioning and he ran. Fugitive. Wrong and illegal. Now he'd have to prove he didn't kill the girl.

Before Portage, Mick needed to learn what Grace and JJ knew, but right now neither one was in any mood to talk to him. They'd get over it. He started the car and headed back to the highway. He'd stop again when they got closer to home, when their anger had passed, when they could pool information.

• • •

They made it about a half hour into Montana before JJ asked Mick to pull over for a bathroom break. Mick thought there'd be something in Troy but it was close to dawn and the town was completely buttoned up. Ten or fifteen minutes later they hit a rest area at the intersection of Bull Lake Road.

JJ was out of the car immediately, heading for the Women's. Grace was asleep. Mick's head ached and his eyes burned from straining to watch for animals crossing the dark two-lane. A good-sized buck could wreck a car. He rested his chin on his chest and shut down for a minute.

JJ opening the car door jerked him awake.

"Where's Grace?" JJ asked, sounding tired herself. "She go in the bushes?"

Mick spun around. Gone. Grace was gone. They both jumped out of the car and scanned the parking area. There were two other cars. They checked those first. Single men, asleep. JJ went back to the toilets, searched them. Nothing. Could she have gotten in a car that had already pulled out? Mick had been so wiped he hadn't noticed other cars when they arrived. It was possible.

JJ hustled back to the Bonnie, leaned on it. "Hang on," she said, catching her breath. "I don't think she trusts men enough to hitch a ride in the dark or even wake those sleeping guys. I watched her. She only goes with guys she chooses. She's out here somewhere, gonna wait till light to find somebody to take her back to Coeur d'Alene. That's her best bet."

They calmed down and looked the rest area over more carefully. The truck parking area was empty save for a Forest Service pickup with a man in the driver's seat eating a sandwich. Neither Mick nor JJ thought Grace would hitch with a government person. They'd ask him later if they needed to. Moved to a different vantage point and saw behind them, across the parking lot from the toilets, a metal enclosure for the dumpster. JJ motioned Mick to follow and sneaked over.

It was too tall to see inside, but when JJ opened the gate, Grace was sitting on the far side on a pile of balloony orange plastic trash bags. She rose without speaking and walked directly to the women's bathroom. JJ went with her and Mick started the car.

56

WHEN GRACE got in the front seat Mick could smell onions, probably fast food remains from the garbage area. She looked beat, hopeless.

JJ got in beside her. Crowded but workable for a short distance. "We need to get off the highway and talk."

Mick wheeled the car out of the rest area and onto Bull Lake Road. A mile down, took a right on a dirt road and pulled off shortly at the entrance to a range gate. Parked and left the car to stretch for a minute. He came back to JJ and Grace standing beside the car, talking. Interrupted.

"Me making the 911 wrecked it," Mick said, voicing what he'd been thinking. He looked at Grace to get a read.

Her hands were clasped in front of her, her eyes on the ground. "You should've let me alone," she said. "I can't go back, now."

"What do you mean?" Mick asked.

"I was working with them before. Now they're going to be suspicious."

"Them who?" JJ.

"Hammond and all his guys."

"Doing what?" Mick asked, but while his stomach churned, something else slid into place. "Do Hammond and his guys have these, wear these V-rings?"

Grace nodded. Said, "I think so."

"Like who?" Mick asked.

"Cookie told me Sam Hammond started it back in high school after the school football and basketball teams won their league."

"Started it with . . . ?"

"Teammates, I guess. Greer, Bolton, Cassel, maybe Mackler."

"What does—?"

"God! Leave me alone." Grace turned away, reached in, snatched the folded tarp from the car floor, and hugged it in front of her like a shield.

Their questions were interrupted by a low-grade noise back toward the highway. They saw the cloud of dust before they saw the vehicle. A quarter mile away, Forest Service green pickup. They left the Bonnie and walked out to meet it as if they had nothing to hide. "It's the breakfast guy from the rest stop," JJ said. "Say we've been visiting friends in Bonners Ferry, just needed a driving break."

Mick nodded. That would work.

When the truck stopped they saw their mistake. Government insignia had been painted over. The truck had been bought at auction.

The man behind the wheel set down the paper sack he'd been sipping from, reached over and lifted a twelve-pack off his seat. Gestured like "want one?"

JJ headed around the far side of the Pontiac. Mick shook his head. Grace was motionless beside him.

The man turned off his engine, stopping his truck in a position that blocked their car's path back to the road. Stepped out carrying the box of beer. "Too hot for work, even early in the morning, huh?" He reached in the box, came out with a can, and pitched it to Mick.

Mick stepped aside and let the can fly by, hit the ground and roll.

"Well, if you can't catch, I'm damned sure going to hand one to the lady."

"We're not drinking," Mick said.

"I saw your little dance back there at the stop. Thought the little lady might need some help."

Grace shook her head. "No. An argument. I'm fine."

"Say the word." The man tipped his hat back and wiped his forehead with his sleeve, even though it was just past dawn and far from warm. When Grace didn't speak, he started again. "You broke down?" The man drew out another beer, popped the top, and took a long swallow. "Hell of a place to be busted," he said. "Nothing around except the Merrill spread and I'm the best grease monkey he got."

"We're fine," Mick said. "Just taking a break."

"One boy, two ladies, whatcha do on your break? Getting frisky? I wouldn't mind some of that."

Mick looked the man over more carefully. What was he missing? Was he just drunk or was he dangerous? Guy was unshaven under his battered cowboy hat. Bowlegged, wiry, sun-beat, with a crafty narrow face that made Mick think of a ferret. Looking for a gun or a knife on his belt, Mick finally spotted the crowbar, hanging from a belt loop and lying close to his leg.

"Lot can happen out here fifty miles from Jesus," the man said. "You don't want to get crossways with a Good Samaritan. That'd be arrogance. Be costly."

Grace walked a couple of steps away, bent over and picked up a fallen limb from a tree they were parked near. It was dry, over two feet long and thick as her wrist. Held it at her side.

Mick saw JJ making a looping circle past the back of the man's truck and then walking toward them talking on the cell phone.

"His license number is 41-1130," she was saying. "Green Dodge. He's about fifty, slim, five eight or ten, one sixty. We're just off Bull Lake Road past Troy about a half mile south of the rest stop on 2. You want to talk to him?"

The man was listening, mouth open. Took a step back as JJ continued to walk toward him, now holding the phone out. "Who's that?" he asked, glancing back at his truck.

"My uncle, Lieutenant Cassel, Highway Patrol."

The man turned and left without another word.

Watching the truck's tailgate disappear over a short rise, Grace turned to JJ. "Nobody, right?" she said.

JJ clicked the phone shut. Smiled. "No service."

Mick had been going to bull-rush the man, hit him like a tackling dummy. Now he was reconsidering. Thought maybe his dad had taught him the wrong kind of fighting. Thought maybe he should ask JJ to teach him some brain-fu.

"So it could be any of those guys at the river," JJ said. "Who drove you home the night before we went swimming?" she asked Grace. "Was it Hammond?"

"She's seeing old men?" The picture of Grace with somebody like Hammond gave Mick's insides another crank.

"Shut up!" Grace slammed the limb down and whirled to face them. "You guys made me come back. I told you what I know. Now drop it!"

"You only tell us what you want us to know." Mick, not going to be put off again. "You leave us, me, holding the bag for this and I tell Paint and Cassel about California. Get you sent back."

Grace laughed. "You don't know anything and you'll never find out, so it's not gonna happen."

Once again, Mick's rage flashed. He'd been willing to give up his home for her! He could strangle her, choke her out, close that mouth for good.

JJ broke in. "So one of the V guys dumped the girl. And whoever brought you home that night, it's probably not him. So could it be Mackler? He's a slimebag. Right?"

Mick missed her question. He was distracted, heading down another track. Going with the fury. The killing . . . what if it was rage? Like he himself a second ago. Who could get angry enough with Evelyn to kill her? Who had a V-ring and a violent temper? Scott Cassel, probably. Larry, so he'd heard. Mackler? He hadn't met the man. Tim? Cunneen? But would those two have a ring like that?

57

GRACE HALF LISTENED to Mick and JJ discuss a plan she wasn't going to follow. She was dazed, off in an entirely different direction, and Mick's threat had triggered it. She couldn't believe she hadn't seen it before. *Her mother hadn't filed a missing person report!*

If her mom got the police involved and Grace was found, the information about the incest might come to light. Couldn't have that. Wreck her brothers' lives? The scandal would affect her parents' reputation. They could lose their jobs. Her mother wouldn't take any of those risks. She'd let sleeping dogs lie. Grace saw it clear as day. Her mother didn't want Grace back. Ever.

As much as she disliked—hated—her mother, that awareness brought tears. Her mom didn't care about her. At all. In a way she was an orphan like JJ. Might as well be. Grace made herself yawn. Rubbed her face with her sleeve to cover the sorrow.

• • •

When the sadness passed, freedom remained. Neither Cassel nor Paint could get anything on her. They couldn't find out her real name or where she was from. They couldn't send her home! Whole new game.

Grace would call Hammond as soon as possible. Be straight. Tell him the killing freaked her out and she ran. Admit she was there when they found the body but say she had no idea what had happened or who did it. If he had any questions, she'd answer them. Tell him she was ready to go back to work.

After that, she'd call the restaurant. Blame Cunneen and Tim Cassel for scaring her. Say she couldn't think straight. Tell Cookie they threatened to hurt her and she ran without sorting out the consequences. Apologize. Say she needed the job and her placement with the Stovalls so she could eventually be independent. Beg her boss to take her back.

Hammond would probably pull the strings to make that happen. He'd want her close by to keep tabs on her. Actually, her return would probably reassure him. She wouldn't knowingly put herself in his grasp if she was trying to hide something.

But Mick and JJ couldn't include her in this ring thing. If Hammond found out she knew about the ring, all bets were off. So she had to go back to town first. Before JJ and Mick. She needed some separation to make her story credible. She needed Hammond to think she'd split from the other two. Broke away. She'd say she hitched home with a tourist. Hammond might believe it. Might. It was a story he couldn't check.

She had to get JJ and Mick to agree. JJ probably would. JJ'd lie so Grace wouldn't get hurt and so would Mick. Especially if she made up to him. Poor dope. And no sense telling him that his father was the one who'd brought her home that Monday night. He didn't need to know Fitz went out with both her and Ev.

She hadn't thought about Fitz and Ev. Would he kill her? Grace had refused sex with Fitz, Ev had said yes. No motive. And he'd had all the chance in the world that night he'd taken Grace shooting. If Fitz was going to force a girl, hurt a girl, that was a great opportunity. Out in the country, drinking, holding a gun . . . no, Fitz wasn't the guy.

Larry had his eye on Ev, too. Ev was polite but distant and Grace knew the girl didn't warm to him. Somebody may have warned her. Larry had a rough reputation. In spite of the money, Ev wouldn't date him. How *would* Larry Cassel take "no" for an answer? Was that what she'd overlooked that bothered her earlier? Immediately she could see how it happened!

Larry follows her from the café as she drives home to Plains. He runs her off the road. She tells him one more time she won't do it with him and he goes ballistic and kills her. He's the one. Ring, motive, temper!

That changed everything. Larry would be her winning lottery ticket. Mick and JJ could do whatever they wanted. Grace didn't care. She was homed in on her target. The end game. She might be just hours from real freedom.

The Women's Homeless Refuge in Coeur d'Alene had given her the key. She no longer needed Gary's. As soon as she got a bit more money she could go to a homeless shelter in Billings, lie about her age, pick a new name, and they'd begin connecting her with services. Housing, employment resources. She'd be a new woman, with her stash to finance a career as soon as the staff stopped paying attention. Her stash? She'd brought twenty-four hundred from Portage and earned another twelve in Coeur d'Alene. If Larry would spring for a thousand to get rid of her that'd be enough to start something.

She regretting pulling that dumb hiding stunt back at the rest area. Now Mick and JJ were wary. Be difficult to phone Larry without their hearing, but she could find a way. Especially if she agreed to all their ideas.

She needed Larry's work number so she could she leave a message at his office. Show him how dangerous she could be. Would he have a secretary? She didn't think so. It was risky, so she'd have to be casual. Something like "Found your ring on the river and thought you might want it back. Call me." Afterward, she needed to hide and wait for his response.

Best place to do all that was . . . the restaurant? No, going there might bring Hammond and Scott Cassel into the mix. She didn't know Cookie or any of the waitresses well enough to go to their homes. But how about the Conoco? Mick's dad? He wouldn't hurt her, had kind of a bond with her. Plus, she had something on him if she needed it. The guns, the underage dating. She'd call him after she left her tease message for Larry. Wouldn't Fitz let her use the service station's phone number and hang out while she waited for the return call? Flirt a little. No problem.

58

GRACE BROKE IN ON MICK AND JJ'S PLANNING. "They'll give my job to some other girl, like permanently, if I don't check in at the café today. By lunch shift. I probably have to do the motel, too." She'd keep harping until they caved and did what she wanted. Actually, her scheme fit pretty well with their idea about how to ID the ring's owner. Mick was ready to rush back, get to Sheriff Paint first before anything else got messed up. JJ only disagreed about the order of things. She thought they ought to make their ring calls before contacting Paint.

Grace showed her agitation, paced, fiddled with her hair. Said since they made her come back, she couldn't have Hammond and his friends getting more and more upset. She had to get to Sanders County ASAP, call the restaurant and arrange her return to work. Neglected to mention that a local phone book would tell her the county building inspector's office phone number as well as the Conoco.

Mick bought Grace's performance. JJ was more suspicious. She'd never heard Grace be so concerned about her work. Neither JJ nor Mick wanted to give Grace too much room to set them up for more trouble, but they both thought that going back to the café might keep her from doing something more dangerous for money. Maybe it would settle her down again. They couldn't keep Grace with them all the time. If she wanted to split, she'd find a way.

The decision? Grace got her phone numbers and made her calls about an hour later when they reached Noxon. They stopped in Trout Creek for a snack and were on the outskirts of Portage well before noon. Mick went as far as Pond Street on Main and dropped Grace at the corner. She walked downtown toward the café stretching her arms over her head, apparently glad to be out of the car and in the sun.

Grace had promised to get back with them at closing. The three of them together would go to Dovey's and set their "insurance" plan in motion. They'd give the woman the ring and ask her to call Sheriff Paint for a truth-telling session. If Grace blew them off, they'd tell Paint she'd been tricking like Ev and doing other "special" work with Hammond.

Mick and JJ watched her. She didn't turn around to check on them, didn't seem furtive or nervous. Good so far. They took the less traveled Maiden Lane a mile east across town to the garage JJ knew. It was practically on the river and reasonably close to their own compound. Mick hid the Bonnie on the far side of the wooden building.

"We can go in if you want," JJ said, pointing to a weathered back entrance. The door itself looked sturdier than the building. JJ knew the combination to the heavy-duty lock.

Mick could not have been more surprised. He'd expected a single hanging lightbulb, spiderwebs, stained cardboard boxes, ancient rusted tools. Instead, as soon as JJ flipped on the fluorescents, he saw clean, bright blue outdoor carpeting and a polished four-wheel-drive Ford Bronco with the big engine, oversized tires, roll bars, and a winch. An orderly workbench surrounded the car on three sides, shelves above stacked with labeled metal canisters.

"Gary said he bought this place and the dope shed on the north side when he first came to town. I don't think Tina even knows he has it. I know Grace doesn't." JJ, smiling. She sat on a tall stool and leaned against the workbench.

Mick shook his head. His dad would love this place. He pointed to the Bronco.

"Off-roading," JJ said. "Gary hardly ever does it anymore, but he likes it. Drives to back lakes. This is the car we took to Missoula on that trip I told you about to the planetarium. This is like his travel car. Or maybe a getaway car if he needs it. His secret."

Mick felt like clapping. Gary was full of contradictions. The horrible way he handled Jon versus the kindness and protectiveness he could show Tina and the others. The ever-present Visine. The carefully hidden SUV.

"When it's too cold for the river, I come here to be alone," JJ said. "Even got a toilet." She pointed to a closed-off area in the far corner. "Got an electric door." She pointed above their heads to metal rails that helped raise and lower the sectioned roll-up in front.

Mick had an unfamiliar jolt of playfulness. He wanted to hug JJ, celebrate with her. Celebrate what? He couldn't say. But they were alive, damn it, and they had a plan. And Mick might just be getting out from under some baggage that had been weighing on him for years. He could live without his dad and he knew it.

Mick didn't hug her. Didn't even look at her. But he wanted to and it baffled him.

"Sanders County Bank, how may I help you?"

"May I speak to Mr. Greer?"

"May I tell him who's calling?"

"I'm a friend of his family," JJ said, glancing at Mick to see how he thought she was doing.

Mick nodded his encouragement.

"Robert Greer."

"Mr. Greer, I found part of your V-ring up on the Salish. Would you like to meet me to get it back?"

"I'm sorry, Miss . . . uh, miss, but you're mistaken. I'm looking at my ring as we speak and it's fine."

JJ hung up, looked at Mick, sighed. Dialed the next number.

"Sanders County Superior Court."

In a few minutes they'd contacted everyone. Scott Cassel demanded to know who was calling. Greer and Mackler denied any problem with their rings. Bolton suggested a meeting in person to see if he could identify the setting. JJ broke the connection. No one she talked to seemed alarmed. She had to leave a message with Hammond and Larry Cassel. Neither had called back.

Mick was disappointed, the calls useless, their plan a failure. "We have to see if Dovey knows who has a ring like that. We just haven't found the right guy yet. He wouldn't tell the others, so they'd have no reason to be bothered by our questions." He touched JJ on the shoulder to get her attention. "I keep thinking about how the killing happened."

JJ looked at him funny, like who hasn't?

"No, I mean, what kind of guy would do it."

"Anybody could do it."

"Okay, but look, it wasn't planned. Right?"

"Why?"

"If somebody planned to kill Ev, they would've done a better job. Hidden the car, really hidden the body, or even made it look like an accident. It was a rush job."

JJ nodded, dubious.

"So are there guys we know who might get angry and kill her? Not plan to. Maybe not even mean to. See what I'm saying? Would Hammond be the kind of guy to put himself in that situation and act that way? Would the judge? Or the Social Services guy? The bank guy? I don't see it. But how about Larry or Tim or Cunneen? They might."

"I get it, but it's such a huge guess. It's not even fair."

"We need to ask Dovey, find out exactly which people have those rings. That's what we know that other people don't, the connection between the ring and the murder. That's our edge."

"But that's another huge guess. We don't really know the ring and Evelyn are connected. Not for sure."

Mick heard her. That was true, but he had a feeling about this. The rage, the ring, he was getting closer to the answer.

• • •

JJ needed a break, fresh air. She walked out of the garage into the summer afternoon. Into the tree-lined street and the quiet neighborhood. This town had become her home. It used to feel safe. Larry, Tim, Cunneen? She didn't like any of them, but that didn't make them killers. She sat on the curb, looked at the sky. Where was the ghost moon when she needed it? A soft breeze off the water and the warm sun made her sleepy. Figuring out who killed Evelyn was impossible.

At closing time, Mick and JJ waited for Grace in the parking lot behind the café. Fifteen minutes, twenty, she didn't show. Both were angry at themselves. Fooled again. JJ went inside to ask what time Grace had left work. She got puzzled looks. Grace? Grace was gone. Left town a couple of days ago as far as Cookie knew.

59

MICK AND JJ RETURNED TO THE GARAGE, parked the Bonnie beside it, and sneaked along the river a few blocks toward town and Dovey's trailer. Duckwalked low behind her deck rails and tapped on her door. It was late for a surprise visit but it couldn't be helped.

Dovey's eyebrows rose when she opened her door, but she let them in without a word.

Mick started before they even sat down. "I didn't do anything,

Ms. Crabtree. Except run. That was stupid. JJ and Grace didn't do anything at all except come with me. I can prove I'm innocent. I was just hoping you'd be willing to call Sheriff Paint and ask him to come here and talk to me."

JJ stepped to Mick's side as if her solidarity would support that Mick was telling the truth. "We shouldn't have run," JJ said. "We were scared that Tim or his father would hurt us."

Mick wanted to argue, embarrassed that JJ would think he was scared. Noticed that worrying about how JJ thought of him was a new phenomenon.

Dovey had retreated a few steps into her living room as they came in. Now she looked from one to the other. No smile, no welcome.

Mick knew something wasn't right. Did she disapprove of his taking the girls out of town? Or his running out on Paint? He swallowed away his discomfort. It had never occurred to him that Dovey wouldn't be in his corner. He wanted to apologize but had no idea what to say. Noticed JJ at his side, inching even closer, as if she'd also noticed Dovey's chilly reception.

"You did the right thing to come back," Dovey said, pensive, looking away as if that helped her recalibrate her thinking. "I don't know that running was a bad idea at the time. Tim and his punks were loose. Nobody knew who was going to do what." She moved a couple of steps farther away from them, close enough to pick up the phone if she needed. "A lot's happened since you left." She addressed Mick. "You know your dad was brought in for the girl's murder?"

Mick's chest got hollow.

"Cassel had him in lockup by Saturday. He was talking to one of the public defenders this morning, so he may be home tonight. If they let him go it'll be a very short leash. Your father won't be able to leave the county. I don't know if he still has his job."

Mick didn't know what to say. In a terrible way, he'd felt glad to hear his dad had been nailed for something. A long time coming. But killing the girl? He couldn't imagine it.

"Cardwell's been asking a lot of questions. Asked Tim and his buddy Cunneen about why they'd harassed you. Talked to Hammond and the restaurant manager about the Edmonds girl. He's got motel records, tracked down tourists and truckers through here that Monday. He and Cassel don't exactly cooperate, so I don't know what Highway Patrol has besides your dad." Dovey gestured to her couch but no one sat.

She picked up the phone, pushed the buttons, and waited. Her eyes shifted like somebody answered. "The Fitzhugh boy's with me" was all she said before hanging up and returning to the sitting area, to her rocker by the window.

Mick and JJ were frozen, uneasy, but uncertain what they should do. First Grace, now this, so different than they'd planned.

Dovey pulled the cord on the blinds, opening them to a view of the dirt lot and the trailer across. "The night you left, Jon got loose. People saw him stealing a soda at Skinny's but couldn't catch him. Next morning their breakfast cook found him asleep in the pantry, probably snuck in and hid before closing. Anyway, the woman noticed the cuts and bruises on his wrist. Phoned Cardwell. Cardwell went straight to Protective in Helena. Kept our local politics out of the mix."

JJ moaned.

Mick didn't think she realized it, didn't seem to notice the water in the edges of her eyes.

Dovey pointed to the Stovalls' trailer. "Did you know about this?" she asked. They stepped forward and looked. Mick saw a different car in front of the studio. A primer-spotted Chevelle with mag rims. His dad's kind of vehicle. It wasn't till JJ gasped that he noticed the yellow crime-scene tape across the Stovalls' trailer door, visible even fifty yards away at night.

JJ tore out of Dovey's and sprinted toward the trailer.

Mick chased her but couldn't catch her.

On her porch in a few seconds, JJ grabbed the doorknob and pushed through the tape, but the door was locked. When she yelled, no one answered.

Mick waited for her by the steps until she gave up.

ON THE WAY BACK to Dovey's they were cut off by a Highway Patrol car sliding to a stop in front of them. Scott Cassel got out, came around the front of the car. "Over here, hands on the hood," he said, his voice as hard as Mick remembered.

JJ complied, moving like a zombie.

Mick wanted to argue but was cut short by Cassel's speed as the man grabbed him by the shoulder and shoved him onto the front of the cruiser.

"Right now, I want to hear why you fingered my son for Edmonds."

Neither Mick nor JJ could find their voice.

"Can I help you, Officer?" Dovey was standing on her porch, holding her cell phone like she might be taking a picture.

"Not your business, Mrs. Crabtree."

"Ms.," Dovey corrected. "I wasn't aware this was MHP procedure with unarmed citizens."

"I'm investigating a murder. Sheriff's got a warrant."

"I have no idea what you're doing, Officer, but I haven't seen paperwork on this young woman cross my desk, no bulletins on my scanner. I believe her civil rights remain intact. And since when did you begin serving Cardwell's warrants?"

"Butt out, Crabtree. This is way out of your jurisdiction."

"Sheriff Paint'll be here in a minute or so, and he'll be grateful you've decided to do some county work. Course there's all the forms and whatnot. He'll make sure you're comfortable in his office."

Mick could feel the heat coming off the man standing behind him. A couple more barbs from Dovey and Cassel was going to spontaneously combust.

Dovey went on. "If you proceed in this manner, I'll advise these children to remain absolutely silent until their attorney arrives to speak for them. You'll have to charge Mick to keep him and he'll be lawyered up from that point on. Neither you nor Paint will get one speck of usable information."

Dovey came down off her porch and walked closer. "The evidence behind that warrant is circumstantial, the result of a highly suspicious phone call. Do you think Bolton is so flameproof he'll keep an adolescent locked up for that flimsy drivel?"

"He signed the goddamn warrant. He'll stand."

"Mick's lawyer will have this case thrown out so fast you'll be a laughing stock and you'll have soiled your main witness. Wonder how Helena will view that conduct?"

"SHUT UP!"

"I already called him. Paint is coming for the boy right now. He'll be pleased to see you working for him. Would you like him to review your interrogations of other suspects, like Larry and Tim?"

Dovey reached JJ's side and put a hand on the girl's shoulder. "Let Cardwell make his arrest and we'll have these young people in your office by nine-thirty tomorrow morning, ready to cooperate."

Cassel looked like he wanted to shoot her. Checked the parking area to see if there was anybody watching. Rolled his neck around his shoulders. "All right," he said, taking a step back. "As you were."

That language had no meaning to Mick or JJ. They didn't move.

"You can stand up," Dovey said.

"These two and the Herick girl are coming in for questioning," Cassel said.

"Haven't seen the Herick girl," Dovey said.

"You?" Cassel nodded first to Mick, then to JJ.

They shook their heads.

Mick didn't trust his voice.

"No idea," JJ said.

"I'm holding you and your office responsible," Cassel said. "They don't show, I'll bring obstruction charges."

Dovey didn't respond and no one moved until the cruiser rolled away.

Inside, Mick and JJ sat this time, tired now, struggling to understand these developments. Within seconds Mick bolted up, strode to the window, squinting to examine his studio apartment more carefully. A light was on inside. He hadn't noticed that before.

They'd only been in view, over to Stovalls', for a few minutes. How could Cassel have known they were at Dovey's? The answer? His dad told. Saw JJ and Mick in the parking area and called Cassel. Used some phone! No one else could have seen them. Nothing else made sense. His father had made some kind of agreement to get out of jail. Informing was part of it.

Mick didn't share his thoughts, but he didn't have to. The others watching his face made the connection. "What evidence? What warrant?" he asked.

Dovey didn't answer. Went to the kitchen for a tray of corn muffins, put them on the coffee table in front of Mick and JJ. Closed the blinds and sat in her rocker. Looked at the carpet as if its color and texture interested her. Within seconds a knock brought her back to her feet. "Cardwell," she said. "Must have been close by."

But it wasn't Cardwell. Hammond stood at the door in a tweed sportcoat carrying a briefcase like it was too valuable to leave in his car.

Mick realized he'd never given what people wore much of a thought. Girls in skimpy clothes, sure, but men? Nope. He and his dad and Gary were jeans and T-shirt guys. Hammond's gold neck chain caught Mick's eye. The rest, a close-fitting white shirt, pressed slacks, and fancy shoes. Spiffy.

"Good evening, Mrs. Crabtree," he said, "may I come in?" He looked past her to the couch.

"I already have company, Mr. Hammond," Dovey said. "If you have business, please bring it to the courthouse in the morning."

"Not exactly with you, ma'am," Hammond said, taking a step forward toward the threshold and offering his free hand as if to shake.

Dovey didn't retreat.

During this exchange Mick remained seated, but JJ stood and walked closer to the door.

Hammond glanced at her but continued speaking to Dovey. "Don't be paranoid, Crabtree. I wanted to welcome Ms. Herick back to town and meet her friends."

Dovey closed her door slowly but firmly. Locked it.

From the sound of it, Hammond stood facing the door for another minute. Left as headlights swung into the dirt lot.

Sheriff Paint.

While they waited, Dovey asked the obvious question. "Where's Grace?"

Mick was distracted, having trouble thinking, strung tight by this talk of evidence and warrants and arrest.

JJ filled in. "We let her off at the west end of town about noon. She was supposed to go straight to work and we were supposed to pick her up at the café at closing time and bring her here with us, but she no-showed, skipped. She'd told us she'd called them but she hadn't. She's in the wind. Maybe gone for good."

"Oh, I don't like the sound of that," Dovey said.

Mick and JJ looked at each other. They'd thought she fled. They hadn't considered the other possibility.

61

MICK HEARD THE CAR DOOR SLAM. Paint was seconds away from the front door. Warrant. "Sheriff's got a warrant" was what Lieutenant Cassel said. That meant arrest. Much bigger than questioning. Something happened. Did his dad point the killing Mick's way? He'd already told Cassel that Mick was back. He wouldn't rat out his own son on a warrant . . . unless his own neck depended on it.

So Paint was arresting Mick for fleeing? Was that all? What if Paint had decided Mick killed the girl? If he ran, Dovey would think he was a liar and Paint would be sure he was a murderer.

Did a double-wide have a back door? Mick thought so. Backside in the middle was the best bet. He grabbed JJ's leg and squeezed, launched himself off the couch and ran for the kitchen already imagining the lock it would have.

Dovey's backyard was small, bordered by thick bushes, room for two lawn chairs and a gas barbecue. Mick crashed through the thinnest patch in the foliage and ran for the river to retrace his and JJ's earlier route. Gary's garage. Nobody would look for him there and JJ wouldn't tell, but he had to get there quickly and switch out the Bonneville and the Bronco. Couldn't leave the Bonnie visible when cops would be combing this area.

In less than a minute he was at the side door, jerked it but it wouldn't budge. Locked. The rolling door in front would need one of those push-button electric remotes. He couldn't remember, was there a window? Made a circuit. A three-by-four locked shutter on each side. Gary wouldn't want anybody looking in and deciding the place had valuable equipment. At the back, though, a two-foot-square double window, frosted, for the bathroom. Also locked.

The window was old-fashioned, wood-framed, like Mick had seen in some of the places he and his dad stayed. Those older double windows usually had a clasp atop the bottom frame that slid into a lip on the bottom of the top frame. To open them from the outside you needed something strong and thin to slide into the seam and trip the clasp where the two frames met. A screwdriver probably wouldn't work. Too thick, create too much pressure. A knife or a metal ruler or a shim like his dad had used to steal that pickup. What were the odds he'd find something like that lying around. Zero.

Wrong. He'd seen something usable, but he hated to go back for it. What if Paint was already tracking him? Couldn't be helped. He sprinted for the spatula resting on the sideboard of Dovey's barbecue.

62

GRACE WAS A BLOCK from the Conoco when she felt a car pull alongside her. Heard an electric window buzz down.

"You called?"

Larry. She continued walking as he rolled along beside her.

"Hey, you disappeared. I was worried about you. I thought something happened."

"You know why I called?" she asked, turning to him, wondering if she'd see a pistol pointed at her.

"Something about a ring? Nope, but I'm glad you did. I missed you." He smiled. "Let me pull in, talk to me a minute," he said, pointing to a driveway between stores that connected the street to the alley in back.

He made a right into the passage and stopped the Town Car a few feet in. Hard to see now from the street.

Grace followed as far as the back door on his side. If he tried to get out, she could beat him to the street and run to the service station. Fitz would protect her. "I told you I found something of yours," she said, suddenly wondering if she should ask for two thousand and safe passage to Missoula.

"Can't think of anything I'm missing, hon, but whatever it is, I 'preciate you returning it."

"Like the jewel in your ring?" Grace said.

"My ring?"

"The V-Club thing."

"That right there is amazing. Who told you about the Vs?"

Grace ignored the question. "More important, guess where I found it?"

"You got me," he said, continuing to smile, leaning out the window a few inches to see her better.

"The river?" Grace said, planting her front foot, getting ready to sprint.

"Can't say I've been up there recently," he said.

Up there! "How'd you know which river I meant?" Grace asked, feeling unprepared for such a risky conversation so soon in the negotiation.

"I'm a guesser. Always have been. Helped me make a lot of tackles."

"I'll give it to you for three thousand," Grace said, suddenly deciding it would be worth at least that to him.

"Well, it's a relief I won't have to pay it," he said.

He's going to kill me right here. Grace took an involuntary step toward the back of the car. "Why not?"

He stuck his hand out the window and Grace flew for the street.

She stopped when she reached the sidewalk because she didn't hear the car door open and she knew he wouldn't shoot her down in plain sight. When she looked back, his hand was still sticking out the window . . . Looking closely she saw sparkle on his finger. Not his ring!

She was an idiot. She'd played her cards in front of the wrong person. Now he, they, whoever it turned out to be, could plan how to deal with her. Could get rid of anything incriminating, like the ring with the missing stone. Could even replace the ring if that was simple. She'd given away her edge and put herself at major risk at the same time. That thought made her sick and the ham-on-white she'd eaten in Trout Creek rose in her throat till she swallowed it back, spit.

"Hey!"

Grace jumped, ready to run again.

Larry had pulled his arm back inside the car, stuck his head out the window in its place. "Not to worry. Probably easy to find out who lost that. I'll help you." He smiled and lowered his voice. "Look, I know you're scared. You should be. If it can happen to Ev, right? I'll tell you something. You were heading to the café? I don't think I'd do that. If somebody's looking, that's the first place he'd go."

Grace found herself listening to him in spite of her misgivings. She hadn't been going to the café, but let him think that. She knew Ev wouldn't date Larry because he couldn't take a no, but Grace's experience had been different. He had been unusually generous and always respectful of her limits. If anything, he and

Grace seemed to understand each other. Each out for what they could get. It was possible . . . he could be an ally instead of a dupe. Maybe they could each make some money on this and then he'd help her get away. She'd have to be totally careful, but it was worth checking. If he'd wanted to hurt her, he could have done that already.

She walked back to the Town Car, to the passenger side.

He leaned over the front seat and opened the door.

She looked in, hands braced against the door in case he tried to grab her. "Give me your gun," she said, holding out her hand.

His eyebrows went up. "What?"

Grace kept her hand out, didn't respond.

Larry thought it over for several seconds. Shook his head. Reached under his seat and retrieved a black automatic pistol, handed it to her by the trigger guard.

She took it by the grip, held it at her side. "Now the other one," she said. She'd looked through his car one night on one of their outings when he'd gone in a store to get more beer.

His smile disappeared briefly but he put it back. "You *got* it," he said, turning both hands up empty, showing her.

She continued to stand outside the car, one hand out. Waited.

"Goddamn it!" He scooted to face her directly, his face coloring now with irritation. "Stop dicking around. Get in or forget it. See how you do on your own."

Grace didn't move, pleasant look on her face. Patient. Back in control.

Larry sighed. Smiled again. Let the tension dissipate from his muscles. Leaned to open the glove compartment, brought out a tiny gun so small it looked like a toy.

She pursed her lips. Question.

"Derringer," he said as if that explained it. He pinched the gun by the handle and gave it to her.

Grace took it, put it in her pocket. Slid her purse off her shoulder and put the larger gun in it.

"Safety's on," he said, nodding at her purse. "The other won't fire unless you cock it."

Grace got in, ignoring the safety belt. No way she was going to strap herself down. "Where we going?" she asked.

"Someplace beautiful," he said, steering the car slowly toward the end of the alley.

Grace loved the Lincoln's black leather seats, the way they smelled, the way they felt. Everything about the car was luxurious. She leaned against the headrest and let herself notice how good-looking Larry was, his tan arms, his strong hands . . . Was that ring the same kind JJ'd shown her? Larry's black stone had an upside-down V on the top overlapping a V on the bottom, making a diamond-shaped box with a small capital G in the middle. That's not right. And why was the car stopping?

Grace woke up in a room so dark she couldn't see her hands.

63

JJ WAS MORE STARTLED than Dovey when Mick ran. She didn't get it. What about their plan? She looked to Dovey for an explanation, but Dovey was opening the door for Sheriff Paint.

"Your boy just flew my coop," she told him as he stepped inside, took his hat off, rubbed his hand over his hair.

Paint took a phone off his belt and told dispatch to scramble all available to Dovey's neighborhood. "Young male, six two, two twenty, dark hair, wearing . . ." He looked to JJ.

"What does he ever wear?" she said. "Jeans and a T-shirt."

Paint relayed that, added the Bonneville info. Asked Dovey for a glass of water and went to her dining room for a straight-backed chair.

Paint waited for Dovey to come back and sit, then turned his chair around and tried to straddle it. Gave up. Sat regular fashion. "Smart thing to come here," he said to JJ. "I trust her, too," nodding at Dovey. "Where have you been?"

"Coeur d'Alene for a day or so," JJ said. "Why are you after Mick? He didn't do anything."

"Some think he did. There's evidence he needs to explain. Know where he went?"

JJ looked away. Not enough practice lying.

"Is he safe?"

"Probably." JJ was pretty sure he went back to Gary's garage. When he couldn't get in, maybe he'd jump in the Pontiac and disappear. Maybe he'd call JJ later but she couldn't think how.

"Tell me anything that'll help about the Edmonds girl."

"I didn't know her," JJ said.

Paint looked to Dovey for confirmation.

"Five or six years older, different schools. I never saw Evelyn around here," Dovey said.

"So anything at all." He bent over slightly, rested his elbows on his knees, made his voice even softer. "Her family's miserable. You understand that."

JJ got it. Mick didn't need protecting. He was innocent. And Grace? Who knew what that girl was doing?

"You want me here for this?" Dovey asked.

Paint nodded. "Witness."

"It wasn't Hammond," JJ said, bringing puzzled looks.

"Who said it was?" Paint asked.

"We thought . . . I found this jewel and we . . . it probably . . ." JJ stopped, sensing Paint's confusion.

Paint shifted in the wooden chair, trying to get more comfortable. "Tell me the whole thing. From the start. I got Jon before they took him to placement. I know you all found the body."

"I didn't," JJ said. "But I found this." She brought the black stone out of her pocket and tried to hand it to Paint.

He leaned away, fumbling for a handkerchief so he could accept the stone without adding any more prints. "Found this where?"

Dovey leaned over to see it better. Caught her lip between her teeth and sat back.

"I went for a walk that day. It was in the dirt above those big rocks, upstream from the girl."

"In the dirt . . ."

"At the riverbank. At the water, where you could put in a boat, a canoe—"

"By a break in the willows," Paint said. "You wear a nine shoe?" He was looking at JJ's feet.

"I thought it was beautiful. Like something a king . . . I put it in my pocket and kind of forgot. I was going to ask Gary . . ." JJ ran down.

"Didn't tell anybody?" Paint asked.

"Mick and Grace. A couple of days ago," JJ said.

"You know what it is?"

"Now, I think," JJ said. "The stone from somebody's ring?" She looked to Paint for confirmation. He was still, but Dovey nodded.

"Grace said it was probably Hammond's, or maybe a couple of other people had one like it," JJ said. "So I looked. When he was here. I checked for it." She mimicked his gesture, the hand coming forward to shake Dovey's. "He was wearing a ring with a black stone, tiny diamonds all the way around the outside. Silver V with another diamond in the middle. Pretty much the same kind as the one I found, so I don't think it was Hammond. He has his."

"Do you know anything about rings with a V?" Dovey asked. JJ shook her head.

"You do," Dovey said, nodding to Paint. "How many people have those?"

Paint shot her a look like not here, not now.

"Please," JJ said. "This is really important for my friends."

Dovey ignored Paint's signal. "A long time ago, twenty-something years, the Trappers took state, football and basketball, back-to-back years. The best players were Sam Hammond and Scott Cassel, but Greer was the point guard, Bolton and Mackler were starters. They made some kind of vow at the end of their junior year. Got written up in the paper. They said they were going to do the same thing their senior year and then, after college, come back here and build a winning town, like a business hub for northwest Montana."

Paint was shaking his head, remembering, or annoyed with Dovey's revelation? "That was the rings," he said. "Each kid had one. Patterned after Sam's father's masonic ring. A V with a diamond chip in the middle. V-Club. Stood for victory."

"I was pretty new in the clerk's office at the time," Dovey said. "I don't think anybody took them seriously, but it was . . . what? Inspiring? The kids, the hope for the future." She sighed. "Anyway, they did it. They won the next year, too, and even more amazing, they came back. Became community leaders."

"Of a sort," Paint said.

JJ thought his face looked redder than it had before. "So does anybody else have these rings?"

"Not that I know of," Dovey said, "but if Hammond's got one with diamonds around the outside, then he has a new one." She looked right at Paint. "You should find out what happened to the old one."

64

MICK WAS INSIDE THE GARAGE AND SWEATING. Had to get the Bronco out and the Bonneville in and hidden before one of the deputies spotted it. He'd found the button to raise the garage door, but could he start the Bronco? Would the keys be in it? No. So where? It was a secret. Gary'd never mentioned it earlier when they talked about needing a car. If Gary carried them, someone might see the Ford key, so he would leave them here. Convenient. Mick thought about his dad saying anything under a doormat or floor mat was begging for theft. Same for under flowerpots or up on ledges above doors. He looked around the garage, a zillion places, one as good as the next. But Gary smoked a lot of dope. He needed something he could remember.

The car. Somewhere by or in the car. The Bronco was sitting on outdoor carpeting. Mick knelt beside the driver's door and checked the blue mat for seams. None. He looked for a magnetic box inside the bumpers, the top of the wheel wells, between the hood and the windshield, under the front and rear frame. Nope.

He tried the driver's door. Unlocked. Okay! The ashtray, the glove compartment, under the seat, under the lip of the dash. Looked for a toggle switch down by the fuse box that meant you didn't need a key. Nope. Felt in the air vents and the slit for the cassettes. Turned the sun visors down. Realized he was too nervous, making this too complicated.

Mick sat in the driver's seat and thought for a minute. Arm's reach away. Down. Nothing. To the front behind the steering wheel. To his right, on the passenger seat, a dark blue bandanna. Lifted it . . . Yes!

The SUV rumbled to a start on the first try, which was a surprise after the fact because Mick realized he should have thought to check whether the battery was connected. He jumped out, pressed the garage door button, backed to the street. In a minute the Bonnie was inside with the door shut and Mick was searching the building for a phone or a weapon and anything else he might need. Like a sandwich. When was the last time he ate?

Mick didn't have much information but he had some key pieces. V-ring near the place where the body was found. Probably not a coincidence. Hammond's friends had those rings. Only people he and JJ hadn't heard from were Hammond himself and Scott and Larry Cassel. If the highway patrol guy had killed the girl, he should have done a world-class job of covering it up. Hammond didn't seem like the rageful type. Would he kill some girl when he could fairly easily lure a lot of women with his style and money?

Larry was the prime bet, but Mick didn't think he could go against him alone and come out on top. Gary might help, but with crime tape on the trailer, Mick had no idea where Gary could be. So, who had the balls to stand up to Larry Cassel? Mick could think of one person. Fitz Fitzhugh. And his dad had pistols. That could help. But he couldn't go back to the compound tonight while Paint was there. After the sheriff left, deputies would be cruising, watching the shack. He'd have to see Fitz tomorrow at the Conoco.

Even with the Bonnie safe, Mick couldn't afford to sit around. The only useful things from his search were a set of coveralls he could pull over his clothes and a beat-up straw cowboy hat to cover his hair. Tonight he'd get a cheeseburger and go looking for Tim Cassel. Set him straight about JJ and this "Cassel's girlfriend" misunderstanding. Get him to call off his mastodon, Cunneen.

65

"WHY DID YOU SAY CASSEL DID IT?" Paint asked, abruptly changing direction.

"I didn't," JJ said. "I saw the body in the river. I just asked, 'Isn't that Cassel's girlfriend?'"

"Which Cassel?" Paint again.

"Larry . . . I mean, I saw them talking a few times. It just came out of my mouth. I don't—"

Paint held up his hand to stop her. "Don't lie to me!"

JJ's lip trembled.

Paint studied her. Believed her.

JJ had never considered herself a suspect. Didn't know how

to deal with Paint's abrupt questions. She was afraid she might get Mick in more trouble and she needed to tell him what she'd learned. There were probably only five possibles, six at the most if Hammond had given away his old ring. Why would he do that? No idea. Who would he give it to? A woman he liked? He was too old for that kind of thing. His son? That thought made JJ feel cold.

Paint moved on. "Who else talked with Evelyn? A close friend? We haven't found one. Lived with her folks in Plains. Only high school pardner got killed in Afghanistan."

JJ shook her head. "I only knew about Larry. I don't know if they were even friends. Grace said . . . Grace would know more."

"Why wouldn't they be friendly?" Paint pressed her. "I hear Evelyn was looking to make a little traveling money. Wasn't she friendly with several men?"

JJ had no idea.

"Maybe somebody put a bee in her bonnet," Dovey said.

"What do you mean?" Paint asked.

"The Copy Shop, Legal Aid, Tirrell's Bookkeeping are in my building," Dovey said. "I hear talk about local men. Scott and Larry Cassel, Mackler, Baker at the pharmacy. The younger women say these guys won't take no for an answer. Larry's particularly persistent. Course he's not alone. I've heard that about Baker, too."

"Hammond has all those imports," Paint said. "Don't think he partakes of local women anymore."

"Imports?" JJ wasn't following.

"He brings in Internet women," Dovey said.

JJ couldn't digest that. It didn't seem possible. Seemed like a movie.

"True," Paint said, "so his dance card's pretty full."

JJ felt a little dizzy, out of it. Did she walk around in a fog? Did she know anything about her hometown?

A sheriff's car came into the lot, lights flashing, and Paint stood, went out to meet it.

"Wait! What happened to Gary and Tina?" JJ to Paint's back, but he was already through the door.

"You should have told me," Dovey said.

JJ knew what was coming. Looked at the floor. "I didn't know what to do. None of us did. Jon was . . . I should have. I was afraid." She waited for Dovey to say something.

Silence.

"I don't have any more relatives. I'd be—" Her voice broke.

Dovey went to the kitchen for a dish towel, set it on JJ's knee. Waited. Started talking as JJ dried her face. "Gary's being held at the jail here until fingerprints come back from Helena."

"Fingerprints?" JJ asked. "Why? They took Jon away."

"Jon told them about the marijuana, about the hiding places outside the trailer. The deputies collected several bags. It's not usable evidence unless they tie the drugs to his prints."

"Can I get him out on bail?"

"You have a deposit?"

"I have money in my college account." She watched Dovey's eyebrows lift, surprised that JJ had any money or maybe that she was planning on college.

"For Gary?" Dovey sounded like she disapproved.

"He's not a bad person. He took care of us—me, Tina, Grace. The stuff with Jon was cruel and stupid but I don't think he knows any better. What would you do with Jon?"

Good question. Dovey admitted she'd never seen anyone be able to direct or reason with the kid and make him mind. Said, as far as she could tell, Jon wasn't exactly crazy. Probably a fetal alcohol kid, agitated, wild, whole nervous system irritated. She'd thought he needed one of those residential programs. Well, he'd get one now.

"He's in Helena and the state will deal with him for the next few years. Tina's detoxing in Missoula. My guess is she's headed to permanent residential."

"If I get the money, can you get Gary out?" JJ again.

"Maybe. Tomorrow afternoon," Dovey said. "We have to think where you're going to stay. You might be a ward of the court at this point."

"Do Mick and I need a lawyer?"

"Sounds like Mick does."

66

MICK IN COVERALLS AND HAT was anonymous if he stayed in the Bronco. At Skinny's he did the drive-through. Fries and . . . a cup of water. Forgot. He put his last two dollars together with loose change from Gary's ashtray and covered the bill. Maybe there was some canned food back at the garage.

He parked near the road under the Skinny's sign where he could see both the drive-in and the street. He'd come and go for the next three hours. Odds were he'd see Tim cruising. What was there to do in July in Portage? Keg party at Taylor's once a week over on West River or park-and-pussy at the overlook. Mick had no idea if Tim had a girl or girls. Probably. But sooner or later he'd come tooling down the main drag, more than likely pull into Skinny's if it was still open.

He lowered the front windows and turned off the engine, wished he'd asked for salt and ketchup. A distant crackle of laughter got his attention and he scanned for the source. In the far corner of the lot shaded by large tamaracks, a knot of teenagers were circled around a black convertible and sitting in nearby pickup beds like an impromptu party. Tim's Mustang was black. Mick wished he had binocs. He searched the console, looked in the rear seat on the off chance, but no luck.

He walked the long way back around the drive-through, moving slow like he was older and sore from a hard day's work. Stopped behind a dumpster where he had a good look at the action. Mustang, all right, and Tim holding forth, telling some story, his arm around a girl that looked like the blond softball pitcher. Fifteen or twenty kids from the high school in hearing range. Mick recognized several, didn't know names. He'd wait. Keep his distance. If Tim stayed with that girl, he'd have to take her home at some point. Her folks wouldn't let an NCAA-class pitcher stay out all night. At least Mick didn't think so.

• • •

The group kept its momentum till Skinny's closed at eleven. The pickups left, ferrying people like open-air buses. Some cheerleader-types drove out in a big Lexus SUV full of giggling girlfriends, followed by the Mustang with Tim and the blonde. Mick tailed them to the river park where they got out and took a waterside bench, kissed and diddled for another hour. He was a few hundred yards behind when they returned all the way through town and took a right onto Blue Hills Road toward the country club. Mick stopped when they made a left onto Sylvan Circle. He set the straw hat in the seat, got out, waited for Cassel to finish his goodnighting and come back to the intersection.

"The hell do you want?" Not much of a greeting but at least he'd stopped, let his car idle in the street beside the Bronco.

Mick crossed in front of the car over to Tim's side. "I want to explain how JJ got crossways with you and Edmonds."

"There is no me and Edmonds!"

"I know." Mick held his hands up like surrender. "I've told Paint and so has JJ." Probably not true but it would be soon.

"Tell my dad, dickwad. He's in my face every day and he doesn't know shit."

"I will. It was a mistake."

Tim was staring a hole in Mick but at least he was listening.

"I'm sorry. Okay? Tell Cunneen and your stubby buddy to back off. We're fixing it."

"You tell him. The suck's gone."

"What . . ."

"Some scholarship. You believe a high school scholarship? Sports? Cunneen'll be a senior. Yeah. He's moved." Tim was shaking his head. Looked like a mix of anger, disbelief, disappointment. He rammed the car in gear and spun around the corner, tires pelting Mick with gravel.

PAINT WAS INSIDE, sitting again. Rubbing his hands on his pants like something had gotten them dirty. "They found a car. Turned out to be the wrong one. Unlucky kid who was driving may have to have his pants dry-cleaned."

Dovey smiled. JJ didn't. What if they got her and didn't realize she was the wrong one?

Dovey filled him in. "I told her about Gary and Tina. Puts her in a tough position. What do we do here?"

"We keep her out of Mackler's hands."

"I know, but what's her status? Does Bolton determine that?"

Paint snorted. "You have a place to stay for a week or two while we sort this?" he asked JJ.

She shook her head, coughed to cover her mix of embarrassment and fear.

"What the hell? What do we have?" Paint to Dovey.

"Domestic violence shelter or the Methodist basement," Dovey said. "Neither seems . . . how old are you?"

"Sophomore," JJ said, not really lying, avoiding the question. She watched a look pass between the elders.

Turned out Dovey had an extra toothbrush to go with an extra bed. JJ didn't mention her things were back at the garage. Wondered how Mick was doing. Tried to put it out of her mind.

JJ woke in the morning to the smell of coffee and cinnamon bread. Note on the table. *Meet at lunch—courthouse steps.*

The shower felt great. JJ wolfed the bread and burned her mouth on the coffee. Couldn't wait to get to the garage.

She noticed the Bronco had taken the Pontiac's place parked at the far side. Good news. Dialed the combo lock and found Mick using a screwdriver to jimmy the locked metal cabinet. It wasn't working. The look on his face when he saw her was worth burning her mouth twice over. He was glad to see her. She could tell. It was more than the smile. He'd missed her. Was that a first? Made her wish she had taken some time with her hair or face or something. She had no idea how she looked. Probably like a lumberjack.

"You have keys for this thing?" Mick rapped on the cabinet with his knuckles.

"No. What're you looking for?"

"Rifle, handgun, bat. Anything that'll even the odds when I find Larry Cassel."

JJ watched his face. He was kidding, wasn't he?

Mick didn't smile.

"Gary had that rifle at the trailer."

"The shotgun?"

"I guess so. Paint's giving me the key this morning. I'll look for it."

"Want me to meet you there?"

"You'll get caught."

"No way. I found some scissors on the workbench. Help me cut my hair. Coveralls and this straw hat? Instant farmhand."

JJ could picture it, thought it would work.

"I got to talk to my dad."

"Why?" Didn't sound like a good idea.

"I think I'm going to need his help."

68

THE HAIRCUT MADE THE HAT FIT BETTER, sit lower. Perfect disguise. Mick parked off Main beside the Conoco, watched for a couple of minutes to spot a stakeout. Didn't see anything that made him suspicious. Walked behind the station around the fence that secured used tires, around the side of the garage where two cars sat waiting for repair. Guessed the owner was in the office with the cash register and phone.

Mick had time to think this through. Knew what he wanted to say. Approached his dad, who was over a fender, leaning into an engine compartment.

Fitz grunted, something gave, and he glanced up holding a rusty water pump. Didn't seem surprised to see Mick. Set the pump on the floor and went back to work.

Mick came closer, close enough to talk, but not close enough to get hit by the closed-end wrench his dad was using. "I thought . . . we had to leave. Right then. Nothing to take but the Bonnie." It was a poor start. Not the way he had planned.

Fitz ignored him.

"I'm sorry I took your car without telling you."

Fitz swore at a belt that was in his way.

"You called Scott Cassel when you saw us last night. We don't do that."

That brought Fitz out of the engine compartment. "Are you nuts? Cassel thinks I could've killed that blond bitch. I wouldn't call . . . Piss off."

Mick thought about that. Who called if not his dad? . . . Went on. "I'm getting my stuff out of the studio."

"It's locked."

That was a lie. Mick had never seen his dad lock a door. Always said: "Somebody wants in, they'll get in, and then you got to replace the glass or frame." If this kept going badly, there was a possibility Mick might not talk to his dad again. Was there anything else he needed to say? He wiped oily sweat from his forehead, remembered he hadn't showered for days. "Uh, thanks for taking care of me all this time," he said.

No response.

"You didn't have to," Mick said. "I appreciate it."

Fitz cursed at the engine.

"I'm in a lot of trouble now. I might need your help."

"Tough tits, Bucky Boy. Shoulda thought about that a few days ago."

"No, I mean it." Mick looked around to be sure this conversation was private. "I think Larry Cassel killed that girl we found."

Fitz stopped work. Rested forearms on the car fender, listening.

"We, uh, JJ found something there on the river. Pretty sure it belongs to Larry. He's strong enough. Temper. Big ladies' man. I think the girl refused him and he snapped and killed her."

Now Fitz straightened. "Not my business. I got his dad running checks in Idaho and Oregon trying to sew me to a whole mess of trouble. If he connects the dots, I'm doing time." He waited for Mick's reaction. Mick didn't give him one. "I can't leave the city limits."

Mick realized he'd often wished for something like this. Do the crime, do the time, something to knock his dad out of this stupid life. But not now. Not today. Today he needed his dad hard and ornery. "Grace is missing," he said. "Larry may have got her, too."

His dad pulled a red shop rag out of his back pocket and began wiping his hands.

"I'm going to find him and make him tell me what he's done," Mick said.

His dad snorted.

"I have to. Otherwise they'll pin it on me."

"You set me up," his dad said, pitching the rag in a laundry barrel, "somebody set you up. Goes around, comes around. Little late for begging."

Mick thought about wishing his dad good luck. Realized he didn't mean it. Walked out.

69

MICK LEFT THE BRONCO in an empty driveway a couple of streets over, walked to the studio. The door was unlocked, like he thought. Went straight to his bed and felt under the mattress for his paychecks. Lifted the whole mattress. Looked like his dad had helped himself. Okay, so Mick was keeping the Bonnie if it didn't get impounded. Wasn't much else in the studio worth his time. His winter jacket, winter boots, a better pair of jeans, a couple of button shirts. As usual, everything he wanted fit in a grocery bag.

By the time he got to the Stovall trailer, JJ had it open, airing it out. He called her name at the porch steps so he wouldn't startle her, and she came to the door, clothes dirty, smudged face, wet rag in one hand, Pine-Sol in the other.

"Guess what? This place is a pigsty." She rubbed her nose with the back of her hand to keep sweat from dripping.

"I remember," Mick said. "Never knew how you and Grace could stand it."

JJ winced at the word "Grace." "Get used to anything." She stepped out of the way. "Come in before somebody sees you."

Couch and furniture cushions leaned against porch banisters in the sun. Inside, the place smelled like disinfectant. JJ had swept the rugs and mopped the linoleum. The bathroom door was propped open, the kitchen counter was clear. Gary's table was empty and the garbage was gone.

"Wow. Somebody could actually live here," Mick said, nodding appreciatively.

"Yeah. Me. Course, there's two bedrooms."

That reminded Mick. "You got Gary's cell? I want to call Larry's office. I've been driving around looking for Grace, looking for Cassel's Lincoln. Didn't see either. You know anybody that's seen Grace since we let her out?"

JJ shook her head.

"I think he's got her."

"Why?"

Mick went back to his theory about the ring owners and who would be the most likely person to have killed Evelyn in a burst of anger.

"There's a loose string," JJ said. "Dovey says the ring I saw Hammond wearing is a new one. He upgraded."

Mick frowned, not understanding.

"More diamonds. So, did he lose the old one's setting when he dumped the girl at the river, or did he keep his old one and it's in his jewelry box, or what?"

"Did Paint or Dovey tell you anything about those rings?"

"Yeah, V-Club for sure. Like Grace said, from a long time ago, high school. Hammond, Scott Cassel, Greer, Bolton, and Mackler."

"What else did Grace say when you first showed it to us?"

JJ looked away, trying to remember. "She named Hammond and somebody else from that group."

"Didn't she say Larry had one?"

"I don't know . . . hey, I couldn't find the shotgun. Probably the police."

"That's okay. Maybe it's better without it."

"I'm meeting Dovey for lunch and then I'm getting money out of my account to bail Gary. He'll help us."

"Your account?"

"Long story." JJ looked around the trailer, assessing what still needed to be done. "Hey, give me a hand? I finish wiping stuff here in the living room, you go through the fridge and toss anything that doesn't look right?"

Mick's first reaction: wrinkled his nose. Second, resistant. Didn't want to get sidetracked from his search for Grace and Larry.

"Leave their bedroom and sheets till I can stand it. Help me finish the kitchen, I'll get cleaned up, you make your calls. Deal?"

Hard to argue.

While JJ showered, Mick found a phone book, got the number for the county building inspector. When he called, he got a phone message: Out of the office for the rest of the week. Leave name and number. His message: "This is Mick Fitzhugh. You've got Grace and I'm coming after you." He hung up wondering if that was another mistake. His dad would have said so. "Never let them see you coming."

Mick fidgeted while JJ showered and dressed. When she came out of the bedroom, he was a little surprised. Had she gotten taller lately? She looked good in T-shirt, jeans, and sandals. He hadn't had that thought before. When she turned to close her bedroom door, he added to his appraisal. Still looked like a boy from behind, but . . .

He dropped her off a block away from the courthouse. Couldn't sit still. Started a street-by-street grid search of Portage. After fifteen minutes he parked. Too much territory, too much gas, and Cassel could be anywhere. Back to the ring. Hammond? Still didn't fit Mick's theory. Damn it, what had Grace said? Hammond got Larry on as inspector. What else did Larry do? Mick had seen him try to intimidate Dovey. Looked pretty good at it. With no son on the horizon, would Hammond give Larry that ring and make him an honorary club member? Just might.

The question Mick kept avoiding: Was Grace already dead?

70

COULD SHE EVEN MOVE? How could someplace be this dark? Grace was scared of the answers. How did she get here? She felt her pulse climbing. Breathe!

She'd disarmed Larry, gotten in the car with him. A car accident? Is this the morgue? Do they think she's dead? She heard herself cry out. Didn't mean to. And then she did. Started yelling her head off. Stopped, afraid she was lying on something she might fall off of. What if Larry had put her in a well and she was balanced on a ledge, squirm and she'd tip over and drop the rest of the way? She needed to move very carefully. Get some information.

Her left hand first. The right seemed like it was wedged between her body and a wall. She felt her hip, then up to her stomach. She was dressed. Down to her butt. She was on something leather or vinyl. Felt like a wood frame beneath. What? Too flat and hard for a couch. What are those places in cemeteries? Slots for bodies in a big marble building? Her grandmother'd been put in one. Forced her mind off that. A shelf or a table? What kind of table would have a little padding covered by leather? None she'd ever seen.

She pressed her head down. Felt like a thin pillow. Pressed her feet. Same thing. Lifted her hand. Nothing above her that she could feel. She would sit up. When she did, her right hand came up short against a metal chain. A handcuff. Attached to . . . a pipe running along a cold wall. Should she swing her feet over the side? Feel for the floor? Good questions, but what she really wanted to know right now was how long would her bladder last? She closed her eyes and focused on hearing and smell. She needed more information about her predicament.

A sharp sound jolted Grace out of uneasy sleep. A door opening. It took several seconds for her eyes to adjust. The light hurt, wavered, finally formed into an image. Hammond, standing in a doorway in a chichi tracksuit. Now Grace could see she was lying on a massage table, cuffed to a drainpipe in a wine cellar.

"Larry thought you might want to use the powder room. My bad. Should have thought of that before."

Grace took him in: gold chain at the neck, tracksuit, BOSS brand on the sweatshirt, matching pants, tan leather Air-something-or-others. He looked like a Nordstrom's ad from her hometown.

"Sorry about the cuff. Didn't want you to hurt yourself. We'll explain everything whenever you're ready."

"Where's—?" Grace's voice was rough. She stopped and tried it again. "Where's Larry?"

"Upstairs."

"What did he do to me?"

"Nothing. He didn't touch you. Really. Odorless. Like chloroform. We needed to have a serious conversation. Someplace private. Needed your cooperation."

Grace watched as his face colored. That was a first. "This is the way you get cooperation?"

Hammond's face hardened. "There's a lot you don't know. Things you need to understand. You want to hit the can or not?"

71

JJ AND DOVEY WAITED FOR GARY on the sidewalk in front of the jail. When he appeared, JJ hardly recognized him. He looked smaller, older and crippled. Shuffled as he came toward them like he'd recently been badly beaten.

Dovey stepped back, letting JJ greet him. "Grace is missing,"

JJ said. "Maybe she's run again, but I think Hammond or one of his people took her to shut her up."

Gary shook his head like it was going to take him a while to readjust to brighter light and pot-free thinking. "Hammond . . . that'd be crazy."

"Maybe," JJ said. "Or maybe she knows something and those guys don't want her around anymore."

Gary grimaced like he was getting a headache, said, "Don't mess with those guys."

"You'd know?" Dovey asked. Didn't sound like she expected an answer.

"Just making a living," Gary said, scanning the nearby area to see if anyone was looking or listening. "I got people that depend on—" He stopped talking as Bolton walked out the front door, saw him and scowled.

"Let's go home," Gary said. "Talk there."

This wasn't the Gary JJ knew. If he was going to be super-careful about Hammond, then he couldn't help her.

"You two be okay?" Dovey asked, looking at her watch.

"We'll walk home," JJ said. "I'll call you tonight."

"You can't sleep there with him in the trailer."

Gary glared at the woman.

JJ thought she understood. Dovey's deal with Paint to keep JJ out of the system for a couple of weeks. "So let me know when you're home and I'll join you."

Dovey thought it over. Nodded.

"Question?" JJ looked at Dovey for permission to ask it.

"Depends."

"I need to find Larry Cassel. Is he working?"

Gary reacted. JJ shushed him.

"You want to know something, let Paint ask Cassel," Dovey advised. "But no, he's not working this week. Sign on his office says back next Monday."

"How about Hammond?"

"Haven't seen him."

Gary was tugging on her arm and JJ left reluctantly, more unsettled than before. What she was thinking seemed impossible, but when they were all traveling together, Grace had seemed genuinely afraid. Would Hammond actually kidnap her? Get rid of her? Could he do that?

JJ kept checking each street and driveway for Cassel's Lincoln. She asked Gary what kind of car Hammond drove but got no response. Wished she'd looked out the window the night before when he'd been at Dovey's. Gary hobbled as quickly as he could, but it still took almost thirty minutes to get to the trailer. Alone, JJ could have made it in half the time.

Once inside, Gary turned on her, so mad he was sputtering. "Goddamn it, shut up about Hammond. You don't know what you're doing." He looked like he wanted to hit her.

JJ hadn't seen Gary panicked before. Had never seen him like this, even with Jon. She fought an impulse to run to her room and lock the door.

"I'm not going back to jail! Not! Never!" He wheeled abruptly and gimped to his bedroom. If he'd noticed the cleanup, he made no mention.

JJ continued standing just inside the door, shaken, trying to think.

When Gary came back he was carrying a suitcase that he set by the door as he passed and went to Tina's TV. Cursed. Jerked the plug out of the wall and lugged the TV to the kitchen table, rummaged for a screwdriver.

JJ had always assumed the TV case was solid plastic but Gary had the back off in less than a minute. At that point he got careful, got a wooden spoon from the counter and used it to dig three packages from the mess of wires. Out on the table it was clear two were money. Hundred-dollar bills. Stacks about an inch thick. Gary shoved them inside his shirt. Third package was much smaller, a transparent bag with gray powder. Gary dumped a small mound on top of his hand near his wrist. Snorted. Shook his head. Sniffled. Tucked the bag in his shirt pocket and rummaged in his tool drawer again. Came out with a key ring.

"Mick has the Bronco," JJ said.

Gary stopped in his tracks. Nailed JJ with a look that made her shiver.

"The hell. Miss Two-shoes spreading the wealth?" He clomped out of the trailer, stopping long enough to jam the money packets in the suitcase.

JJ could hear him swearing and banging things around the side. Looked out the window.

He brought a battery to the Chevy, set it on the ground while he opened the hood. Left and came back with a metal box. Un-rolled its electrical cord and plugged it somewhere around the porch. Attached its hose to a front tire.

JJ could hear a rhythmic pumping begin.

Gary left for the side of the trailer again, came back with a heavy red jerry can. Unscrewed the car's gas cap and poured.

It worked! JJ couldn't believe it. All this time she'd thought the Chevy was a junker. No, it was one more piece of Gary's getaway plan. All these years. Made her wonder what else she didn't know about him.

It took him another half hour to inflate the tires, connect the battery, put water in the radiator, add quarts of oil, and spray starter fluid in the carb. When he cranked it over, the wreck rumbled blue smoke for a minute and then calmed into an idle. He came back inside for a final look around, grabbed the suitcase, and left without a word.

JJ yelled, "Hey! My money!"

If he heard her he didn't care. Slammed the car door and rolled out of the compound without a backward glance.

No way. Yes, she bailed him out to help her, but no, she wasn't going to let him skip with her college fund. Call Dovey! But Mick had Gary's cell and the land line in the trailer was dead. Looked like time to start getting in shape for school sports. She lit out across the parking area to the alley and up to Main. Saw the Chevy speeding east toward Plains. Going to get Tina? Didn't matter. She headed west toward the sheriff's office at a fast jog.

Paint immediately ordered roadblocks on the three highways north, south, and east of Portage. While he was busy with that, JJ went to Dovey's office and told her what Gary'd done.

"The tank's pretty hard on child abusers and he looked awful when he came out," Dovey said. "No reason for him to stay. Hammond's probably already severed their association. He wouldn't want anything public that would tie him to illegal activity."

JJ'd wondered whether to tell her what Mick was up to, worried he was going to get seriously hurt. "He's going after Larry Cassel."

"Gary?"

"Mick. He's asking his dad to help him."

"You think you can find him? Talk sense?"

"Maybe. Unless he gets to Larry first."

"Well, according to the note on his office, Larry's off somewhere."

"So I'll start looking."

"Wait for me to close up. I bet Cardwell's got an idea about this."

72

MICK DIDN'T WANT TO STAY parked in one place too long. Couldn't afford to attract attention. Something his dad had said was bothering him. They'd been talking about finding Larry and Fitz said, "I can't leave town," or near that. Why would that matter?

Was Cassel out of town? Or Hammond? Mick realized he didn't know where either of them lived. Should have thought of that.

Who would know? Dovey? Would she tell him? Probably not. Phone book? Where could you find one anymore? The motel on the west end of town that Hammond didn't own? He went there first. The front door tinkled when he entered and shortly an older woman with obviously dyed black hair came to the counter from the apartment in back. She was happy to give him the book to look at, but neither man was listed.

He didn't realize he'd groaned.

"What's the matter?" Soft voice, reaching out as if to touch him.

"I need to talk with Sam Hammond or Larry Cassel about a . . . county problem, uh, but they're not in their offices and this doesn't have their home phones."

"That's common," she said. "Most public officials don't list private lines."

"Well, I'd leave them a note in their mailboxes but I don't have their address."

"Let's see," she said, turning around and yelling through the apartment door. "Lester? . . . Lester? Didn't Scott Cassel's boy buy one of those places west by the river? Other side of the highway from the country club?" She waited for an answer but none came. She returned to Mick, said, "I'm pretty sure he did and that's a new area, aren't that many places, so somebody out there ought to be able to tell you which one's his."

"Thanks. I appreciate—"

"And Hammond," she went on, "everybody knows that. He's

on that island east of town. First big one. Only one that anything's built on. Gets across by boat. I want to see it one of these days. His dad had it built. They say it looks like one of those lodges."

"You've been won—"

"You want to stay for a cup of coffee, I don't mind," she said, smiling, hopeful.

"Another day," Mick said, already at the door. "You've been great." He didn't hear her exact words, but it seemed like she was still talking as he started the car and headed for Larry's neighborhood.

She was right. There weren't many houses yet, and half of the streets had staked lots ready for construction. He asked a grizzled man in a ball cap who was putting a hasp on a new backyard gate.

"Across the street and two down, but I ain't seen him past couple a days and I been out here a lot. No lights. Probably up at the lake. He likes them casinos."

Okay. Hammond. Was Mick ready?

73

BAIL SPECIFIED GARY COULDN'T LEAVE THE COUNTY. He might have forgotten. The powder he'd inhaled came on stronger as he crossed the Salish, reminded him to give himself another toot. He slowed to sixty for Plains, goosed it again after on the straight two-lane. He would be in Missoula in less than an hour.

Fortunately for its citizens, the streets of Dixon were summer mid-afternoon empty when he blew through a half hour later. Deputies argued whether Gary saw the roadblock a few miles out of town, just past the Sanders County line. Most said it didn't seem like it. Others said he had to have but that he was too far gone to care. Whichever, he hit the seam between the two cruisers parked nose to nose. Going close to a hundred miles an hour, he shot through his own windshield and sailed another fifty feet before hitting the fence that nearly tore him in half.

The news of his death didn't reach Portage till evening.

74

MICK SLOWED AS HE PASSED THE CONOCO. After three his dad could probably take the rest of the day off. Was it worth another try? He turned on the side street and found a shady spot to think about it. A few hours ago he was never going to talk to his dad again. His dad stole his checks. Mick guessed he couldn't get too worked up about that since he'd stolen his dad's car. If he kept the Bonnie it was worth more than six hundred dollars. So were they even?

His dad hadn't been anyone's idea of a model father. He'd made Mick join him on two or three major jobs. If they'd been caught, Mick would *still* be in juvie or on some work farm and he'd have a record that would mess up the rest of his life. On the other hand, his dad had kept him. That hadn't been exactly convenient, dragging an anchor you had to take care of.

Had he been a decent son? Mick wasn't sure. Was Fitz proud of him? Didn't seem like it. Did he love him? Hard to tell. But it wasn't the worst relationship. Did his dad beat him? Had, sometimes. Did he literally scare the pee out of him getting mad and sticking a pistol in his mouth? Yes. But he'd done some good things, too. Especially when Mick was younger. Made lunches to take to school, washed his clothes, babied him when he got sick. Were they even? Mick guessed with family you never ever got even.

He would ask his dad again for a couple of reasons. One, he was scared to go against either Hammond or Cassel, more afraid if they were together. Two? His dad was a rugged guy, good at going against people. Sometimes too good.

Mick walked around back into the garage and froze. His dad was in a pissing contest, trying to stare somebody down.

JJ had her hands on her hips, not buying it. "Look at me hard as you want, you know I'm right."

"Bullshit. I don't owe you and I don't owe him. You guys pulled the pin when you ran. Screwed Gary and Tina, dropped me in the shitter. May have got Grace killed. Now you want me to fix it. Too late, Buttercup."

He turned back to the car he was fixing, saw Mick in the process. "Bloody hell, the Bobbsey Twins."

JJ saw Mick then. Colored.

"You're wrong, Dad. You do owe me. You brought me here. Taught me everything I know. This is the next lesson. Suck it up."

Fitz stared at Mick like he had two heads. Mouth open. Tiniest head shake side to side like: no, no way, I didn't just hear that. Started to say something. Stopped.

Everything stopped. Mick could hear the shop clock go from second to second.

His dad raised the torque wrench he was holding, pointed it at Mick. "If you'd said 'man up' I would have shoved this two feet up your butt."

75

A SHORT DIRT ROAD CONNECTED THE HIGHWAY to a wide gravel parking area at the riverside, creosote posts kept cars thirty feet from the water. Mick put the Bronco between the black Town Car and a slick SUV knockoff he didn't know the name of.

"Don't clip the silver one. It's worth more than the Conoco."

JJ, silent in the backseat, was out first and over to the river. She shaded her eyes. "The house must be over that rise," she said, pointing across the water at a road that climbed away from the island's shoreline.

Mick had imagined a footbridge, had even thought the channel might be wadable. No, that's what the boats were for. Two of them, with ground marks where two others had rested. The problem? A plastic-covered metal cable looped through the eye ring on the front of each boat, ending in an industrial padlock on a thick metal post set in a concrete pad. Hammond didn't want passersby hijacking his ferries.

Mick gave the cable a tug. Even more solid than it looked. He heard an engine start and turned to see his father backing out and rolling away in the Bronco. He was too surprised to yell. Just stood there watching the car disappear.

JJ came to him, reached for his hand, led him to a rock big enough for both to sit on. There was nothing to say.

Mick would have cried if JJ hadn't been there. Helpless frustration. He could try to swim the damn channel but he'd probably drown. That wouldn't help Grace. Nothing to do but sit there and hate himself for not being smarter, more careful, more of a goddamn man.

JJ knew enough to keep the silence.

Ten minutes later his dad was back. Put the Bronco in the same place. Now tears did leak and Mick stood and started walking, clearing his throat to mask a single sob. He stopped halfway to the car, watched his dad pull out a tool kit and buck it to the metal post.

"Can't remember the trick with these," his dad said, sitting on the kit and studying the lock. "Can't just cut 'em. They're case-hardened. Heat 'em first maybe? It'll come back to me."

While his dad considered the lock, Mick and JJ went to the newest-looking boat. Stepped in over life jackets and old fishing rods. The engine was a five-horse Honda with an electric start.

Mick knew it had to be in the water before you turned it on. Checked the gas can chained to the transom. Had more than enough for back and forth to the island. Battery in a watertight case. Spark plug? No. Empty hole. Now what?

Fitz joined them at the boat with a hacksaw in his hand. "Hell with the lock," he said, kneeling at the bow and studying the ring that the cable went through. "Much easier." He began sawing.

"Something else," Mick said, watching him work. "No plug. JJ checked the other boat, too. Hammond pulled them."

"Yeah, that's what I'd do. Careful guy. Smart." His dad glanced back at the Bronco. "I brought some. One of 'em might fit."

76

HAMMOND FOLLOWED HER as Grace climbed steps to a higher floor. She entered a kitchen with a large butcher-block prep island in the middle that had a sink and enough counter space to hold food for a banquet. Light-colored oiled wood cabinets, built-in fridge, another sink, rows of spices and jars of uncooked pasta on two sides. The other two sides opened into a dining and living area with glass walls. The huge rooms were bright enough that Grace needed to squint for a minute or so.

"Ahead." Hammond came to her side.

Pleated couches surrounded a metal fireplace in a far corner. Grace could see two coffee cups on the side tables.

Hammond gestured for her to sit wherever she liked. She took the nearest couch edge, thinking at least she wouldn't be totally trapped, could run from there if she needed.

Larry walked in from another room, picked up a straight-backed chair from the dining room table and sat next to her, blocking the open route to the kitchen. "Sorry," he said, a small embarrassed smile. "Couldn't take a chance. You understand."

Grace hated herself. She did understand. She'd probably have done the same thing.

Hammond joined them, placing a glass of ice water on Grace's side table. "Coffee if you want it."

She would have liked coffee but did not want to be beholden to the bastard. Didn't answer.

Hammond sat across from her. "So, we have a situation." He gave Larry an I'll-do-the-talking look. "This Evelyn thing's not what you think."

Grace glanced away, barricading her feelings against the lies to follow. She'd listen closely enough to maybe glean the truth from what he spun, but she wouldn't meet his eyes, let him see into her. He was too persuasive and she wasn't sure how to protect herself. Instead she'd focus out the window on the jay patrolling the deck and the tree-covered hill beyond.

"Neither Larry nor I had anything to do with Evelyn. In fact, Larry tried to stop it. That's when he lost the ring set. Kicking the punk's ass, but he was too late. She was already dead and in the water."

Grace had not expected that. She had to keep her curiosity

from making her gullible. The first time with her brothers they'd told her they just wanted to see what it was like to kiss a girl. She stayed quiet and let them sit on her bed. Huge mistake.

"So Larry beat the . . . punished the moron that did it, but then what? We, none of us, wanted an investigation that . . . none of us wanted any investigation. Larry brought the guy here and we shipped him off. He'll never hurt anybody in this town again, and that was a pretty good plan until you kids got involved. The boy is clueless and as soon as some time passes we'll undo the trick we did with his little bat, but you, you're too familiar with things. You have to go."

"Disappear me like you did Ramona?" It slipped out and Grace bit her lip. *Now he has even more reason to kill me.*

Hammond sat back for a moment, gave Larry another look. Put hand to mouth briefly, thinking. "Hear me now. Nobody, especially not us, wants to hurt you. But you have to believe what I'm telling you. You can't be around spreading bullshit rumors. Can't. Understand?"

Grace risked a glance at his face. Red and angry. Acid rose in her throat.

"Ramona got . . . okay, Bolton called ICE and reported her. She was getting pretty nosy and I'd given her a job she couldn't have gotten anywhere else. In this county anyway. So she could be close to a friend she came up with. I was the good guy here. And she began snooping. Why? Stupidest thing she could have done. Immigration picked her off the streets. Deported her, same day. End of story."

That was possible. Ramona was pretty, and sweet with the customers, but she had some kind of attitude. Grace never knew her well enough to guess what that was about. Well, she could guess. Mackler.

"So what I'm telling you is that we were fine when you decided to move on. But here you are again, this time bringing the blackmail. It won't fly . . ."

Grace knew this was the important part of what he wanted to say but she was distracted. People, three people, had crested the hill and were walking toward Hammond's house. His back was to them and Larry had a bad angle. What should she do?

77

"ARE YOU LISTENING?"

Grace snapped to, hoped she hadn't given anything away with her eyes. "Yes."

"So we have a good deal. And a bad deal. Which do you want to hear first?"

Grace swallowed, trying to keep the acid down, but the fear was literally making her sick. "Bad." It came out like a whisper. She wanted to do better, appear more confident, but she was losing it.

"Okay, hypothetically. When a person leaves town, runs without a trace, doesn't matter, young or old, people write them off.

They're gone. Never hear from them again. Nobody knows what happened to the person after they went away. After a while, nobody cares. Everybody in Portage thinks you're gone."

Not everybody.

"You were a runaway to start with. You probably run a lot."

Mick and JJ could think I ran this time. I was going to.

"So nobody's going to exactly wonder what happened to you. Nobody's going to worry. You're just gone. Your choice. See where I'm going with this? If Larry had hurt that waitress, no one, ever, would have found the body. There wouldn't be a body. See what I mean?"

Grace was forcing herself to hear his words, but, sneaking glances, she was pretty sure that was Mick and JJ walking closer with some man. Gary? She couldn't tell.

"What the hell's the matter with you?" Hammond looked at Larry again. "You said she was smart."

Larry shrugged.

"I'm listening," Grace said. "I'm just scared."

"Good. That's important. Because that hypothetical situation I said? That could happen to someone. They run away, they're never seen again."

Grace nodded.

"Okay, the good deal?" He waited until Grace looked at him again. "Not so hypothetical. Larry could drive you out of here. We give you more traveling money . . . while you were resting we saw you already got something saved up." He watched her like he was expecting a reaction. "You asked Larry for a loan, right?"

A loan. What had she said? Two thousand?

"Three thousand. That seems reasonable enough. But it comes with a caveat. You know what that is?"

Grace didn't.

"A condition, like a mandate, a word to the wise, shouldn't be ignored. I know you're ahead of me here. You have to get gone and stay gone and keep your mouth shut. Forever. You're young, so that's a long time." He paused.

Grace could feel him studying her.

"Larry thinks you can do it. I'm not so sure."

"Some people are coming down your road." Hard decision. Grace didn't see she had any choice.

Hammond was up in less than a second, scooting to the curtains beside the windows, edging to look, Larry right behind him. "Shit! They won't come up on the deck. Wait for them downstairs."

Larry pulled the larger pistol from the back of his slacks, jacked a shell in the chamber, and headed for the basement steps. "You want to shut her up," he said at the door.

"I got her."

Grace believed that. All her thinking, all her planning, all her work, had brought her to this moment. Six months. And she was got. The freedom she longed for—gone, and she was farther under a man's thumb than she'd ever imagined. She threw up on the couch.

78

HAMMOND HAD JERKED HER by the arm to a nearby bathroom. "Do what you have to and clean up!" He'd slammed the door.

When Grace came out there was a dry towel covering the soiled area and Hammond was motioning to her to come back and sit. He had a shiny chrome pistol beside him and his legs were crossed, waiting for the visitors. Grace could hear footsteps climbing the basement stairs.

JJ was the first one through the door. Brightened and started to run as soon as she saw Grace. Stopped in her tracks when she noticed Hammond. Mick was behind, saw what she did. Frowned and kept coming. Fitz was next, with Larry close enough to do him damage if he tried anything.

Hammond waited till they were all at the couches. "This is not good," he said. "Makes everything just about impossible." He picked up his pistol and motioned for everyone to sit past them on the sectional.

Larry moved to the end and kept his gun trained on Fitz.

"You search them?"

Larry shook his head.

"That's too bad. Now if anybody moves funny you have to shoot first." He shifted his gaze to the rest of the group. "You following this?"

Grace was trying to remember if Hammond had talked like

this before. No. He'd been smooth as butter. Now he sounded like a thug. His civility didn't run so deep. For the first time she wondered if the man had learned this from silent partners outside of town, outside the state, partners who had an even larger interest in gambling and under-the-table deals.

Hammond rested his pistol on his knee. "So what're we going to do here?"

Nobody responded.

"Come on. I know you had an idea when you took one of my boats, right? Had some picture of how things would go down. So tell me. What the hell are we going to do now?"

"Let's start with you killed Evelyn," Mick said.

"That was Cunneen, you dumb shit." Hammond shook his head, disgusted. "And we dealt with that."

It took Mick a couple of seconds. "Sports scholarship? You gave him a reward."

Grace was reeling, having trouble keeping up. Cunneen. She could see it. He was an animal. But a scholarship?

"What were we going to tell Tim? His best friend. 'He killed somebody so we made him disappear'?" Hammond looked at Larry. Took a deep breath. "It's one thing, send a guy away. Four of you? Won't work."

"You killed Cunneen?" Mick was asking the questions that Grace was thinking.

"Hey. I didn't have anything to do with this Evelyn except hire her. And then I had to keep things from blowing up. That's my job. Nobody's talking killing."

That's not exactly what Grace remembered from the "hypothetical" example earlier. That had been a very believable threat.

"So, right now I'm thinking. Spend a little, get a little. I, Larry and I, help this girl get out of town with a . . . a, uh, settlement that lets her start new someplace else. And you two"—he motioned at JJ and Mick with the pistol—"you go back to school. You ever need something, come to me. You know Grace is safe. She can phone you, e-mail, whatever, time to time. You two forget about this stuff. It's over. Handled. We call the law and leave another message saying the evidence on your porch was planted. It's recorded like every 911. Wrecks their case. Larry's dad and Paint? Now they got nothing. Why would you set yourself up? Makes no sense, right? They'd pull you in, talk to you. No big deal. Then they'd leave you alone."

Grace was amazed how well Hammond could think on his feet. An entrepreneur. Easy to imagine how he'd grown his holdings.

"So far so good, but we still have this gentleman. Mr. Fitzhugh, I understand. Lieutenant Cassel says you might have a second job. Might be in the used commercial equipment business. Cassel could be willing to let things slide if we asked him respectfully. You're not operating here? Right? Tell me you're not doing anything here."

Everyone's eyes went to Fitz.

If Grace had to bet, he was. Fitz. That kind of guy, cocky, had to do his thing, stick a knife in the system. That was probably what she liked about him.

Fitz didn't respond.

"I take that as a yes."

Grace could see Larry's hand tighten on the pistol. Hope Fitz noticed it, too, and said something. Anything.

Hammond raised his hand like slow down a minute. "Another idea," he said, looking directly at Fitz. "Pretty nice-looking Infiniti out there, wouldn't you say?"

Fitz didn't speak.

"QX56? What do you think it's worth?"

Fitz shrugged.

"Sixty-three K as it sits. You interested?"

Grace thought Fitz's eyes got a little brighter.

"See, I think we can do business here. Win-win. Let me be straight. What I want? I want this to go away. What you want? You're a businessman. Sixty-three K and you leave, you don't look back. No questions asked. Soon as we get back to the road, gone."

Grace saw he definitely had Fitz's interest. She was learning. Find what people want, give it to them. Anyone. And they're yours.

"Now my Grace, here. I can see her thinking. Sixty-three, and I'm not getting that much. Right?" Hammond smiled at her. "Yeah, it's the P.I.T.A. factor. Know what I mean?"

She didn't.

"Pain-In-The-Ass. You're a young pain, he's an old pain with firearms. Degree of difficulty? Much higher. That's business."

Grace nodded. She got it. Plus, three thousand on top of whatever she had. That would be enough. A new life. "What city?" she asked, confusing everyone but Hammond.

"You tell me," he said, nodding back. "Big and far. Only rule, Larry said he'd be back by Monday. Don't want to raise any more questions."

Fitz surprised everyone by speaking. "Not a good idea. The ride ties me to you. Connects us. Title."

"Documents can be improved, made more accurate," Hammond said easily.

"How about this? You give me a part of your action, point me in the right directions. We split the profits."

"Mr. Fitzhugh, are you stalling for time? This offer doesn't sound like you. From what I hear, you don't do great with partners."

Grace looked at Mick, wondering if he realized his dad was going to get himself shot.

"True," Fitz said, "so how about this. You give me, say, ten times what you're giving the girl. Fifty thousand. Cash. When everything blows over, I move. Out of state. Not a ripple."

"I'm not coming with you." Mick couldn't believe how easily his dad bargained about things that would affect the rest of their lives, how ready his dad was to drop him and move on. Just as Mick was starting to like him a little again. Was his dad stalling or was this for real?

"Acceptable," Hammond said. "Reasonable. So now what? I trust Larry. He keeps the faith. You, you're smart," he said, nodding to Fitz. "You got a lot to lose. Like fifteen or twenty years. Our Grace? Ready to roll, I think. But your son's a crusader rabbit and his girlfriend's an unknown. How do we know they won't blow a whistle?"

"You're going to have other things to worry about." From behind them. The basement door. Sheriff Paint. And then a small flood of deputies moving into the room, guns ready.

79

THE RIVERSIDE PARKING AREA was packed with six sheriff's cruisers. Paint ushered Hammond into one, K-turned, and headed east on 200. Since the Portage jail wasn't big enough to hold and interrogate everyone in isolation, each suspect would be driven separately and questioned in Missoula. Contact between Hammond, Larry, Grace, Fitz, and Mick would be prevented so they wouldn't be able to collaborate on their statements. Paint's phone call to the Montana State Patrol Headquarters in Helena put Scott Cassel on administrative leave until allegations of complicity could be ruled out or substantiated.

Even riding in the back of a sheriff's car, Mick had no words for the relief he was feeling. He'd faced Hammond and Larry and came out okay! Hammond talked negotiation but Mick wasn't at all sure he'd really let them go. Neither he nor Larry had put away their pistols. And Grace was more than okay, still confident-looking, still cool after being kidnapped. That would mess up most people. It was amazing how Paint found them just at the right moment.

Cunneen? Mick didn't see that coming. He'd been so sure it was Larry. But Cunneen was a lot like Larry. Paint would have him extradited. Oh. If he was still alive. A jock and Tim's best friend. He might be. Good athletes could get away with a lot.

When this mess got resolved, Mick would have what he'd hoped for. Almost everything. Hometown, football. He'd be playing in a month! Two-a-days in the August heat and loving every minute of it. Mick would find a new home. Not the studio. He was done with that. Not going to live with his dad again. They'd have a different relationship. More like friends. Or maybe like an uncle, but he'd never had one of those so he didn't really know.

JJ might have an extra bedroom. Interesting. Maybe he and Grace could stay there until Gary got out. If Gary got out. Or maybe Grace would want it by herself.

He'd heard the deputies talking, using words like accomplice and kidnapping. Mick didn't see how Hammond could evade everything Paint would discover, so he was going to need a job. He bet Dovey would give him a recommendation. Somebody would hire a strong back and a decent attitude. It had been easy enough in Coeur d'Alene. He could do it again.

Would Grace be grateful he'd saved her and want to be with him? He thought about that while road noise washed over him, while he breathed the smell of the patrol car: bleach and old vinyl, dust vibrating off the floorboards. Out his window to the south, summer wheat looked ready for harvest, and farther, the Bitterroots, long empty of snow, were dark with fir.

No. Grace wouldn't be grateful. She probably didn't even realize he'd been trying to save her. She wouldn't want to stay at JJ's with him. He didn't have any money and he wasn't smart enough for her. Grace had been going out with older men before this all went down. She was so hot and so . . . hidden. He could live a million years and never know her. A really good daydream, a piss-poor girlfriend.

80

JJ WAS SURPRISED to find herself in the back of a sheriff's car. Why her? She'd been the key to the arrests. Dovey thought of the transmitter, but JJ'd worn it. Who'd think? She didn't notice her cruiser alone had turned toward Portage.

The rest of the summer should be fun. There hadn't been any other applicants when they hired her, so her job was probably still open. Didn't seem like Gary was coming back anytime soon and JJ was too young to be responsible for Tina or Jon. She had no idea where they'd wind up or what would happen to them but she called herself a Stovall, Tina's niece, so wasn't the trailer hers? If they caught Gary, what would happen to the money in the suitcase? Maybe she could afford a really good college after all.

JJ didn't believe Grace would stay in Portage. Her home and

job were messed up and her benefactor would be gone. In some ways she'd outgrown the town, but JJ hated to think of her prossing in a city. Would she do that? Like always, Grace was hard to predict.

Mick? He was easier. He'd stay, find some work and play ball when school started. That's what he'd talked about. She wasn't sure where he'd live. Didn't seem like he'd be with his dad anymore. And he'd left his bags of clothes in her trailer. Right now Dovey was like JJ's temporary guardian. She probably wouldn't let JJ and Mick stay together even with separate bedrooms, so a lot was up in the air.

JJ caught herself humming. Felt happier than she remembered being since she was back with her real mom years ago. Finally! She had a clean place to stay. Dovey's or the empty trailer. That was big. And Mick. They'd pal around when everything settled down. Maybe even go swimming again. Someplace different. And when school started, a new ball game. Literally.

She'd not only be a little older, she was already stronger, taller than last year. Even if they didn't return her bail bond since Gary ran away, she still had a little money left in her college fund. And she'd decided. She was going to get a scholarship. Hammond said Cunneen got a sports scholarship and he was mainly big and mean. She was coordinated. She hadn't tried much volleyball but she would this fall, and if she worked on it, she knew she'd start. Same with swimming in the winter. And softball? More hitting practice and she could be all-state. Now that was a plan!

The driver's radio squawked, interrupted her thoughts, reminded her what a tense afternoon this had been: dealing with Gary, running to Paint's office, making the scary undercover plan, arguing with Fitz, stealing a boat, getting caught by Hammond and Larry. That was enough excitement for one day.

Ahead, she caught glimpses of the pale moon barely visible on the eastern horizon. Right now it was a ghost moon. Good luck just when she'd needed it! But in an hour or so, while it was still low in the sky, it would become a butter-orange smile. The next cycle after the Dead Girl Moon. What would this one be?

Silly. She wanted to call it the Mick Moon, but that would never do.

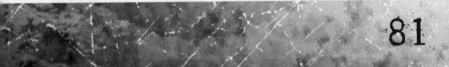

81

SINCE THEY WERE EACH IN SEPARATE CARS, Grace couldn't ask Mick or JJ what had happened, how Paint knew where she was. She could guess. Larry didn't search them. Big mistake! Mick or Fitz wore a wire. Fitz might have cooperated with the sheriff if he'd made a deal to get out from under the interstate theft investigation. Mick could have cooperated in order to beat whatever charges Paint had filed. She could hardly wait to have a moment alone with JJ and find out which it was.

JJ. Poor girl. Put herself in danger schlepping after Mick. Some girls just didn't have it. Never would. She liked her younger roomie, but JJ would always be a follower. Never do anything on her own, always staring at the moon, never dealing with what was right in front of her. Grace wished she'd taught her how to be sneaky. Well, she'd learn or she wouldn't.

Grace felt like she was recovering from a virus. The last few hours had been . . . she hadn't thought she'd make it out alive. Hammond's best move would have been to get rid of the four of them. Anyone could see that. She'd hoped if she warned Hammond about Mick and JJ coming, he'd trust her again and take care of her. Didn't work out that way.

Originally he might have sent Grace away like he outlined in the "good deal," but as she watched Hammond think through his possibilities with Mick and Fitz, she'd realized that bringing more people into it had eliminated that option. He'd just been blowing smoke. He'd never risk turning Mick and JJ and Fitz loose. He didn't know them, couldn't be sure they'd hold up their end. And he'd wonder if Grace had a bigger alliance to one of them than to him. He wouldn't take that chance. Grace had to go, too.

Would he really have done that? Kill or get Larry to kill four people? She thought so. Would Larry have gone along with it? Maybe. Probably. Self-preservation. In too deep to quit. In a way, Mick and his dad saved her life by giving the sheriff time to find her. She hoped they never discovered she'd ratted them out. Actually, Mick would forgive her. That'd be a quick fix. Kiss or two or a little more.

Fitz. He'd be a problem.

She'd had a couple of narrow escapes. She could be in a California prison for killing her brothers. She could be decomposing, scattered in bits and pieces around the Cabinet Mountains Wilderness. Did the sheriff have anything on her? She was safe from the runaway complication now that she knew her mom would never have filed a missing person. And Grace hadn't done anything too illegal. One way or another she'd earned the money she'd saved. She was small potatoes compared to Hammond.

When she got to Missoula they'd ask her a bunch of questions. She'd play dumb. Afterward, they could release her right there as far as she was concerned. The main thing was getting her money back and leaving. She didn't really need the extra three thousand Hammond had offered. She already had enough to go someplace and start a business.

Earlier when Hammond had left the destination up to her, "somewhere big and far away," she'd realized she wanted to get out of state. Get distance from these people. Everybody. Someplace she couldn't be found. Denver sounded good. Or maybe all the way to Phoenix. Lot of older people there that might want her services.

Let's say Phoenix. How hard would it be to find another obit? Some college girl in a neighboring state. Take the name. Grace Herick would disappear and the new person could enroll in a university. Maybe even transfer courses if the other girl had been a decent student. New school, new city, new work. Piece of cake, really. Grace thought she might be pretty good at a career in law enforcement. So many possibilities in a field like that.

ACKNOWLEDGMENTS

The idea for this book emerged as I drove down a small town's alley toward the Clark Fork River and was surprised by the living conditions I encountered not fifty feet off a manicured main street. I imagined the people I'd met in schools and hospitals who might wash up on such shores, and *Dead Girl Moon* began. I owe a great deal to teenagers who literally inspired me with their bravery, perseverance, and resourcefulness. The setting depicted, the community, and its business and politics are fiction.

I am most grateful to my editor, Wes Adams, for his encouragement, savvy recommendations, and humor that makes each literary project a many-smiled collaboration. Also, to Karla Reganold and FSG's superb copyediting staff for helping make this book accurate and cohesive, and to Jay Colvin for proving you can tell a book by his covers.

Huge thanks to my agents Tracey and Josh Adams at Adams Literary, whose elegant support and advocacy I cherish.

I received finely tuned feedback from the world's best writing group: Jim Dowling, Kathryn Gessner, Carla Jackson, Melinda Kashuba, and Robb Lightfoot. I'm lucky to have a larger writing community: Steve Brewer, Chris Crutcher, Tony D'Souza, George Rogers, Bill Siemer, and Jamie Weil.

Special appreciation goes to northwestern Montana Highway Patrol officers for their strategic information, to Dr. Paul Swinderman for relevant medical consultations, and to Manuel J. Garcia, Attorney, for advice pertinent to the story's legal areas.

I'm forever endebted to and enriched by the loves of my life. My darling psychotherapist/artist wife is always my first reader, and my bright, beautiful daughter, Jessica Rose, edits from afar in Portland.

Which of your characters is most like you?

In ways, I was alienated as a boy, like Murray in *Dead Connection*, but I had a much, much better time in school.

When you finish a book, who reads it first?

My wife, a psychotherapist and avid reader.

Are you a morning person or a night owl?

I'm not a big fan of early mornings. If the sun is still asleep, we should be, too. I love the daylight, love being outside, shine or rain, but I have trouble giving up the night. I am nearly always reluctant to go to bed and end it.

What's your idea of the best meal ever?

Lebanese-spiced barbecued meats, hummus, baba ganoush, cayenne-spiced rice, multiple crusty breads, green salad with homemade ranch, *and* lemon icebox pie for dessert.

Which do you like better: cats or dogs?

Dogs, by a mile. I like their relentless good cheer and loyalty.

What do you value most in your friends?

Integrity and openness, humor, original thinking.

Where do you go for peace and quiet?

A river or mountain lake.

What makes you laugh out loud?

A zillion things: my daughter, my wife, friends, movies, magic, our many human foibles, differences of opinion along gender lines.

What's your favorite song?

The Beatles—"With a Little Help from My Friends."

Who is your favorite fictional character?
I loved the plucky Scout Finch in *To Kill a Mockingbird,* and I admire Josh Arnold, the boy who became a young man in *Red Sky at Morning.*

What are you most afraid of?
I'm a big guy, and I hate being tightly enclosed on all sides, like crawling through a narrow passage in a cave. I'm also afraid of people willing to kill for their opinions.

What time of the year do you like best?
Winter: rain, quiet snow, leather jackets and wool shirts, crystal night skies, blustery storms.

What is your favorite TV show?
Right now, it's *Friday Night Lights*—rich characters and bold explorations of controversial issues.

If you were stranded on a desert island, who would you want for company?
My wife and daughter! And a good friend for even more fishing, singing, and basketball playing. Four people can have loads of fun together!

If you could travel in time, where would you go?
I've always been curious about the Neanderthal people. What were they like? What happened? I'd start there and move toward Babylonia, Egypt, and possibly sail with the Phoenicians around 500 B.C. to Brazil. No, I take that back. I'd go crazy cooped up that long on a boat. Ancient Greece. I'd want to see that, for sure. Socrates and his questions.

What's the best advice you have ever received about writing?

My first editor, Deborah Brodie, told me "write dessert first." Which means write what fascinates you, what you believe in, and what you are curious about, and sweat the details later.

What do you want readers to remember about your books?

The characters: their courage, their personal dignity, their struggles, the risks they were afraid to take but did.

What would you do if you ever stopped writing?

Play more music, write more songs.

What do you like best about yourself?

The ability to do a lot of different things fairly well.

What is your worst habit?

Driving too aggressively.

What do you consider to be your greatest accomplishment?

Turning away from drinking and drugs. I didn't get in trouble with the law, but I was a party-hard kind of guy. My father died from alcoholism. I didn't think it was possible to fully enjoy life without drinking. It is. Second is being chosen unanimous all-state tackle, offense and defense, in Montana in the '60s.

What do you wish you could do better?

Play the piano.

What would your readers be most surprised to learn about you?

Perhaps, that I often cry. I cry from joy at the love I feel or see. I cry from sadness at the hideous ways human beings treat each other over differing beliefs. I cry for our seeming inability to learn from history. I cry for the way we sometimes squander the gift of life. I cry because, from time to time, I feel things so strongly I cannot contain the emotion.

Murray is a kid with the strange ability to converse with those who are buried in the cemetery where he lives. His "power" is sometimes more a curse than a blessing. And when he is forced to use it to help solve a brutal crime, it turns out to be downright dangerous—for others, as well as himself.

THE DEAD CAN TALK TO MURRAY.
AND THEY ARE ASKING FOR HELP.

DEAD INVESTIGATION

CHARLIE PRICE

Keep reading for a sneak peek.

Living in the cemetery lawnmower shed turned out pretty well. Murray had gotten used to the uninsulated prefab and its peculiarities. Sure, the concrete floor leached warmth from anything it touched and the place reeked of motor oil and industrial cleaners. The window rattled when a city bus passed on the street. The little hut was an iceberg during cold spells, and yes, its seams made an eerie whistle when the wind gusted. Nonetheless, it had only one serious drawback.

The shed sat atop a foundation that had been mistakenly poured eighty or ninety years ago over an old woman's grave, and she complained nonstop to anyone who'd listen. It was enough to drive a person crazy.

If you parked the riding mower under the front utility shelf, there was room in back for a cot and a milk crate that held a battery lantern so you could read yourself to sleep. Murray preferred it to home and was very grateful to Pearl for suggesting it, and to her dad, the cemetery caretaker, for making it available.

Saturday morning was chilly but not shivery. Murray washed his face in a metal basin, put on jeans and pulled a hoodie over his sweatshirt, grabbed an apple from the grocery bag he kept on the tool bench. Breakfast. He'd get something at 7-Eleven for lunch. Candy bar, orange, something easy. What was cheap and built muscles? A banana? Murray noticed his T-shirts were tighter. But he wasn't fat. He might be getting some muscles. Made him wonder why. All the walking he did? Genes from whoever his father had been?

And he'd grown taller in the last few months. He could

tell because his pants were too short. Time to visit Salvation Army. And his face? Pimples were rare now. His messy hair almost fit current styles. His nose was still too big, but his face wasn't actually frightening. No horns. No fangs. Girls looked at him sometimes.

In February nothing needed mowing, but there was always trash to be bagged, stuff that visitors left behind, plus cups and wrappers the wind blew in off the street. Murray was picking a fast food sack out of the hedge at the cemetery's north border when he heard somebody jogging through the leaves and downed branches behind him. Unusual. Most people were somber and dignified in cemeteries. He looked up and was surprised to see Pearl. Ordinarily she was quiet. She'd been known to sneak up and startle him just to watch him jump. So . . . in a rush today. Why?

Pearl didn't seem like a cemetery caretaker's daughter. Her skin wasn't pale green, her head didn't do three-sixties. She looked . . . well, gingery blond hair, tight curls, a decent face that didn't need makeup; medium tall, a girl jock with muscles and the start of a figure. Actually, Murray thought she looked kind of pretty. But dangerous. Smart and stubborn. Went after what she wanted like a torpedo. Could get you to do things you'd rather not. Murray braced himself.

"Hey, Ghostbuster. I need your help."

"I'm busy."

"You'd rather pick up trash than talk to me?"

"Um . . ." At least half the time Pearl came around she had something she wanted Murray to do that was borderline risky. He'd learned to be careful about what he agreed to. "What kind of help?"

"Your special thing. Like the others." Pearl held out a dirty wool stocking cap.

Murray didn't get it. "What others?"

"Others with the gift. Clairvoyants."

Murray stepped back onto the garbage bag and heard it rip. "Dang it, Pearl, don't use that . . . I don't . . . Leave me alone."

"You just probably haven't tried it before." She pushed the cap toward him. "They hold something that the person wears or handles a lot and they get information."

"What information?"

"Tell me where to find that down-and-out guy who walks around outside the gate all the time."

"Try outside the gate."

Pearl stuck out her tongue. Glared. "I have stuff for him."

"Uh, why?" Murray couldn't imagine.

"You know the ratty sleeping bag he carries? Dad and I got him a new one and a coat and some canned meat. I'm pretty sure he sleeps up in these hedges sometimes."

Murray nodded. Both Pearl and Janochek did kind things for people all the time. Murray was one of them. "Okay, I'll tell him."

"Have you seen him lately?"

Murray tried to remember. "Probably not for a week. Ask at the mission."

"I did. Nothing. They didn't recognize him."

"How would they? You don't even know his name, right?"

"That big red bump on his forehead? Like an infected boil? Pretty hard to miss. They said they'd never met him."

"Yeah, so, what could I do? I'll tell him you have stuff when I run into him."

"No, you could actually find him." Pearl held out the stocking cap again.

"You're nuts. Even if that's really his, you want me to read the label and tell you where he bought it or something?"

She stuck the cap out closer to his hand. "Just hold it and tell me what comes to you."

Where do you even start with a request like that? Murray had never done anything like it. Would never do anything like it. Felt queasy just thinking about touching the smelly thing.

"I've been reading," Pearl said, rummaging in her backpack like she was searching for a book. "Clairvoyants can hold somebody's favorite pen and know where they're hiding."

Murray retreated another step, hearing paper and cans crunch under his feet.

Pearl shook her head, pursed her lips. "Don't be such a pussy. Give it a shot."

The last time Murray had helped Pearl he got shot, literally. Spent days in a hospital and got hauled into the police station to explain how the two of them found a missing cheerleader's body. And then, somebody talked. Maybe a cop told his family at dinner or a reporter leaked it. Something. Somehow. The story got around school that Murray Kiefer thinks he can talk to dead people. He went from being a mostly invisible loser to a well-known certifiable wacko.

Big problem: it was true. He *was* friends with a lot of dead people, and he learned things from them. The cheerleader, for example. "A lot happens in your last second. You're so mad that you're dying, and so scared, but there's also this relief . . . and it hits you all at once like lightning. I couldn't say anything quick enough before I was gone."

Maybe Murray could have guessed the fear and anger part, but relief? That was a surprise . . . and then it wasn't. Living is probably hard for everybody.

"When you realize it's really the end, everything gets clear," Blessed Daughter told him. "In that moment I knew who I really loved and who I didn't, what I was proud of and what I wasn't. It was surprising. I loved my dog as much as I loved my parents. I don't know why. Riley was always bouncy and happy. Didn't understand how quick I was dying away. I didn't have to watch his face crumple."

As far as Murray could tell, Blessed was as sharp and sensible as a lot of adults even though she had died of a brain tumor when she was only eleven.

"And the school grades I worked so hard for? I was prouder of my swimming medal, 'cause they said the tumor would wreck my swimming but I made the team anyway. And I won a fifty-yard backstroke before the cancer messed my timing."

His older friend, Dearly Beloved, told him she didn't miss her family very much. "It was back in the fifties. Mom and Dad mostly paid attention to my brothers. 'Stay a virgin till you're married.' That and 'Wear clean underwear when you go to town' was the only advice I ever got. I wish now I'd moved out before the darn car accident."

Dearly had gone through the windshield when her date hit a tree.

"When I croaked, what I missed was the life I'd saved money for. I'd earned enough to bus to San Francisco. I thought if I winked and smiled I could maybe get a job at a bookstore in North Beach."

Dearly was light-hearted, and wise for her twenty-five years. Almost like a mother to Murray.

"Don't worry about me and the others," she said. "The grave isn't uncomfortable or cold or anything. Really, you don't even feel it."

That was good news, because Murray couldn't imagine being an adult. What would he do? He didn't drive, didn't have money, couldn't think of a job he could hold except caretaking this cemetery, and Janochek already had that. So Murray was pretty much ready to die. He had his tombstone picked out, charcoal granite with silvery flecks. He was paying for it by keeping the lawns and hedges and grave sites free of trash. And he had his words:

Murray Kiefer
May 12, 1997–
Friend to the Deceased

He knew he'd miss Pearl and Janochek. That's why he hadn't died yet. Well . . . and there was one more reason. He was happy in the cemetery. Mostly. Except it had started again. Voices. People he didn't know and wasn't talking to. Moaning. Mumbling. Hurting. East, just past the back fence, probably on the hill between the rodeo grounds and the rear hedge. He'd heard them last week and again this morning when he was picking up trash. More than one person at the same time. That hadn't happened before. He knew they were dead. But they were outside the cemetery. Not his people.